SAM FISHER

RE
APE

SCHOLASTIC PRESS / NEW YORK

Library of Congress Cataloging-in-Publication Data Available

ISBN 978-0-545-74497-3

10 9 8 7 6 5 4 3 2 1   15 16 17 18 19
Printed in the U.S.A.   23
First edition, March 2015

The text type was set in Apollo MT.
Book design by Phil Falco

For Sue
and everyone who loved her

CHAPTER 1

THE DARKEST PLACE

The house, when they finally found it, was like nothing Morton had ever seen in the city. Tucked away at the end of a winding gravel driveway and veiled in curtains of tangled ivy, it loomed behind a dense row of trees like an ancient lost monument.

"Here we are," Dad announced cheerily as they pulled up to the end of the driveway. "Eighty-eight Hemlock Hill. Our new home."

Morton felt a jolt of excitement wash away the tensions of the long journey. Could it be true? Could this immense old house really be their new home? He clambered forward from the backseat to get a better view. To Morton it looked almost like a small castle. There was a tall round turret at the front and long wide porches wrapping around the sides. It had countless windows of all shapes and sizes, and there were at least two large upstairs balconies. Morton began to get so excited he felt he might burst. It had to be three times bigger than their old house.

"You've got to be kidding me!" a morose voice intoned

from beside Morton. It was Melissa, his sixteen-year-old sister. "That's not a house, it's a ruin."

"It does look kind of run-down," agreed James, Morton's thirteen-year-old brother, who was also squashed uncomfortably in the backseat.

"I hate it!" Melissa added, as if declaring a guilty verdict at a trial.

Morton turned to look at them in bewilderment. "What are you talking about? It's perfect!" he exclaimed.

"Well, of course you'd like it. You're a freak," Melissa scoffed.

"What's that supposed to mean?"

"It's ghastly, creepy, and almost certainly haunted. In fact, it's like something right out of that horrid comic you read all the time."

Morton looked up at the house again. It was true; it did look a little neglected. Some of the windows were cracked, shingles were missing, and the paint was peeling here and there, giving way to green mildew, but surely that was all part of the charm.

"I told you it was a stupid idea to buy a house without seeing it," Melissa said with a scowl.

Dad ignored Melissa's comment and climbed stiffly out of the car to gaze up at the old building. Morton wriggled over to the front seat and bounded out after him. Melissa and James followed suit, throwing the back doors open wide and stepping out onto the gravel driveway.

"I suppose it is a little worse than it looked in the picture," Dad admitted, in his clipped British accent. "But it's not that bad. Anyway, it wouldn't be any fun if we didn't get to fix it up and make it our own, would it?"

"No offense, Dad," James said, stretching his arms and legs, "but you're not exactly the world's best handyman."

Morton had to agree with James on this point. Whenever Dad tried to do anything around the house he inevitably bungled it, and it had always been Mum who'd swooped in with a big smile to save the day. But now . . .

"Don't they have normal houses in this freak show of a town?" Melissa pouted.

"But it's a cool house," Morton said, feeling irritated by Melissa's barrage of pessimism. "And what's wrong with the town?"

"Didn't you see that sign as we drove in?" Melissa went on. "It said, 'Welcome to Dimvale, the Darkest Town in the Civilized World.' What's that all about?"

Dad began rubbing his temples. "I'm quite sure I've explained the situation to you at least a dozen times," he said, trying to sound patient. "Astronomers need absolute darkness to get good results. Dimvale is one of the few places left in North America that has bylaws controlling light pollution, which is why I jumped at the chance to work at the Dimvale Observatory."

"'Bylaws controlling light pollution'? What does that even mean?" Melissa asked suspiciously.

"It means no neon signs, no office buildings spilling light into the sky, no unnecessary street lights. . . ."

"No street lights! Are you sure this place actually is civilized?"

"I assure you it has everything you need. It has a cinema, a library, lots of restaurants. It even has a school."

"Oh, a school! So glad you didn't overlook that little detail. I'll bet they don't have any good shoe stores," Melissa said, crossing her arms and sinking into a big sulk.

"Melissa, it's going to be just fine," Dad said soothingly. "Come on, let's explore inside."

After being stuck in the car for five hours, this, at least, was something everyone was happy to do. They followed Dad along the path to the sagging porch at the back of the house. Dad produced an old key from under the. doormat and clicked the lock open with a satisfied smile.

Morton thought the inside was even better than the outside. True, there was a lot of cracked plaster, and several of the rooms had ugly wallpaper, but the grand, high ceilings and beautifully preserved original woodwork more than made up for that. Everything smelled of furniture wax and mothballs, and Morton felt instantly at home, which was odd because the house couldn't have been more different from their clean, sterile, modern place in the city. Morton decided this had something to do with the fact that the movers had already delivered all of their furniture and boxes, which had been neatly arranged in the appropriate rooms.

Dad immediately led them on a brief tour, and both James's and Melissa's moods seemed to pick up when they saw their new spacious bedrooms. James was particularly pleased because he and Morton had always had to share a room up until now.

"You've got to admit, it's pretty cool," Morton said to James as they trooped through the house.

"I guess it will be nice not to have to listen to you snoring all night," James said, ruffling Morton's wavy hair.

"I don't snore," Morton protested, and then James laughed for the first time since Morton could remember.

"Just kidding," James said.

"And last but not least," Dad was saying, "this is Morton's room."

The three kids followed Dad to the very end of the narrow upstairs landing into a large bedroom at the back.

"Whoa! This is awesome!" Morton said, pushing past the others to get a good look. The room was at least twice the size of the one he used to share with James, with two large windows and a small door leading to one of the balconies he'd seen from outside. Not only did he get his own balcony but now he'd also have more than enough room for his large collection of comics and toys. Morton threw his arms around Dad's waist and squeezed him tight. "Thanks, Dad. I love it."

Dad looked over at James and Melissa. "You see," he said, raising his eyebrows. "Not so bad, eh?"

James nodded appreciatively while Melissa kind of

shrugged and chewed her nails, which was as close as she'd come to agreeing with Dad.

"Now," Dad went on, "how about you lot start unpacking the small stuff, and I'll see about fixing us some lunch." And he paced off down the stairs, leaving the three kids alone.

Melissa glared at James and Morton. "Living in this place is going to be a nightmare. You know that, right?"

"I dunno," James said. "My nightmares don't usually have spacious bedrooms with balconies overlooking the flower garden."

Melissa sneered. "There you go again."

"What?" James said.

"Trying to make jokes about everything."

"I'm being serious," James said, with a teasing smile. "I've never had a nightmare about flower gardens."

Morton braced himself for this teasing exchange to explode into the now familiar all-out fight, but to his relief Melissa bit her tongue and stomped off down the hallway to her new bedroom.

James shrugged. "It *may* actually be a nightmare with her around," he said.

Morton didn't reply. Things had been so tense between James and Melissa recently that it was pretty much unbearable any time they were in the same room together. James couldn't seem to resist winding Melissa up, and Melissa had become more petulant and moody than ever.

"What's up?" James asked, as if sensing Morton's mood.

Morton sighed. "I don't know," he said. "It's just, why do you two always have to fight? It's not fun anymore."

James reflected on this for a moment and then snapped his fingers. "You know what *is* fun?" he said. "Attic hunting. There's sure to be one in this old house."

Morton hadn't even thought of that. He'd seen the large peaked roof from the outside, but Dad hadn't mentioned anything about an attic on the tour. That would be fun, he thought, and moments later he and James were racing around the upstairs, looking in all the corners and cubbies. They soon found a narrow, dusty staircase hidden behind what appeared to be a door to a small closet.

"Whoa!" James said. "Jackpot."

Morton peered up. The stairs vanished into complete blackness. James flipped a tarnished old brass light switch mounted just inside the door with no result.

"Looks like the bulb's gone. Maybe we should wait until . . ."

But Morton wasn't about to wait. All his life he'd wanted to live in a house with a big old attic. He bounded up the bare wooden steps, his eyes rapidly adjusting to the dim light, until he arrived on a narrow landing at the top.

James hesitated below.

"Come on," Morton called. "Your eyes get used to it pretty quick."

"Aren't you afraid of the dark?" James said, timidly following him up the stairs. "Most kids your age won't even go to bed without a night-light, never mind dash up into a strange attic."

"You can't be afraid of something that's not there," Morton said matter-of-factly.

James arrived on the landing and stood next to him. There was a second door, much older than the first, with a large ragged hole in the woodwork, and Morton could see dim shapes in the attic beyond.

"But darkness is there," James said. "I can see it."

Morton shook his head. "Darkness is the absence of light. It's not actually anything, and you can't be afraid of nothing."

"I can," James said, looking through the hole in the door. "In fact, I'm very good at it."

"I learned a trick from *Scare Scape* issue 275," Morton said. "The story about the boy lost in an abandoned mine shaft. He had to find his way out in the complete dark and he kept telling himself that darkness was nothing, but it still made him afraid, so he started shouting, 'I *am* afraid of nothing, I *am* afraid of nothing.' And then he realized that was the same as saying he wasn't afraid, so then he wasn't afraid, get it?"

James scratched his head. "You know, that almost makes sense. Not quite, but almost."

"So now you don't have to be afraid of the dark either," Morton said, and without pausing he pushed the broken door open and stepped into the gloom beyond.

The attic couldn't have been more perfect. It had tall

sloped ceilings, rough-sawn rafters covered in cobwebs, and an uneven planked floor scattered with old discarded objects. There were moth-eaten suitcases, a moldering baby carriage, and several old wooden trunks. Strangely, like the rest of the house, the attic had an air of familiarity to it. Yet this time Morton realized exactly why.

"Hey, this reminds me of another story in *Scare Scape*," Morton said excitedly. "The one where the lawyer gets an infestation of Flesh-Eating Cockroaches in his attic. You must remember that one?"

James stepped timidly into the attic and gave a thin smile. "Ever think you might be getting too old for that comic, Morton?"

Morton sighed, feeling a pang of disappointment. *Scare Scape* had once been James's favorite comic too, but over the last few years his interest had waned completely. Some of Morton's fondest memories were of the times they'd stayed up late reading and talking and making up their own creepy stories. In fact, it had been James who first showed him the comic, and it had been James who bought Morton his first mail-order monster, starting off his prized collection of *Scare Scape* toys.

James didn't seem to notice Morton's disappointment and turned to look at the tiny, cracked windows that were casting hazy shafts of light across the room. "How do you suppose they all got broken?" he asked.

Morton shrugged. "Kids throwing stones?"

James shook his head. "We're too high up for that."

Morton looked again at the disheveled attic. A standing lamp had fallen and smashed, several boxes were on their sides, and sawdust had spilled from a large wooden crate in the corner. This really was like something from one of the creepy stories in *Scare Scape*.

"You think somebody might have been trapped in here?" Morton said, in an excited whisper.

"Uh, maybe we should go," James said, his mood suddenly shifting. But before either of them had time to turn, a sudden scratching noise made them freeze on the spot. Something was moving behind one of the old trunks. Morton and James stared at each other.

"Mice?" James asked hopefully.

"Uh-uh," Morton said. "Too big for a mouse. Could be a Visible Fang."

"A what?"

"Visible Fang. You know, the creature with a transparent body, likes to hide in attics and basements."

James looked around nervously. "You do know those creatures in your comic aren't real, right?"

Morton grinned. This was starting to be fun.

The scratching noise came again, and this time it seemed to be coming from inside the trunk, not behind it.

"Well, it's definitely too big for a mouse," Morton repeated firmly. "So I don't know what else it could be."

James swallowed hard. "Why would Visible Fangs be in an attic anyway?"

"Don't you remember? They like to live near people. They creep down into their houses at night and hypnotize them."

"Oh, yeah, what was all that about? They'd hypnotize you and then steal stuff?"

"No, you're getting them confused with Swag Sprites," Morton replied. "The Visible Fang paralyzes you with hypnosis so it can eat your heart out while you're asleep."

"Oh, right," James said, a distinct tremor in his voice. "Now I remember."

"Didn't they used to be your favorite?" Morton asked.

"No. That was the Toxic Vapor Worms. They were the coolest."

"Hey, you never read the issue where the Visible Fangs and the Toxic Vapor Worms teamed up, did you?"

"I don't think so."

"It's awesome. Do you want me to lend it to you sometime?" Morton asked, a hopeful note in his voice.

James opened his mouth to respond but the scratching noise came again, and this time there was no doubt that it was coming from inside the old trunk.

"It can't really be a Visible Fang, can it?" James whispered, looking genuinely afraid now.

"Only one way to find out," Morton said, and without even thinking about it he stepped swiftly forward and threw the lid open. There was a sudden screech and the fierce rattle of claws scratching on wood. Morton heard

James let out a shriek and saw him fall to the floor just as a fast-moving gray blur flew out of the trunk, bounded onto James's leg, and then rushed to one of the tiny windows. Morton spun quickly around to see the creature's body silhouetted in the cracked glass. A small head with a curved body and a large fluffy tail. It was a fat gray squirrel. It chirped angrily at them before disappearing through the hole in the broken window.

"It was just a squirrel," Morton said, surprised to feel his heart pounding against his ribs.

James lay motionless on his back, his face as white as chalk. For a moment Morton couldn't interpret James's expression, then quite unexpectedly he began to laugh. Morton felt a wave of relief and started laughing too, and before he knew it, they were both rolling around on the dusty wooden floorboards, practically suffocating with laughter.

Just like the old days, Morton thought, and for the first time in months he dared to hope that things were going to get back to normal.

James finally stopped laughing and stood up. "Come on, Squirto," he said, offering his hand to Morton. "We'd better go help unpack or Dad will give us one of his long speeches about pulling our weight."

Morton grabbed on to James's hand and got to his feet.

"Hey, I know which box that Toxic Vapor Worm and Visible Fang issue is in. Do you want me to get it for you?" Morton asked as he followed James down the stairs.

"Sure," James said, "but I should get started unpacking." The two of them stepped back out onto the wide landing.

"I'll bring it to you," Morton said eagerly.

"Okay, then, but don't get lost in this big creepy house of ours," James said with a wry smile. "And look out for Kamikaze Cobras."

Morton chuckled again and sprinted to his new room at the end of the hallway. Since Morton had insisted on packing his moving boxes himself, he knew exactly what he was looking for. He quickly found the box marked SCARE SCAPE, ISSUES 200 TO 400 and ripped the tape from its lid. The familiar, comforting smell of old musty paper filled his nostrils. He pulled issue 237 from the box and was about to run from the room when he noticed something odd about the front cover. It had a shadowy illustration of a girl who looked exactly like Melissa. She was tall and skinny, with jet-black hair and dark brown, almost black, eyes. The girl was screaming, terrified of a giant centipede-like creature. Funny, Morton thought, he must have seen this cover a hundred times but never noticed the resemblance before now.

He put the lid back on the box and rushed down the hall to James's room. The door was closed, but he burst in without knocking.

"Hey, I found that issue, and it's the weirdest thing — the girl on the cover looks just like Melissa. . . ."

Morton stopped short. James was huddled in a corner over an open moving box, with his hands covering his face.

"James?" Morton asked softly.

After what seemed like too long a pause James turned around, wiping his face with his sleeve. "Oh, wow!" he said, putting on a crooked smile. "The dust in this place is out of control. Just look at me, allergies totally gone berserk!"

James's eyes were bright pink and his cheeks were wet.

"Here's that issue we talked about," Morton said, wishing suddenly that he'd knocked first.

"Oh, yeah, thanks," James said, holding the same crooked smile, and without even looking at the comic, he took it from Morton's hand and placed it on his small desk. "I'll read it later."

Morton nodded and began to shuffle awkwardly out of the room. "Yeah, I better go, uh, unpack," he said, and a moment later he was standing in the hallway with his back to the wall as an odd choking feeling seemed to envelop him.

No, not like the old days, he thought. It had been stupid of him to even think that. It would never be like the old days again.

CHAPTER 2

THE GARGOYLE

It didn't take Morton long to unpack, despite the fact that there were almost a dozen boxes in his room. In no time at all his comics were neatly stacked in numerical order on the shelf unit at the foot of his bed, and his monster toys adorned every remaining surface like specimens in a macabre museum. For years now he'd been buying toys from the back pages of *Scare Scape*, and his collection was almost complete. Two-Headed Mutant Rodents, Zombie Twins, Flesh-Eating Cockroach pods, Toxic Vapor Worms, Ten-Eyed Salamanders, Acid-Spitting Frogs, a Visible Fang. He even had a clock in the likeness of a Shark Hound that gnashed its teeth on the hour and howled at midnight on the full moon (although Dad had made Morton turn that feature off after the first month).

Morton flopped back on his bed to admire his work. It was as though he were in a parallel-universe version of his old bedroom. The comics, the toys, the furniture, even the rug was the same, and yet everything felt different. The big old Victorian house, with its jagged, cracked ceilings and peeling flakes of paint, somehow made it seem like Morton's toys, instead of being detailed and lifelike, were plastic and fake. Even the King-Crab Spiders, which he'd always thought were the most realistic of all, suddenly looked rubbery with garishly painted eyes and squishy foam bodies. Maybe that's why James had lost interest in them, he thought. The toys just didn't live up to the really cool stories in the comic. If only . . .

Morton's train of thought was interrupted by a sudden shriek from Melissa's room.

"It's not fair!" she screeched, in a voice that sounded hysterical even by her standards.

Morton decided to investigate. He found Melissa standing in her room surrounded by half-emptied suitcases of clothes and shoes, confronting a very tired-looking Dad.

"I need a room with a walk-in closet! Honestly, it's bad enough that I've lost all my friends in this stupid move, I don't see why I have to lose my walk-in closet too."

"Melissa, calm down," Dad said. "There aren't any big closets in this house."

"What do you mean there aren't any big closets?"

"They just didn't need large closets in Victorian times because they didn't have a lot of clothes."

A look of abject horror came over Melissa's face. "Then what exactly am I supposed to do?"

"Just leave your clothes in the cases for now, and we'll figure something out."

"When?" Melissa said suspiciously.

"Later," Dad said, rubbing his head wearily.

This was the wrong thing to say. Melissa's eyes became narrow slits. "Later!" she shouted, releasing several hours of pent-up anger. "It's always later with you! Nothing ever gets done. We all know you'll forget about us as soon as you start work."

"Melissa! That's not true."

"Yes, it is true! You don't care about anything except your stupid telescope and those stupid Quasi Star things you're always going on about."

"Quasars," Dad said, correcting her.

Melissa's face became as hard as stone. "See?" she said. "You're not even listening to me!" She stormed out of the room, pushing Morton angrily aside. A moment later the bathroom door slammed shut. Dad sighed heavily and scratched his head with a perplexed look on his face. Morton puffed his cheeks and gave him what he hoped was a sympathetic smile. Dad attempted to smile back, but he didn't seem happy. In fact, Morton couldn't remember Dad ever looking quite so run-down.

"I've finished unpacking," Morton said, in an attempt to brighten the mood. "Do you need help with anything?"

Dad's face softened into a half smile. "You know, there is one important job you can help me with. I'll even pay you to do it."

A few minutes later Morton found himself standing on the edge of a very overgrown lawn. Dad was filling the lawn mower with gas.

"It's going to take a lot of work to get this lawn back

into shape," Dad said. "But you'll have the honor of doing the first cut."

Morton had mowed lots of lawns over the last couple of years, which was one of the ways he'd managed to save up enough money for his monster and comic collections, but this looked more like a wild prairie than a lawn. He wasn't even sure if the small, frail-looking, gas-powered mower was up to the task. But if he knew one thing about Dad, it was that he loved his lawn. Mum had always said it was a British thing that they'd never understand, and even though Morton was sure there were more-pressing jobs, he knew a neatly mowed lawn would make Dad happy.

"Are you sure this will work?" he asked, looking at the dense knots of brambles and knee-high grass.

"Just do what you can," Dad said, heading back toward the house. "And be careful around the well."

Morton looked around and for the first time noticed a circular stone well with a winch and a rotten wooden bucket. It reminded him of a drawing he'd seen in a book of nursery rhymes. He fired up the mower and launched bravely into the long grass. The mower stalled several times at first, but he was determined to make Dad happy, so even though he was sweating and his arms began to ache, he forced himself to go on. Eventually he got the hang of it. As long as he went slowly, and kept raking away the freshly cut grass and brambles, things progressed smoothly. At least for a while. He had almost cleared all the way to the old stone well when there was a terrific clang. The motor backfired, making a sound like a gun-shot, and a filthy cloud of black smoke spewed out of the small exhaust.

He'd hit a rock. Not only that, he'd twisted the blade of the lawn mower so badly that it was poking out at an ungainly angle from beneath the wheels.

Morton saw a large gray hump half buried in the dirt. He bent down to clear away the tightly wound vines and began to uncover the object. At first it looked like a large, circular paving slab, but as he dug around it with his hands he realized it was some kind of statue. A garden ornament, perhaps? Whatever it was, it had been buried upside down in the middle of the lawn so that only its base was protruding. Morton dug more rapidly and soon unearthed what looked like a stone animal with a ghastly face and three horns sticking out of its head.

Quite suddenly James and Melissa appeared behind him.

"What the heck was that noise?" Melissa asked, all traces of her earlier tantrum vanished. She then spotted the smoking lawn mower with the twisted blade sticking out like some menacing metal claw. "Uh-oh! Dad's going to blow his top now. That lawn mower was his most prized possession. He loves it far more than he loves us, you know."

"More than he loves you, maybe," James said, winking at Morton. "What have you found, anyway? A creepy garden gnome?"

Morton brushed some dirt from the statue and took another look. It had three goatish horns; a nasty, mocking grin; and hollow but somehow penetrating eyes. It sat squatting on three stubby legs and, most curiously of all, it was holding out its left hand.

"I think it's some kind of gargoyle," he said.

"There's writing on it," Melissa pointed out.

Sure enough there was a small stone plaque gripped in the claws of one of its feet. Morton wiped the damp earth away to reveal a short stanza. They all read in silence.

> *Break a finger, make a wish,*
> *But selfish thoughts you must banish*
> *Choices made without due care*
> *Will plague forever — friend, beware!*

"Break a finger?" James said. "What does that mean?"

That's when Morton realized that the outstretched left hand was holding up three fingers, only they were so encrusted in mud that you could hardly see them. He began pulling away the clumps of mud to reveal the details of the hand. As he did so, he heard a slight cracking sound and realized that he'd broken off one of the delicate stone fingers.

"Oh no! I broke it," he said.

"Oh, cool," Melissa said glibly. "That means you get a wish. Well, you better not waste it. What do you want most in the world?"

Morton's arms and back ached from the strain of mowing the long grass, and he wasn't really in the mood to humor Melissa. "I don't know," he said, but Melissa was being strangely hyperactive.

"Quick, quick, before the magic blows away!" she teased.

Morton looked up at James, who seemed disinterested and distant.

"I guess I'd wish for my monster toys to be more realistic," Morton said, hoping Melissa would just calm down and stop being so irritating. Unfortunately she didn't.

"That's a lame wish," she said. "I've got a better one." Then, to Morton's utter amazement, she blithely reached forward and with surprisingly little effort snapped a second finger clean off.

"I want a giant walk-in closet, complete with the latest and greatest fashions," she said.

James jerked suddenly to attention. "Are you out of your mind?" he blurted, sounding genuinely annoyed. "This might be some kind of antique."

"Oh, come on," Melissa said. "It's just some ugly old statue. And anyway, Morton already broke it."

"I didn't mean to," Morton said defensively, looking guiltily down at the broken gargoyle. It now had one solitary finger remaining on its outstretched hand that pointed directly upward in what could only be described as a very rude gesture.

"But that's an act of vandalism!" James said, scowling angrily at Melissa.

"Who cares?" Melissa intoned.

"Not you, obviously," James said. "That thing might have been valuable, and now you've turned it into something obscene."

"Oh, stop being such a mummy's boy!" Melissa said mockingly.

Morton felt his breath catch in his throat.

James's face became suddenly twisted, and his eyes turned hard as glass. He looked like he was trying not to cry, and Morton thought for a moment that James might even hit Melissa.

Just then Dad emerged from the house. "What the blazes was all that noise?"

James glanced over at Dad approaching and then at the gargoyle. Without any warning he roughly pushed Melissa aside, snapped off the remaining finger, and stuffed it into his pocket.

"I'm not a mummy's boy anymore, am I?" he said in a pained, angry voice, and stormed into the house.

Melissa looked pleadingly at Morton, as if seeking forgiveness for her thoughtless slip. She opened her mouth in an attempt to speak but no words came out, just an odd croak followed by a stream of tears running over her cheeks. Then she too ran back into the house, brushing past Dad without a word.

Dad looked questioningly at Morton. "I don't suppose there's much point in me trying to talk to them," he said. "Any idea what started it?"

Morton had no desire to recount the scene. "It's nothing. Just the usual stuff," he said, hoping it would all blow over without Dad getting involved.

Dad sighed and turned his attention to the gargoyle. "Well, what have you found?" he said, crouching down to get a closer look. " 'Break a finger, make a wish.' I've never seen a statue that encourages people to break it before." Dad pointed to the three broken stumps that remained at the end of the gargoyle's hand. "Too bad somebody gave in to the temptation. Looks like a genuine stone carving."

Morton tightened his fist around the stone finger in his hand and decided not to mention their part in defacing the curious artifact.

"Looks like you did a number on my trusty old lawn mower too," Dad said with a hint of regret in his voice.

"I'm sorry," Morton said. "But it was buried and I didn't see it."

"Yes, well. My fault. I was in too much of a hurry to get my lawn under way." Dad rubbed his hand over the gargoyle. "You know, this little fellow looks like he could be part of your monster collection. Maybe we should clean him up and put him in your bedroom, what do you think?"

Morton had to agree that the gargoyle did look like it could be part of his monster menagerie, but somehow he didn't want it anywhere near his bedroom. In fact, he thought, as chills ran inexplicably down his spine, he'd be happy if he never laid eyes on it again.

"Um, no, thanks. It's not really my style," he said, hoping Dad wouldn't sense his sudden unease.

"No, I suppose not," Dad agreed. "Come on, I think we could all use a spot of lunch."

Half an hour later Morton, Melissa, and Dad sat around the kitchen table eating some strange mashed-up fishy substance on partially burned toast. James however refused to come down for lunch, insisting he wasn't hungry.

"He must still be exhausted from the trip," Dad said.

"It wouldn't be so bad if you didn't squash us into the backseat like sardines," Melissa blurted out.

"I am sorry about that," Dad replied in his best attempt to sound reasonable. "But as you know, the front air bags are dangerous for children. Remember that story in the newspaper about the child who had his head blown clean off in a supermarket car park?"

"Dad, firstly, it's a parking lot, not a car park. A car park sounds like a place where you take your car for a walk."

In spite of himself, Morton almost laughed out loud at this comment, although he didn't really like the way Melissa always teased Dad about his accent and his funny British ways.

"Secondly," Melissa went on, "*I'm* not a child; and thirdly, that never happened. It's an urban myth."

"Unbelievable as it sounds, I did see the photo," Dad said. "The child's head ended up in some poor woman's shopping basket. Quite shocking for the old lady. She never ate cabbage again, so the article said."

Melissa growled with frustration. "Dad, those aren't real newspapers. They make all that stuff up."

"In any case," Dad said, "I can't let you sit in the front until you're eighteen. Would anyone like more toast?"

Melissa pushed her plate into the middle of the table. "No, thanks," she said, and excused herself.

"Morton?" Dad said.

Morton shook his head. "No, thanks. I'm full," he said, and he too headed up to his room.

He was halfway up the stairs when it happened.

A blue pulse like a ball of lightning appeared suddenly all around him. He felt a prickling heat, as if a thousand hot needles had pierced his body, and heard a terrific throbbing drone. The drone got louder until it was almost more than he could bear and then all at once, with a fierce whiplike crack, the light and the noise exploded away from him and vanished, leaving him trembling and confused.

Before Morton even had time to react, James flung his door open and stood there, his face drained of blood and his eyes wild with shock, holding the stone finger in his hand. Morton knew at once that James had experienced the very same thing. A split second later, Melissa's door also burst open and a breathless and deathly pale Melissa looked frantically out at them.

"Did you, uh, I mean . . ." Melissa struggled for words, obviously trying to remain calm.

"A blue light?" James said.

Melissa's already wide eyes grew even wider, and she nodded silently.

Morton pulled his own stone finger from his pocket and looked at it. "You don't suppose . . . ," he began, but he couldn't really bring himself to say out loud the thought that was crystallizing in his head.

Then, quite surprisingly, Melissa's bewildered expression vanished and a look of cold anger crossed her face.

"Oh, wait a minute. Now I get it," she said. "You two are in this together. This is one of Morton's pranks, isn't it?"

James and Morton exchanged confused glances.

"Me?" Morton said. "Why do you think it has anything to do with me?"

"Because, Squirto, you're the mail-order menace around here. You've always got some ghastly trick up your sleeve. Exploding lipstick, acne-inducing soap, remote-control spiders — to name just a few that I've experienced personally."

There was no denying that Morton had played his share of pranks over the years, but it seemed obvious to him that this was not in the same league.

James obviously had the same thought. "Hold on a minute," he said. "Stink bombs and smoke pellets are one thing, but what we just experienced wasn't some cheap trick."

"I'm not stupid," Melissa said. "I should have figured it out sooner. Morton didn't dig that gargoyle up. He bought it from the back pages of his hideous comic and then pretended to find it as soon as we got here, hoping to freak me out. You two have probably been planning the whole thing for weeks."

"Melissa," James said in a pleading tone. "Try to be rational. How could Morton hide a twenty-pound stone gargoyle in the car without you or Dad seeing it?"

"I don't know, but obviously he did."

"I didn't!" Morton pleaded.

"Oh, so it's all magic is it?" Melissa said in a derisive tone. "Well, let's see," and she marched down the hall, straight into Morton's bedroom.

James and Morton followed curiously. Melissa gestured at Morton's grizzly display of toys. "If it was gargoyle magic, then Morton's toys would be more realistic, wouldn't they?" she said, grabbing a tangled handful of black rubbery eels and throwing them directly at Morton.

Morton caught the eels and looked down at them. In the comic these were the Electric Killer Eels, fearsome creatures capable of packing a six-thousand-volt charge. But these toys had smudged, poorly painted eyes and a disappointingly dim blue light in their tails that came on when you flicked a switch on their backs. There was nothing vaguely realistic about them, nor any of his other toys for that matter. Melissa had a valid point. "She's right," Morton said, feeling more confused than ever.

Melissa gave a victorious grin and turned to leave. "And I already checked my closet, which still isn't big enough for a coat hanger. So, nice try, but guess what? I'm telling Dad."

"Telling Dad?" James said. "Telling him what?"

Melissa paused in the doorway and seemed to have second thoughts. "Okay, maybe I won't bother telling him this time, but if you idiots try anything else, I'm going to make sure he grounds you both for a month."

Melissa stomped dramatically out of the room, slamming the door behind her. James and Morton exchanged befuddled glances.

"It wasn't you, was it?" James asked tentatively.

Morton shook his head. "No, I swear," he said. "I didn't do anything. I was just walking up the stairs when it happened. Did you . . . ?" Morton trailed off.

James flexed his fingers and stared at his hands in an unusual manner. "I was just lying on my bed, reading that comic you gave me. Actually, I wasn't even reading it, I was looking at the picture on the front, you know, the one with the girl who looks like Melissa."

"Maybe you made a wish," Morton said. "I mean, maybe the magic doesn't work until all three wishes have been made. I read a story like that once in *Scare Scape*, it was about this guy who —"

"But I didn't make a wish," James interrupted. I was just looking at the cover when . . ." He stopped midsentence, and for a moment a look of total horror flashed across his face.

"What is it?" Morton asked urgently.

James shook his head. "Nah! That would be stupid. I didn't make a wish. And anyway, your toys still look like plastic junk, so it can't be that, can it?"

Morton felt a little stung by James's comment about his prized collection but realized he was right.

"It's probably nothing," James added, but he didn't seem to have convinced himself, and he certainly hadn't convinced Morton. Something strange *had* happened, and Morton had an odd, guilty feeling — as though they'd opened a door to a forbidden room and released something sinister into the world.

CHAPTER 3

THE BLIND MAN

The fact that nothing unusual happened over the next few days further convinced Melissa that the boys had been playing a prank. By Friday even Morton was beginning to doubt that anything had actually happened, and slowly but surely life began to slip into a comfortable rhythm.

On the Sunday night before their first day of school, Dad reminded them that he'd be working nights on a regular basis at the Dimvale Observatory. He'd always be home at breakfast and supper though, so while there was nothing normal about his schedule, things would at least feel normal most of the time. Then the subject of babysitting came up. Morton had never liked the fact that Dad worked nights, but the one thing he, James, and Melissa agreed on was that they didn't want a babysitter. Just before the move they'd had a nanny stay with them on the nights when Dad worked. She'd been next to useless, eating all the snacks, leaving dirty dishes everywhere, and staying up late watching television with the volume turned up loud. Melissa was particularly adamant that she was too old to need a nanny and made that very clear to Dad.

"Well, I suppose I'm willing to see how things go without a nanny," he said, "but on one condition: you all agree that Melissa's in charge."

"What!" James protested. "Why her?"

"Because she's the oldest, obviously," Dad said.

"That's not fair!" James said.

"I agree," Melissa said, surprising Morton. "It's not fair. I don't see why it can't be every man for himself. I mean, James is only a couple of years younger than me, and we all know Squirto likes to live alone in his creepy alternate reality."

"That's not true!" Morton said in an outraged squeal. Although he knew he *had* been spending far too much time reading his comics lately.

"It's not up for negotiation," Dad said. "Somebody has to be the responsible party, and if you don't think you're up to it, Melissa, then a nanny it will have to be."

Melissa glowered at Morton and James as if they were her archenemies.

"Do I have to make them a bedtime snack?"

"Yes, and make sure they do their homework and get to bed on time."

Melissa pressed her lips together and pondered the situation. Morton knew this would be a difficult choice for her. Taking care of others was hardly in her nature, but for some reason she seemed to hate the idea of a nanny more than anyone.

"Fine!" Melissa snapped, after a long pause. "But I'm not singing any lullabies."

"There you go," Dad said, giving Melissa a hug that she didn't seem to want. "I knew you had it in you. Now, I start work tomorrow night, after you come home from school, so we'll treat it as a practice run. I'm sure you're going to do fine."

"Isn't tomorrow a full moon?" Morton said.

"It is, as a matter of fact," Dad said. "How do you know that?

"My Shark Hound clock. It always knows when it's the full moon."

"Oh yes, I remember that ghastly thing," Dad said. "Anyway, the full moon's not ideal for stargazing, but it will give me time to calibrate the scopes. Tomorrow night will be a sort of test run for all of us I suppose."

Morton looked over at Melissa, who was chewing her nails and gazing sullenly at the floor. He wasn't sure this plan was going to work out.

When Monday morning finally came it was warm and sunny, which Morton dared to hope was a good omen. He and James, who were in the same middle school, walked together, while Melissa, who was going to Dimvale High, went off alone in the opposite direction.

As they strolled along the wide streets, the trees glowed with flashes of fall colors in the early morning sun and Morton's spirits began to lift. James seemed to be feeling the same thing and commented several times on how nice the houses were and how great it was to walk to school without battling constant traffic.

The school was a pleasant, old brick building with tall, narrow windows and a large fenced-in yard. Morton and James arrived just as the bell was ringing and a jumble of running, screaming, laughing kids were jostling into orderly lines and shuffling in through the main entrance. Morton and James followed the crowd.

Just inside the door, a stocky man with short gray hair, a walking stick, and a clipboard was supervising the kids. Morton and James must have stuck out like sore thumbs, because the man spotted them immediately. "James and Morton Clay?" he said, limping toward them.

The two boys nodded, and the man handed them each a pile of papers that included a map of the school.

"You're in homeroom SG9 on the top floor," he said to James, "and you're in SG5, down here on the first floor," he said to Morton. "Don't worry, the school's not as big as it looks. You'll soon get used to it. If you have any questions, come and see me. I'm Mr. Brown. You'll find me in the school counselor's office, which is also marked on the map."

Morton and James both thanked the man and continued following the crowd down the hallway.

"What do you suppose the 'SG' stands for?" Morton asked.

"Smart geniuses," James said with a playful grin. "Somebody must have told them that the Clay kids are smart geniuses. Hope they don't find out the truth!"

Morton laughed. The truth was that if there were a "smart genius" class, James probably would be in it, although he'd be the last to admit it. "Well, I guess I'll see you at recess."

James nodded. "If I can find my way out of this labyrinth," he said, turning his map upside down and squinting comically.

Morton laughed again and went off to find his classroom.

Later that morning Morton's homeroom teacher, Mr. Rickets, a very distracted, bald man, showed him where his locker was and gave him a quick tour of the school, including the gym, cafeteria, and library. After that he had biology, which promised to be Morton's favorite subject because the teacher, Mr. Noble, announced there would be lots of dissections, and they spent most of the class talking about gastropod mollusks (otherwise known as slugs) and looking at different species with a large magnifying glass.

At recess Morton was very excited to tell James about Mr. Noble's class, but strangely, James was nowhere to be seen. Morton searched the school yard and even wandered through the halls past all the lockers, but there was no sign of him. That's when Morton realized that he didn't have any friends and, for the first time in his life, began to feel self-conscious. He ended up spending the whole time standing alone with his back against the wall with the uncomfortable feeling that everyone was talking about him. He was relieved when recess was over, even though the next class was math, his least favorite subject.

At lunchtime James still didn't show up, and Morton

felt a sense of panic rising from somewhere deep inside. Thoughts of the gargoyle and the strange experience with the blue light began to crowd his imagination. Even though nothing had happened for days, he couldn't shake the feeling that they'd done something wrong. And there was something about the way James had behaved when Morton asked him if he'd made a wish. . . .

"Hey, is that a *Scare Scape* bag?"

Morton turned to see a scrawny kid in a torn T-shirt and dirty jeans eyeing his schoolbag from across the yard.

"Those are limited edition," the boy continued. "Only four hundred of them ever made."

"Oh, are you a collector too?" Morton asked, walking over to the boy.

"Not really. I guess I'm the opposite of a collector. I sell stuff."

"What kind of stuff?"

"Anything I can make money on. Mostly I find old things, fix them up, and then sell them. It's crazy what people throw out. I'll give you twenty bucks for that bag. Lots of kids around here are into *Scare Scape*."

Morton shook his head. "I don't want to sell it."

"I don't blame you. It's worth at least fifty bucks. I'm Robbie Bolan, by the way," the boy said, wiping his nose on his sleeve and offering out his hand.

Morton shook Robbie's hand. "I'm Morton."

"You're new, huh?"

"Yes. We just moved here."

"I was sitting behind you in biology class this morning," Robbie said. "You really liked those slugs, huh?"

Morton grinned. "Yeah! Slugs are cool. Did you know they used to be snails that lost their shells and that most of them are vegetarian, but a few years ago they found a real flesh-eating slug called a ghost slug that eats worms? It's almost exactly like the Flesh-Eating Slugs in *Scare Scape* issue 319."

Robbie let out a sudden and surprising laugh. "It's like you know more than Mr. Noble. Are you some kind of slug fanatic?"

Morton felt his cheeks go red. He always had to remind himself not to get carried away when he was talking about obscure creatures and *Scare Scape* monsters.

Robbie obviously noticed him blushing.

"Oh, I didn't mean it like that," he said apologetically. "I think it's cool that you know about that stuff. I mean, most people spend all their time learning about what movie stars eat for breakfast and they think that's normal. Learning about rare slugs sounds much more interesting to me."

"Well, it's not just slugs," Morton said, feeling suddenly very friendly toward this Robbie character. "It's pretty much any kind of animal. Although, to be honest, I'm not really interested in the tame ones like guinea pigs."

"No, I figured being a *Scare Scape* fan, bunnies weren't really your thing," Robbie said dryly.

Morton laughed. "So you say lots of kids here are into *Scare Scape*?"

"Yeah, there's Timothy Clarke and . . ." Robbie stopped short. At that moment a tall, heavyset boy, who looked too old to be in middle school, called across the yard in a deep, hostile voice. "Hey, Robbie! You little barf bag!"

"Uh-oh, it's Wall of Noise," Robbie said, and he ran off at lightning speed, disappearing from view behind the school. The heavyset boy was flanked by two other boys, and Morton noticed that all three of them were wearing identical T-shirts, which had the words *Wall of Noise* written in jagged, migraine-inducing, fluorescent orange and green. The three of them ran around the back of the school, presumably chasing after Robbie. Once again Morton found himself standing alone in the school yard.

For the rest of the day Morton kept his eyes peeled for Robbie, wondering why exactly the "Wall of Noise" boys were after him. He finally caught sight of him running down the hall after last period.

"Hey, uh, Robbie," he called, running after him.

Robbie slowed down and looked back suspiciously at Morton.

"Oh, it's you," he said in a gravelly voice.

"I just wanted to see if you were okay," Morton said. "I mean, those guys are about three times your size, and there were three of them, so that's like nine to one, so I was a bit worried."

Morton had expected Robbie to laugh at this, but instead he just stood in total silence, staring right at him as if trying to read his mind.

"You don't look hurt, anyway," Morton said, feeling uncomfortable under Robbie's gaze.

"Nah, don't worry, those punks will never catch me," Robbie said, turning away and continuing down the hall.

Morton followed him. "Who are they anyway?" he asked.

"They're punks."

"Yeah, you already said that."

"No. I mean, they actually are punks. They have a punk band called Wall of Noise. They take themselves way too seriously, especially since the local radio station has started playing their songs. The big one, he's Brad. He failed eighth grade twice."

"Oh, that explains why he looks so old," Morton said, picking up his pace to keep up with Robbie. "But why was he chasing you?"

"It's a long story, but the short version is Brad is a moron."

By now the two boys had arrived on the street and Robbie slowed down. "Uh, where do you live?" he asked.

"On Hemlock Hill," Morton said.

"I have to go past there to get home," Robbie said. "Come on, I'll show you the shortcut."

"Great," Morton said.

A few minutes later they were rustling their way along the leafy sidewalks.

"So, do you have a lot of *Scare Scape* comics?" Robbie asked.

"Almost a full set," Morton said. "And I have nearly all the monsters too."

"You must spend a lot of money on that," Robbie said. "Those are expensive toys."

"Yeah, I do," Morton admitted. "I had to mow a lot of lawns and deliver a lot of papers to pay for it all."

"So, how long you been into *Scare Scape*?" Robbie asked.

"Well, James and I used to read it when we were younger, but it's only since . . . er . . . well, it's only recently I started to get really into it."

"Who's James?" Robbie asked.

At that moment Morton stopped dead and slapped his hand on his forehead.

"Oh no!" he groaned.

"What's wrong?" Robbie asked.

"James is my brother. I was supposed to walk home with him."

"Well, we can go back for him," Robbie said, but it turned out they didn't need to. At that very moment a voice echoed down the street and they both turned to see James clutching an enormous pile of books and running toward them.

James quickly gained on them and stood panting for a minute.

"I'm sorry," Morton said. "I didn't see you all day and I wasn't sure where you were."

"I got detention," James said, still panting. "Had to stay in at recess and lunch."

"Detention! On the first day?"

"Let me guess," Robbie said. "Mrs. Houston."

James nodded. "How did you know?"

"She likes to pick on new kids, put them in their place."

Morton introduced James and Robbie to each other, and the three of them resumed walking.

"Still, there has to be a reason," Morton inquired a moment later. "She can't just put you in detention because you're the new kid."

"We had a, uh, disagreement," James mumbled, looking sheepishly at his feet.

"Oh no," Morton groaned. James often got on the wrong side of teachers, not because he was badly behaved exactly, but because he couldn't stop himself from pointing out their mistakes. "What was it this time?"

"Mrs. Houston seems to think the full moon causes the high tide. But I told her our dad's an astronomer and he said it's not that simple. You get a high tide twice a day, but a full moon only happens once a month. So she's really talking about spring and neap tides, but even there you get a spring high tide when there's a new moon, too. I mean, that's obvious anyway."

"You didn't say that, did you?" Morton asked.

"Say what?"

"You didn't say, 'that's obvious anyway'?"

James's scratched his head and looked away. "I don't remember. I might have."

"Sounds like you got off lightly," Robbie put in. "I'd tread carefully with Mrs. Houston."

Several minutes later they arrived at the ivy-covered stone pillars that stood at either side of the driveway to 88 Hemlock Hill.

"Well, this is where we live," Morton said, slowing down.

Robbie stared in sudden amazement. "You're kidding?"

"No."

"You live here?"

"As of last week."

"Wow!" Robbie exclaimed, gazing up at the tall circular turret poking above the trees. "That's the Blind Man's house."

Morton and James looked blankly at Robbie.

"Nobody told you about the Blind Man?"

"No," Morton said, feeling a little uneasy about the tone in Robbie's voice.

"This crazy old blind guy used to live here. Rumor has it he fell into the well at the bottom of the yard and drowned."

"He drowned in the well?" James said, looking a bit uneasy himself.

"That's the story. Funny thing is, they never found his body. It's supposed to be a really deep well, leading to some underground stream. Frogmen went down and pulled out one of his shoes but that's all they found. Just a shoe.

Anyway, he vanished and they sold the house, so I'm guessing he must've drowned in the well."

Morton felt a sudden strange prickling sensation at the back of his neck. "I wish you hadn't told me that," he said.

Robbie shrugged. "Sorry, I thought everyone knew."

As they stood there a tall, skinny girl wearing a green dress and matching shoes waltzed around the corner followed by another girl in a white shirt and gray skirt carrying a tennis racquet. It took Morton a moment to realize that the first girl was Melissa. The two of them were so deep in conversation that they trotted down the driveway toward the house without even noticing the boys.

"That's weird," James said.

"What is?" Robbie asked.

"Our sister," Morton said.

"What's weird about her?"

"She only has one friend," James said. "I mean, she's so obsessed with being the most popular girl in school that she never brings home less than six friends at a time."

"It's only the first day," Morton said. "Give her time."

James shrugged. "Maybe, but I have to say, I am honestly shocked."

"Want to come in and see the house?" Morton asked, turning back to Robbie.

Robbie raised his arm and looked at an old hand-wound silver watch that flopped loosely on his wrist. "Nah, I gotta go help my mom," he replied. "Want to hang out tomorrow?"

"Yeah, definitely," Morton said.

"Right, see you in school, then." And Robbie sprinted off down the street.

James and Morton stood at the end of the driveway for a moment and looked up at their new home.

"You don't suppose that gargoyle might have belonged to the Blind Man, do you?" Morton asked.

"The thought had crossed my mind," James said.

Morton shivered involuntarily as an image of the gargoyle's hollow eyes popped into his head. He still couldn't understand why the thought of it made him feel so uneasy.

"Come on," James said, as if reading Morton's mind. "Let's try not to think about it."

When the two of them entered the kitchen a few moments later, Melissa was pouring two glasses of iced water.

"Hey, Melissa, didn't you forget something?" James said, elbowing Morton.

"I don't think so," Melissa replied, handing a glass to her new friend.

"Yeah, you did," James said. "You forgot to bring your fan club home with you."

Melissa smiled at her new friend. "Like I said, boys are so predictable."

"I think the word you're looking for is *consistent*," James said. "Boys are consistent, as opposed to girls who are illogical and fickle."

"I'm not fighting with you," Melissa said in a singsong voice.

She put the jug of water back in the fridge and sat down without offering a drink to James or Morton. James promptly opened the fridge again and made a point of glowering while he poured himself a glass.

"Anyway, you're only jealous because you're too nerdy to make any friends," Melissa said.

"People who follow you around and gaze longingly at your nail polish are not your friends," James retorted.

"And how would you know?"

Morton groaned inwardly at the mounting argument and had just decided to head up to his room when the new girl stuck her arm across the table to shake his hand. "I'm Wendy, by the way," she said.

Morton almost jumped out of his skin. Melissa's friends didn't tend to acknowledge his existence. He was the invisible younger brother. They almost never spoke to him and they certainly, under no circumstances, would ever offer to shake his hand.

He froze and looked at Melissa as if hoping for instructions.

"Well, go ahead, she's not going to bite," she prompted.

Morton was about to reach out and shake hands with Wendy when, quite suddenly, James pushed his own hand forward.

"Hi, I'm James," he said, with an unfamiliar, watery look in his eyes. This too was very strange. James usually avoided Melissa's friends like the plague. Although now that Morton thought about it, there *was* something different about Wendy. She didn't fit the standard mold. She was dressed in a plain white buttoned shirt, straight woolen gray skirt, and white socks. Her glasses made her look studious rather than fashionable, and her voice was calm and friendly. Was Melissa hanging out with a different type of girl now? Or was it just that all girls in Dimvale were like this? If this were a side effect of life in a small town, it might be a good one.

"Wendy's practically our neighbor," Melissa said. "Isn't that great?"

"Yes, it is," James said, nodding vigorously.

"Hey, does that mean you knew the guy who used to live in our house?" Morton asked, curious to find out more about Robbie's story.

"You mean the Blind Man?" Wendy said.

"Who?" Melissa asked.

"Some crazy guy who used to live here," James explained. "He fell down the well at the bottom of the yard and drowned. At least, that's the story we just heard."

Melissa pushed her glass of water away with a sudden sickly expression. "Somebody drowned in our well?"

"Yes, it's true," Wendy said.

"How do you fall down a well?" Melissa asked.

James shrugged. "He was blind. I guess he tripped."

"As a matter of fact," Wendy went on, cocking her head thoughtfully, "there was a lot of debate about that. They never found his body, and the insurance company claimed that he didn't die, that he faked his death because he was bankrupt."

"Bankrupt? That explains why the house is so run-down," Melissa said.

"Why was he bankrupt?" Morton asked, feeling that nervous prickling sensation on the back of his neck mounting.

"I guess he couldn't work after he went blind," Wendy answered.

"You mean, he wasn't always blind?"

"No. That was the real tragedy of the story. He was an artist of some kind. He used to paint, or draw, or something. I don't really know what he did."

Morton was suddenly overwhelmed by the most powerful sensation of déjà vu he'd ever had. Something about the gargoyle and this story touched a nerve, like ice cream on a rotten tooth, and yet he couldn't for the life of him figure out why.

"He was very strange," Wendy continued. "Nobody really knew him very well."

"Like, what kind of strange?" Melissa said, pulling her arms around her as if a chill breeze had entered the room.

"Well, for one thing he was nocturnal. He slept in the day and worked at night."

"That's not so odd," James said. "I mean, our dad does that. He's an astronomer."

"Yes, but what made him especially weird was that he refused to use electric lights," Wendy said, dropping her voice to a whisper. "Before he went blind you'd see him working in that round room upstairs, huddled over his desk with a large flickering candle, like something from an old Victorian painting."

"Ugh!" Melissa said. "That's the room Dad's using for his study."

"How did he go blind?" Morton asked, attempting to stay focused on the conversation despite the still overwhelming sense of déjà vu.

Wendy shrugged. "I don't know. I could ask my uncle if you want me to find out more. He works for the local library. There was a lot in the papers about the guy after he disappeared, or drowned, depending on whose story you believe."

"I don't want to know," Melissa said adamantly. "In fact, I think I'd have been happier not knowing he even existed."

"Not knowing who existed?" Dad said, appearing from the hallway wearing his slippers and bathrobe.

"Dad!" Melissa yelped as soon as she saw him. "Did you know about the freakazoid who used to live in this house?"

"Ah, that," Dad said, scratching his ear nervously. "Yes, as a matter of fact I did."

Melissa's jaw dropped open so wide Morton could see the fillings in her back teeth. "And you still bought it?" she exclaimed.

"Well, it's a gruesome story, but I don't see why it makes any difference. It's a lovely old house. It was cheap too, which doesn't hurt."

"I am never drinking water in this house again."

"Oh, come now, Melissa. The whole street has been on city water for decades. The well is just a decorative relic."

Melissa shivered visibly. "I knew this house would turn out to be haunted."

Dad sighed and shook his head. "Well, while you're indulging in superstitious self-pity, perhaps you should introduce me to your new friend."

"Hello, I'm Wendy," Wendy said, standing up to shake Dad's hand in a very formal and polite manner.

"Wonderful to meet you," Dad said.

"I should get going," Wendy sighed. "I have lots of homework."

She gathered her bag and her tennis racquet and turned to leave. "I'll see you in the morning, then, Melissa."

"I'll be there," Melissa said.

"It was very nice to meet you," Wendy said, looking James directly in the eye.

James suddenly spilled his drink over his lap and broke into an unexpected coughing fit.

"He's clumsy," Melissa said apologetically. "You get used to it after a while."

Wendy smiled. "Nice to meet you too, Morton," she said.

Morton stood up and attempted to smile. "Likewise," he said thinly.

Wendy smiled again and quickly left through the sagging screen door on the side porch. Morton felt his hands trembling and was thankful that all eyes were on James, who was still scrambling to mop up the spilled water.

"Oh, I almost forgot," Dad said as soon as Wendy was out of view. "I've been doing some decorating today, come and tell me what you think."

The three kids exchanged quizzical looks and dutifully followed Dad to the landing at the bottom of the stairs. Dad pointed proudly to a small alcove. "Look," he said.

There in the hallway was a small arched opening where you'd normally expect to see a large Ming vase or a marble bust, only Dad didn't have any vases or busts so, instead, he'd perched the fingerless gargoyle on an old oak telephone table. This was the last thing Morton wanted to see right now.

"It's perfect, don't you think? It even has lights." Dad flicked a switch at the end of the hallway and small spotlights flashed on in the alcove, casting sharp shadows on the grim stone face. Morton's chills grew stronger again.

"It's a bit early for Halloween decorations, don't you think?" Melissa said coldly.

"I thought you'd like it," Dad said, sounding a little crestfallen. "You like it, don't you, Morton?"

Morton made a weak smile and attempted to answer, but all that came out was a tremulous croaking sound.

"Of course he likes it," Melissa said obliviously. "But he doesn't count because he's a monster-loving freak. Personally I think you should throw the ugly thing away."

"I can't do that," Dad said. "It's an antique."

"I doubt it," Melissa said. "Some kid probably stole it

from a graveyard and tossed it on our lawn when he realized how ugly it was."

Dad sighed. "There's no pleasing some people. Come on. I have to go to work soon. Let's have some supper."

At that James, Melissa, and Dad wandered back into the kitchen. But Morton stood as if paralyzed, staring at the rigid face of the grizzly statue. Why did this odd, lifeless figure send chills of fear running up and down his spine? Normally he loved this sort of thing. It made no sense. But there was something . . . something at the edge of memory. . . .

Morton suddenly thought he heard whispering. He turned sharply around, but he was alone on the landing. He turned back to look into the gargoyle's tiny hollow eyes. Is that where the whispering was coming from?

He leaned closer to the gargoyle, straining to listen. An eerie shadow seemed to close in around him. Surely he was imagining things. He leaned closer still, his ear almost touching the gargoyle's cold gray lips. Yes, he was sure of it now. He *could* hear faint whispering, and it was coming from the gargoyle. Morton felt a jolt of fear flash through his body and tore himself away, running as fast as his legs would carry him into the kitchen.

He burst through the door and the others all turned to look at him in surprise.

"Is everything all right?" Dad asked.

"Fine," Morton lied. "What's for supper?"

CHAPTER 4

MONSTER MOON

It was dusk by the time they finished supper and Morton's odd sense of déjà vu had passed, although an unfamiliar grayness still seemed to be clouding his mood. He decided that what he needed was to curl up in bed and read a few *Scare Scape* comics to take his mind off things.

As soon as the dishes were cleared away Dad began racing around the house in a last-minute panic, gathering the papers and charts and piles of books he needed for his first day of work. When he was finally ready to leave, James, Morton, and Melissa felt obliged to walk him to the car and wave good-bye from the driveway.

"My number at the observatory is on the fridge if you need it," Dad said, leaning out of the driver's side window. "And failing that, you can always call Mrs. Smedley."

"Mrs. Smedley? Who's she?" Melissa said suspiciously.

"A nice lady I met who lives across the road. Her number is on the fridge too."

"Thanks, Dad, but I don't think we'll be needing any old ladies to keep an eye on us."

"It's just in case of emergencies," Dad said, then tilted his head at Morton. "And make sure this one doesn't stay up late reading those comics. Melissa, you're responsible for making sure lights are out by nine o'clock, okay?"

"Yes, Dad," Melissa droned.

"If I find any of your grades slipping, I will hire the meanest, ugliest, most unctuous babysitter in the city."

"Don't worry, Dad," James said. "We'll behave, we promise."

"Good, then I'll see you at breakfast."

Dad put the car in gear and reversed quickly up the driveway.

"What does *unctuous* mean?" Morton asked as Dad's car turned onto the street and vanished.

"It means greasy," Melissa said smugly.

"Greasy?" Morton said. "Why would Dad hire a greasy babysitter?"

"Don't listen to her," James said. "She doesn't even know how to use a dictionary."

Melissa clucked her tongue and turned to go back into the house. "Have it your own way, smarty-pants."

James and Morton turned to follow her. The house was now a dark silhouette against a dimly glowing sky. It seemed more angular and crooked than ever before, and moonlit shadows fell across the walls like a veil of black lace. Morton looked up and noticed what he thought were birds flying around the peak of the turret. Then he realized it was too dark for birds. They were bats. Morton knew there were more than a thousand species of bat in the world, and they were one of the few real animals that made a regular appearance in *Scare Scape*. They were definitely one of Morton's favorite creatures. Despite this he didn't feel as excited by them as he normally would. The cloud hanging over him was dulling everything.

As soon as they got back in the house, Morton announced that he was tired and went to bed early to read his comics. It was the first time he'd read them since they'd arrived in Dimvale. He was relieved to find that the grizzly stories about fantastical monsters, human betrayal, greed, and corruption still had the same oddly comforting effect.

All too soon Melissa burst into the room to tell him it was time to sleep.

"Okay. Squirto," she said, tugging the comic rudely from his hands, "you heard Dad's orders. Lights out."

"Can't I at least finish that story?" Morton moaned, not daring to risk grabbing the comic back for fear of creasing the pages.

In answer to the question Melissa stuffed the comic into his bedside drawer and turned off the reading lamp. A silvery moonlight fell into the room, throwing Morton's entire zoo of ghoulish creatures into a web of spidery shadows. Melissa glanced at them and shuddered before heading straight back out of the room.

"You didn't ask me if I brushed my teeth," Morton said.

"Did you brush your teeth?" she said mechanically.

Morton sighed and nodded.

"Good, now get to sleep."

"But," Morton called out, causing Melissa to pause in the doorway. "Aren't you supposed to tuck me in, or straighten my blankets or something?"

Melissa froze for a moment, her face unreadable in the angular shadows. "I'm not Mum," she said finally, and slammed the door behind her.

Morton lay in the darkness and felt a lump swell in his throat as he listened to Melissa's feet stomp off down the hall. Of course he hadn't expected her to make things any easier, but then again, he didn't really expect her to make the situation worse either, which she seemed determined to do. This was always the hardest time, he thought, the time between when the light went out and when he fell asleep. That was the real reason he'd been staying up late reading. It was much easier to fall asleep reading than it was to lie awake thinking.

A moment later Morton's bedroom door creaked open again and the familiar silhouette of James's uncombed head bobbed in the doorway.

"Hey, Squirto, did Mel-zilla tuck you in okay?"

"It could have been worse," Morton said dryly. "At least she didn't stick chewing gum in my hair or bite me."

James chuckled and came to sit on the side of Morton's bed. "That bad, huh?"

Morton made an exaggerated shrug. "No point complaining about tigers."

"What does that mean?" James said, cocking his head to one side.

"I read it in *Scare Scape*. If a tiger was chasing you in the jungle, you wouldn't stop and complain that you were being chased by a tiger. You'd keep running, because everybody knows tigers can't help but be tigers. Nothing you can do to change it."

"And Melissas will be Melissas," James said. "That's pretty good advice . . . from a comic."

"It's like I keep trying to tell everybody," Morton said. "It's not just about monsters."

"No, just mostly," James said, glancing over his shoulder at the shelves cluttered with monster toys. "I still don't understand why these things don't give you nightmares."

Morton shrugged again. He'd never had a nightmare. He'd dreamed about the stories in *Scare Scape* lots of times but they never frightened him. He began to wonder if that was normal.

"Well, sweet dreams anyway," James said, leaving Morton to his thoughts.

"You too," Morton replied, rolling over and pulling his duvet up around his chin.

He had no idea what time it was when something jarred him wide awake. He'd heard a noise. Or had he dreamed a noise? He looked around. The full moon had now vanished behind a thick blanket of clouds, and the room was almost completely dark and deathly silent. He could hear nothing but the whoosh of his own pulse in his ears. It must have been a dream, he thought. But as he was about to roll over and go back to sleep he did hear a sound. He heard a deep growling from beside his bed. Morton recognized it at once. It was his Shark Hound clock. The batteries must be dying, he thought, because he was sure he'd turned off the night mode. Morton fumbled for his reading light but, in his drowsy state, knocked it to the hardwood floor. The bulb popped like a glass balloon. Morton sighed and climbed out of bed and began groping his way along the wall trying to locate the light switch. At last he found it and flicked it on. The intense light blinded him for a second, and he threw his hands over his eyes until they adjusted to the glare.

Nothing could have prepared him for what he saw next. His heart lurched as if someone had just whacked him in the chest with a fairground mallet.

His room was full of all manner of slimy, spiny, wriggly, toothy, twitching beasts. No more plastic toys. No more limp, rubbery replicas. No more fake painted eyes. The creatures before him looked sinewy, muscular, and powerful. He could see the Visible Fang's organs pulsing in its abdomen, he could see the King-Crab Spiders' eyes swiveling around in their sockets, he could see the Electric Killer Eels writhing around in hypnotic knots. They weren't just realistic — somehow, impossibly, they were completely and utterly real.

A loud howl made Morton spin around. It was the Shark Hound clock again. Its teeth were gnashing and its gums frothing and Morton noticed that he could now see a hairy wolf's neck where before there had been only the sharklike face. Then, quite suddenly, a paw emerged from behind the rim of the clock. The Shark Hound was still being born, still being dragged into existence.

He then realized that most of the creatures were in some state of awakening. They were stretching or flexing their limbs as if recovering from a long sleep. The magic of his wish — for that was surely what had brought them to life — hadn't yet fully taken effect. They were vulncrable!

In a flash Morton dashed over to his closet and pulled out a pile of pillowcases. With his heart hammering in his chest he began grasping the creatures with his bare hands, stuffing them into the cases and tying the tops. He quickly filled up all the pillowcases he had, but still wasn't finished. The Zombie Twins, the Gristle Grunts, the Toxic Vapor Worms, a clutch of Two-Headed Mutant Rodents, and several others still remained.

Suddenly the door burst open. A surprisingly calm but nonetheless wide-eyed Melissa stood in her nightgown breathing heavily. Morton was sure she was about to scream, but instead she just said, "You too?" in a thin, tremulous voice.

Morton stared at her. "You mean your wish . . ."

Melissa nodded. "My closet. It's, uh, well, bigger."

At that moment the Shark Hound let out a piercing howl and, with a ferocious effort, dragged a fully formed body completely free of the clockface and leaped onto the bedroom floor. This time Melissa did scream. Morton wasted no time in throwing his duvet over the vicious shark-toothed dog, wrapping it into a tight bundle before it had time to attack.

"What are we going to do?" Melissa gasped.

Morton squeezed his eyes shut, forcing his mind to focus. He knew the thin cotton cases would do nothing to contain the monsters when they were fully awakened. They needed something stronger.

"The attic!" he yelled. "We need a trunk from the attic!"

Morton practically flew down the hall and skidded around the corner to the attic door. The stairs now vanished into utter blackness above and the light switch still did nothing. Melissa appeared behind him. "The light doesn't work?" she asked, glancing nervously over his shoulder.

"Wait here," Morton said, and bravely fumbled his way up the stairs until he reached the top landing. The attic beyond was a dark void. His skin puckered with goose bumps and his legs began to tremble. "I am afraid of nothing," he whispered to himself, and then, feeling his courage return, he inched steadily forward into the swallowing darkness, using memory more than sight. At last he grasped what he was sure was one of the leather handles of the trunk and dragged it across the floor toward the narrow staircase, where light spilled from the hallway below. He was halfway down the stairs when he heard James's voice.

"What the heck is going on?"

James appeared at the bottom of the stairs wearing his tartan robe and stared up at Morton. James's hair was flying wildly above his head and his eyes squinted in confusion.

"It's the wishes," Morton blurted as he dragged the trunk right past him without pausing.

He burst into his bedroom and immediately hoisted the now writhing and twisting pillowcases into the large trunk.

James and Melissa followed him and stood in the door. "You gotta be kidding me," James said, frozen to the spot.

Morton wiped sweat from his forehead as he grabbed the rolled-up Shark Hound and stuffed it into the trunk before slamming the lid firmly. "It's definitely the wishes," Morton said breathlessly. "Only it must be dark magic, because I wished for more realistic toys, not living monsters."

"You gotta be kidding me," James repeated.

"It's no joke," Melissa whined, barely holding on to her sanity. "My closet's bigger too. Actually, it's not just bigger. It's, well, it's not natural."

"You gotta be kidding me," James said a third time, with a completely blank expression on his face.

Morton and Melissa exchanged glances. James was in shock. To Morton's complete surprise Melissa slapped James hard across the cheek. James stumbled backward and began panting fiercely. He looked around as if waking from a dream.

"Whoa! Sorry," James said. "I just . . . I thought I was dreaming." He looked around at the partially wrecked room, then he looked at Morton with an expression of awe. "You single-handedly captured all these monsters?"

Morton was about to explain that they weren't fully alive yet when he noticed a broken pane of glass in his window and realized that the Zombie Twins and several of the others had vanished while he'd been in the attic. "Oh no!" he said. "The Zombie Twins! They got away."

"The Zombie Twins?" Melissa said. "Who are they?"

"They're the smartest ones," Morton groaned. "They're like the ringleaders of the monster world."

"You mean those little floating guys with the skull faces?" James said. "They look harmless enough. I mean, they don't have deadly venom or sharp teeth or claws or anything."

Morton was shaking his head vehemently. "Don't you remember? They can control all the other monsters with their minds. They got away with the Vapor Worms and Gristle Grunts and . . ." Morton groaned again. "This is *not* good!"

"Well, you get the medal for the understatement of the evening," Melissa said. "But how about we worry about the Zombie Twins later and figure out what to do with this trunk now."

Melissa had a point. The whole time they'd been talking, the scraping and growling noises from inside the trunk were growing steadily louder. It wouldn't be long before they scratched right through the soft wood paneling.

"Any suggestions?" James said.

"You didn't use your wish yet," Melissa said. "You can wish the monsters away."

"Uh, I don't know . . . ," James said, glancing sheepishly around the room.

"What do you mean you don't know? Where's the third finger?"

James pulled the finger from his bathrobe pocket and clasped it in his palm.

"Well, what are you waiting for?" Melissa yelled above the increasing din.

James swallowed hard and closed his eyes. "Okay," he said. "I wish Morton's monsters would vanish forever."

Nothing happened. If anything, the gurgling growls from within the trunk got even louder.

"What's wrong?" Melissa said frantically. "Why isn't it working?"

Morton knew. He'd known it from the moment the strange blue light had pulsed through their bodies, and he knew that James knew too.

"James already made his wish," Morton whispered. "Right before that blue light, didn't you, James?"

"I . . . I don't know," James said, clutching his head.

"What do you mean?" Melissa screeched, panic getting the better of her. "How can you not know?"

"I was, uh . . . I don't know, I was thinking about something and that's when the blue light happened and I sort of wondered if I'd made a wish, but I —"

"You what? What the heck did you wish for?"

"I don't know!" James snapped. "And now is not the time to discuss it. We have more pressing matters."

A series of loud snarls flared up, and the trunk began to rattle visibly.

Melissa clearly saw the sense in James's argument and backed down. "Okay, let's drag the trunk outside and burn it," she said coldly.

"That's no good," Morton explained. "Half of the monsters are fire resistant, and some of them give off toxic fumes."

"Then we need to contain them," James said. "At least for a bit longer. How about the basement?"

Melissa shook her head. "They'd find a way out in minutes."

"Oh, wait! Of course!" Morton said.

"What?"

"Melissa's closet!"

"What? Don't even think about it," Melissa snapped with surprising vehemence. "That's my closet, and I don't want it made into a petting zoo for your toothy little flesh-eating pals."

"Melissa! What do you want us to do, dump them at a bus stop?" James pleaded.

"Doesn't anybody have any explosives or something?"

"Oh, let me check my pockets," James said. "Darn, nothing there. Oh, wait! I think I have a few sticks of dynamite in my pencil case. . . ."

"For once in your life will you be serious!" Melissa screamed.

"Of course we don't have any explosives," James barked back. "You think because we're boys we have bottles of nitroglycerin tucked under our beds?"

Melissa didn't have time to respond. There was a sudden splitting sound as a pair of vicious, miniature fangs gnawed a small hole in the side of the trunk. A mouse-size cockroach with razor-sharp teeth and a spiny brown back crawled out.

"What in the devil's name is that?" Melissa said.

"Looks like a cockroach," James said, grabbing Morton's baseball bat from beside his bed.

"Flesh-Eating Cockroach," Morton confirmed. "There's a whole pod of them in there."

"A pod?" Melissa said in an accusing tone. "How many in a pod?"

Morton swallowed, feeling suddenly very guilty about his fascination for gruesome toys. "Hundreds."

Melissa glared murderously at Morton, but the cockroach leaped for her foot, causing her to yelp and dive onto the bed.

James swatted at the oversize insect with the baseball bat and missed. He tried again, but the creature was too small and too fast.

Melissa grabbed a large dictionary from Morton's bedside shelf and bounded down, squashing the bug with one fierce movement. It made a sickening crunch.

"You see," she said, smiling proudly. "I do know how to use a dictionary."

"We don't have much time," Morton said, looking at the hole in the side of the trunk.

"Okay, let's get it in the closet," James said, starting to push the trunk back out into the hall.

"No way!" Melissa yelled, hefting her full weight against the trunk and pushing back in the opposite direction.

"Melissa!" James said in a pleading voice. "Now is not the time to argue."

James pushed on the trunk again.

Melissa pushed back even harder.

"No!" she said, stamping her foot angrily. "This is Morton's stupid wish, and I am not taking responsibility for it. My whole life I have had to put up with brothers who like toy monsters and stupid comics. My whole life I have had to play along with what you want because there's two of you and only one of me. No way am I going to sit back and let you ruin the one truly awesome thing I ever got."

Morton clutched his head and began to groan in frustration. "Do we have to argue about this now?"

There was another splitting sound and suddenly two more giant cockroaches wriggled out of the tiny hole in the side of the trunk. One nipped Melissa on the ankle.

"Ouch! Why, the nasty, filthy little . . ."

Melissa grabbed the dictionary again and started swatting, while James attacked with the bat. This time they each got one of the roaches. A thick yellow and green ooze spewed out of their fat broken bodies like runny toothpaste.

Several more cockroaches scrambled out of the hole, each nibbling the sides of the trunk to make the opening a little larger.

"Here they come!" Morton whimpered.

Melissa and James began swatting fiercely, but no sooner had they squashed one giant insect than two more leaped out. Morton grabbed one of his shoes and joined in the swatting, but within minutes dozens of roaches were running in the hallway, biting at everyone's ankles.

"Forget this," Melissa said at last, dropping the dictionary and storming off to the other end of the hallway.

"Hey, where are you going?" James yelled in protest, but Melissa didn't even glance back.

Morton dropped his shoe and grabbed the dictionary, which turned out to be a much better weapon. But because of the sheer numbers of snapping, biting cockroaches, he kept getting bitten on the hands and wrists, and blood was soon dribbling down his fingers.

"There's too many," James shouted. "We're going to have to run for it."

Indeed it was starting to look hopeless. There were more than fifty cockroaches scuttling in the hallway now, and they were pouring out of the small hole so fast they looked like brown, lumpy liquid.

Just as James and Morton were about to drop their weapons and run, they heard a voice behind them.

"Stand back, boys. I'll handle this."

Melissa stood there wearing safety glasses and head-phones, sporting the power head to the old 1950s Hoover that had been in the family for generations. The saucer-shaped vacuum cleaner was plugged in and ready to go. James and Morton took cover behind Morton's bedroom door as Melissa fired up the antique appliance. It whirred like a defunct jet engine. The power head puffed out dust as the rotating brushes gathered speed and the body began to vibrate. Melissa moved in for the kill. She pushed the power head into the crawling carpet of cockroaches with awesome and horrific results. The rotating brushes cracked the roaches' hard, brittle exoskeletons and pulverized their soft inner bodies. The doomed insects shrieked, almost in harmony with the vacuum cleaner. They ran to escape, but Melissa was surprisingly fast. None managed to get past her. A viscous yellow blood boiled out of the pipe and sprayed from the motor. Melissa's face and arms were spat-tered, and she looked like she was playing a losing game of paintball. But the attack was working. Within a few short moments the last of the vile insects jumped out of the trunk to meet its turbulent end.

Melissa pulled off her headphones and glasses. "We need to block up the hole before something bigger gets out."

James and Morton began to search the house. Morton ran around aimlessly and found himself in Melissa's room. The only thing he could see was a collection of dolls perched on the back of her dresser. There were three of them — two smaller, slender dolls and one oversize baby doll with fat arms and a grotesquely large head. These were, Morton knew, the only remnants of a childhood Melissa now pretended she hadn't had. He grabbed the larger doll and, without really thinking about it, pulled its head clean off. He ran out to Mclissa in the hall, brandishing the find. Melissa snatched the pink hairy lump of plastic and was about to stick it in the hole when she recognized it. Morton braced himself for an explosive outburst, but to his surprise she just blinked at the object.

"Oh. That used to be Mandy," she said. A wave of sadness washed momentarily over her face and then was gone. A grim resolve returned, and she stuffed the perfectly sized stump of Mandy's neck into the hole.

"Now, no more arguments," James said. "It goes in the closet."

Melissa snorted angrily through her nose. "Fine!" she said.

Morton breathed a sigh of relief, grabbed one of the thick leather handles, and began pulling the trunk back toward Melissa's bedroom. Melissa reluctantly joined in and pushed from the other side.

They slowed as they approached Melissa's closet.

"Hold on," she said. "I'll open the door, just, uh, just make sure you don't faint."

James made a scoffing noise and reached for the door.

"No, seriously," Melissa said. "I fainted the first time."

James and Melissa exchanged glances and James stepped aside to let her open the door. Morton took several deep breaths. He had no idea what to expect. Very slowly Melissa pulled the door open and allowed them to peer inside. At first Morton couldn't understand what he was seeing. It was like looking at an optical illusion, or one of those three-dimensional drawings. But then reality came into abrupt focus. What he saw was not so much a closet but an artificial landscape. An immense chamber opened out and stretched off into the distance as far as his eyes could see. The entire space was crowded with racks and shelves and thousands upon thousands of hangers all stocked with brand-new clothing. It was like some surreal department store, arranged in narrow, impossibly long, corridors. Racks of dresses, shirts, skirts, pants, shoes, underwear, coats, and, off in the middle distance, endless displays of purses and accessories went on forever. Morton felt his head spinning. James obviously felt something similar because he grabbed on to Morton's shoulder for support. "How . . . how big is it?" he stammered.

"I don't know," Melissa said. "I walked as far as I could and turned back after half an hour."

"You found this half an hour ago?" James exclaimed.

"Almost an hour ago, actually. But it's harmless, right?" Melissa said in a pleading sort of way. "I mean, it's just clothes."

James shook his head. "I don't think it's going to be that simple. Morton didn't wish for his toys to come alive, did he? He wished for them to be more realistic. Obviously this magic twists things."

Melissa looked at Morton questioningly, as if he were some kind of expert. Morton just shook his head. He might have spent hundreds of hours reading horror comics and stories about dark magic, but this was completely different. This was the real thing. "Maybe," Morton said. "I mean, the magic didn't work until tonight, so I'm guessing that's because of the full moon."

"What does that mean?" Melissa said.

"Well, according to the stories I've read, it means the magic is very old, from a time when people worshipped the moon and the stars."

"Does that make it dark magic?"

"It usually involves some kind of human or animal sacrifice, so I guess you'd call that dark magic."

Morton and Melissa glanced involuntarily at James. They'd both obviously just had the same thought. What exactly was still in store from James's wish?

"Come on," James said, turning away from them. "Let's get rid of this thing."

"Where exactly are we going to put it?" Morton asked, looking at the vast wilderness of clothing ahead of him.

"As far from the door as we can," Melissa said. "I don't want them chewing their way back into my bedroom."

"Good point," Morton said.

They pushed the trunk into the closet and continued pushing for at least twenty minutes. Morton was the first to slow down. The fatigue of the night's events was finally getting to him. His whole body began to tremble. "I can't . . . I can't go any farther," he said.

Melissa and James stood up and stretched their aching backs. James looked around at the hundreds of aisles leading off in all directions like paths in an infinitely complex maze.

"You could get lost in here," James said.

"Easily," Melissa said. "You better follow me out."

Back in Melissa's room they moved Melissa's dresser up against the closet door to make doubly sure nothing escaped, and then they all flopped on her bed utterly exhausted.

"We'll have to do a search of the house," Morton said.

"What, for the Zombie Twins?" James asked.

"No. They'll be gone for sure."

"What exactly is the deal with these Zombie Twins?" Melissa asked.

"Most of the monsters are just like any other animal," Morton explained. "They're pretty much just interested in eating things. But the Zombie Twins are a lot more intelligent and they can control animals using psychic powers."

"You mean monsters, or animals?" James asked.

"There's no difference. They'll control whatever suits their purpose."

"So they're out there right now controlling the monsters that got away?"

"Definitely."

"I can't even begin to imagine what Dad's going to say," James said.

"We're not telling Dad!" Melissa said vehemently. "In fact, we're not telling anybody."

"Oh, and why is that?" James said. "I suppose you want to keep your infinite supply of clothing all to yourself."

"That's not it at all," Melissa said. "Well, not entirely anyway. Think about it. Here we are, barely in town for a week and already we've unleashed a plague of unimaginably hideous monsters. How do you suppose the locals are going to react to that? For all you know they'll lynch us or burn us at the stake for witchcraft."

"I'm with Melissa," Morton said. "What would Dad think if he knew what I'd wished for?"

"He already knows you're crazy," Melissa said flatly.

"Melissa!" James said. "That's not fair."

"The truth is never fair," she said unapologetically.

Morton swallowed hard. How could he argue with her? Would any sane person really have made the wish he did?

James sighed heavily. "Look," he said. "It's getting late. We'll agree not to say anything to anyone for now. But that means we'll have to clean up and, like Morton says, do a thorough search of the house for stray monsters."

To Morton's surprise Melissa agreed without so much as a breath of argument. No doubt she was as tired as he was.

For the next two hours they scoured every inch of the house, checking each and every shadowy corner and dark place. Morton found a few Flesh-Eating Slugs, which were easily disposed of down the toilet, and James had a near fatal encounter with the deadly Kamikaze Cobra, which explodes when cornered. Fortunately Morton came to the rescue and easily outwitted it by shaking a bag of rice to charm it and then chopped its head off with a meat cleaver before it could self-destruct. Aside from that, the house was all clear.

"Well, look on the bright side," James said as they stood in the living room. "Things can't get any worse, can they?"

Morton didn't say anything. He was thinking about the verse that had been carved into the gargoyle. "Selfish thoughts you must banish," it had said. He realized with a sinking feeling that both he and Melissa had made utterly selfish and vain wishes. If the stories he'd read in *Scare Scape* were anything to go by, then that sort of behavior usually spelled disaster. Things probably were going to get worse, he thought. A lot worse.

CHAPTER 5

THE HOUSE OF KING

Morton awoke to the sounds of Dad and Melissa talking downstairs. Wearily he dragged himself out of bed and fumbled into his clothes, buttoning his shirt crookedly twice before getting it right. His whole body ached from the struggles of the night before, and his head felt as if it were full of sawdust.

When he arrived at breakfast he learned that Dad had returned to find all the lights on and Melissa fast asleep on the couch. She claimed to have fallen asleep doing homework.

"What happened to your promise about lights out by nine?" Dad was saying as Morton sat down and helped himself to cereal.

"Dad, you didn't literally mean turn the lights out, did you?" Melissa said. "You just meant go to sleep. It just so happens I went to sleep on the couch — with all the lights on."

"She *was* doing her homework," Morton said, coming to her defense.

Dad looked suspiciously back and forth between Morton and Melissa.

At that moment James appeared at the door, his face deathly white with heavy black shadows under his eyes.

"Good morning," Dad said. "You look a little pale. Are you feeling all right?"

"Yes, I'm fine," James replied, "but I can't find any clean socks."

"Oh yes. Sorry about that," Dad said. "I seem to have broken the washing machine. Too much soap I think. You can borrow a pair of mine if you like."

"Uh, no, thanks," James said. "I'll just wear an old pair."

"I'll tell you what I'll do," Dad went on. "I'll drop the laundry off at Mrs. Smedley's this afternoon. She said she'd help out if we needed anything."

"What?" Melissa said, her eyes widening with horror. "You can't give our dirty laundry to some old bat we haven't even met."

"Please don't call her an 'old bat,'" Dad said in a reprimanding tone. "It's not polite. And anyway, I really don't understand why you have a problem with it."

"Well, it's . . . it's just not right is it? It's personal," Melissa stammered.

"I don't see what's personal about James's smelly socks," Dad said.

"Melissa means we should be doing our own laundry," Morton interjected.

Dad frowned. "I don't think Melissa even knows what a washing machine looks like."

"Of course I do," she snapped. "It's that white thing next to the oven."

"That's actually the dishwasher," Dad said, "but kudos for trying."

Melissa growled. "Well, anyway, Morton's right. It's not fair to ask that old . . . uh, *nice* old lady to do our laundry. From now on we'll do our own, even if we have to take it to the Laundromat."

Dad looked taken aback. "Well, that would be a big help. If you're sure . . ."

"We are," Melissa stated firmly.

"We are?" James said, still looking sleepy and confused.

"Very well, we'll see how it goes," Dad said, and he sat down to join them for breakfast.

At exactly eight thirty, the three kids sauntered off down the driveway together, smiling and waving to Dad as if everything were absolutely normal.

"What was all that about?" James said once they were out of earshot. "I don't want to do my own laundry."

"Oh, never mind that now," Melissa replied. "We've got more important things to worry about, like keeping an eye out for stray monsters."

"That's right," Morton said. "Especially the Zombie Twins."

"I don't even know what the Zombie Twins look like," Melissa said.

"They're really short, like about up to my knees," Morton said. "They have white skull faces with glowing red eyes and they always wear long brown cloaks, so you can't see their feet. Actually, I don't think they even have feet, they just kind of hover."

"Cute!" Melissa said. "I can't wait to meet them."

As they reached the end of the driveway, Morton spotted Wendy waiting on the street. She waved eagerly when she saw them.

"Good morning!" she called.

"If we're going to be friends," Melissa said, approaching Wendy, "there's one thing you have to learn: There's no such thing as a *good* morning, and that's doubly true today."

"Hi, James. Hi, Morton," Wendy said with a glowing smile.

James suddenly began straightening his unruly hair with his hands. "Uh, hi," he said in an unusually high-pitched voice.

Morton grabbed James by the elbow and dragged him off toward school. He seemed to be acting very strangely.

First period was biology again with Mr. Noble. Morton spotted Robbie sitting at one of the long tables near the back and went over to join him.

"Are you okay?" Robbie asked as Morton approached.

"What do you mean?"

"You look like you haven't slept in a year."

"Oh, uh, I was just lying awake thinking about stuff, I guess."

"Well, I know how that is. I lie awake at night all the time. Especially when —"

"Okay, everybody, settle down," Mr. Noble cut in. "Today we have a fun assignment."

Mr. Noble produced a large Styrofoam cooler box and placed it on the desk dramatically. "Today," he continued, "everybody gets to dissect a cow's eyeball."

The class suddenly erupted into a peal of shouts, both of excitement and revulsion. Cries of "Ew!" and "Gross!" were perfectly balanced by calls of "Cool!" and "Awesome!"

"Oh, great," Morton said. "That's all I need this morning."

"What?" Robbie said in a surprised voice. "I thought you loved this stuff?"

"Well, normally I would, but after last night . . . I mean, well, I'm just tired."

"Then this is perfect," Robbie replied. "It will stop you from falling asleep. Trust me. It's the classes where you have to listen to some teacher droning on that are the real killers."

"I suppose so," Morton sighed, and it turned out that Robbie was right. For the next hour they had the best possible time slicing up the gelatinous cow eyes. Robbie proved to be a whiz with a scalpel, and of course Morton knew all the names for the various parts of the eyeball, like the retina, the cornea, and even the aqueous and the vitreous humors. Mr. Noble was so impressed that he gave them both top marks, even though they spent more time laughing and making silly squelching noises than anyone else.

They were still laughing when they got to their lockers at lunchtime. Morton was stuffing his oversize biology textbook onto the top shelf of his locker when somebody slammed the door on his back so hard that he fell right inside. Mocking laughter echoed down the hallway. Morton struggled to his feet in time to see Brad, Sid, and Dave striding away from them making rude gestures.

"Hey, Robbie," Brad called. "Looks like your new buddy can't stand up for himself."

Robbie made a rude gesture in return, but Brad had already turned his back.

"Sorry about that," Robbie said, picking up Morton's books.

"Why are you sorry?" Morton said. "It's not your fault those guys are jerks."

"Yeah, but it's me they hate. They'd leave you alone if you weren't hanging out with me."

"Why do they pick on you anyway?" Morton asked.

"They think I steal stuff," Robbie said solemnly. "Everybody thinks I steal stuff."

Morton wasn't really surprised to hear this. Robbie had a certain look about him. His clothes were wrinkled and his hands were always dirty, but Morton had read enough stories in *Scare Scape* about kids from the wrong side of the tracks to know that you couldn't tell anything about people from the way they dressed. According to what he'd read, it was all in the eyes.

"Do you steal stuff?" Morton asked bluntly.

"Of course not! But that doesn't seem to matter. Every time anything gets stolen, like phones or watches or lunch money, Brad and the others go and tell Principal Finch. Every single time they say it was me, but I never stole anything, ever!"

As Robbie said this he looked directly at Morton with a clear, steady gaze, and Morton decided then and there that he must be telling the truth.

"Well, why don't you tell the principal that they're just trying to cause trouble?" Morton suggested.

"You don't know Finch," Robbie scoffed. "All he cares about is how his school looks in the end-of-year report. 'If someone files a complaint, I have to look into it,' he always says. And then he calls my mom and, well, it makes a lot of trouble."

"That's horrible," Morton said.

"That's my life," Robbie said, looking down at his feet. "You might as well know now that nobody trusts me in this school. So, you know, if you want to stop hanging out with me, I'll understand."

Morton felt very sad and angry at the same time. "I'm not going to let some fuzzy-faced overgrown punk singer tell me who to be friends with," he said defiantly. "In fact, I was going to ask if you wanted to come to our house for supper tonight."

"Really?" Robbie said, his face lighting up.

"Yeah."

"I'd like to see the inside of your house," Robbie said, "but I can't come for supper because I have to do chores. Maybe after supper? I could bring a pie. Mom bakes pies all the time."

"Sure," Morton said. "Actually it's probably safer that way. Dad's cooking isn't so great. It takes a while to get used to it."

"Your dad cooks?" Robbie asked in surprise.

"If you can call it cooking," Morton said. "I take it your dad never cooks, then?"

Robbie's light demeanor changed in an instant. His face went pale, and he just sort of shook his head.

"Uh, my dad's uh, not . . . He's not . . ."

Morton recognized the emotion at once and felt suddenly horribly insensitive.

"Oh no! I'm so sorry. That was stupid of me. I should have . . ." Morton stammered for words. "Look, I know how you feel. Our mum died last year and . . . well, there's nothing you can say, is there? I mean, I know what you're going through."

Robbie looked up at Morton. "I didn't know about your mom. I'm sorry."

"I'm sorry about your dad too," Morton replied, and neither of them said any more about it.

It wasn't until last period that fatigue from the strange events of the night before came back with a vengeance.

The history teacher, it turned out, was Mr. Brown, the heavyset man with short gray hair and a walking stick who had handed out welcome packages on Morton's first day of school.

At the beginning of the lesson Morton thought he was going to really enjoy Mr. Brown's class. He was friendly and managed to get everyone laughing a number of times by telling corny jokes. Unfortunately he had a bad habit of reading enormous sections from the textbook out loud, and Morton found himself repeatedly drifting into sleep. He pinched himself to stay awake and tried breathing deeply, but nothing seemed to work. As the class progressed he slid lower in his chair and began to feel as though somebody had tied lead weights to his eyelids.

The next thing he knew the whole class was laughing at him. His eyes fluttered open, and he found his face stuck to the oak desk in a puddle of drool. Mr. Brown was shaking his shoulder.

Morton sat up and wiped his face with his sleeve. Every eye in the classroom was on him.

"Really, young man, is my class that boring?"

"Yes, sir — I mean, no, sir, of course not."

Everyone laughed again.

"You're Morton Clay, the new boy, aren't you?"

"Yes, sir."

"Well, Morton, I think you better stay behind after class so we can have a word. All right?"

"Yes, sir," Morton said somberly.

When class was dismissed Morton waited until everyone else had left before sauntering up to Mr. Brown's desk. Butterflies fluttered nervously in his stomach. Mr. Brown pulled up a chair and asked him to sit. He turned his own chair around so that he was sitting on it backward and folded his arms on the back.

"Morton," he said in a friendly tone, "I know you didn't really fall asleep just because my class is boring, did you?"

Morton thought for a moment and had to admit that he didn't fall asleep *just* because the class was boring, he fell asleep because he hadn't slept all night *and* because the class was boring. He decided not to share this insight and simply said, "No, sir."

"No, of course not. That much is obvious. You see, Morton, as you know, I'm not just the history teacher, I'm also the guidance counselor. You can come to me anytime you like with any problems you might be having at home or in school."

"Any problems, sir?"

"Yes. And anything you say to me will be in the strictest confidence. Usually if a kid is falling asleep in class, then he's not sleeping at night. And if he's not sleeping, then we know there's something not right, don't we?"

"Uh, yes, sir."

"So what's wrong in Morton's world?"

Morton's head suddenly swarmed with images of Acid-Spitting Frogs, Toxic Vapor Worms, and Zombie Twins roaming the streets of Dimvale.

"It's nothing really, sir, honest," he said. "We just moved here, so I guess we haven't settled in yet."

"Still unpacking boxes, eh?"

"Yes, sir."

"What about those strange cuts on your wrists?" Mr. Brown said, keeping his tone even.

Morton quickly pulled his sleeves down over his hands. He'd forgotten about the tooth marks from the giant cockroaches. "Oh, I was helping my dad clear the garden. It's all overgrown with raspberry bushes. I should have worn gloves."

"Really? That's nice of you to help your dad. Do you like gardening?"

"I mow lawns to earn extra allowance."

"That's very impressive. We don't get all that many entrepreneurial kids these days. Where is this new house of yours anyway?"

"It's a big old house on Hemlock Hill. Victorian, I think. Needs a bit of work."

Mr. Brown, who had been smiling sympathetically up to this point, frowned and shuffled uncomfortably in his chair.

"You don't mean the old King house?"

Morton felt an odd jolt at the mention of the name.

"Uh, I think a blind man owned it before. I don't know his name."

Mr. Brown sat up straight and began to rub his chin. "Yes, that's him, John King."

Morton felt another jolt, only this time he realized why. The name was familiar to him. A wave of adrenaline raced through his veins and his fatigue vanished instantly. Surely it couldn't be . . .

"Was there anything else, sir?" Morton prompted, suddenly eager to get home.

"No, I think we're good," Mr. Brown said, smiling. "We'll just keep an eye on you, shall we?"

Morton didn't like the idea of anyone keeping an eye on him — it made him feel like an insect in a jar, but he smiled and nodded.

"See you next class, bright eyed and bushy tailed."

Morton ran quickly out of the classroom with an increased sense of foreboding. An idea was forming in his mind, and he didn't like the shape of it at all.

He ran all the way home and was sweating fiercely by the time he burst into the kitchen. Without pausing even for a second he raced up to his room, grabbed a handful of *Scare Scape* comics, and took them down to the kitchen to scour through them.

Melissa walked in and saw him flipping pages rapidly.

"Morton! Aren't you cured of those things? I mean honestly, give it a break!"

"I'm doing research," Morton hissed.

"Research?"

"I knew there was something familiar about the Blind Man's story," Morton went on, feeling more anxious by the second. "I'd heard it before, and then when I found out his name was John King, it all made sense."

"It all makes sense?" Melissa said incredulously.

"Well, no, but . . . just hold on!" Morton continued scanning through the comics furiously.

"What's going on?" James said, appearing at the door beside Melissa and dropping his schoolbag to the floor.

"Morton, sibling of sin, is losing his marbles."

Morton ignored Melissa and kept flicking through the comics. At last he found what he was looking for.

"It's here! I was right. This is it."

James and Melissa stared at him blankly. "Look," he said, showing them the introduction to what appeared to be a special edition of *Scare Scape*. There was a fuzzy black-and-white picture of a grizzled old man with an immense mop of greasy gray hair. He was wearing dark, circular sunglasses, a dirty striped shirt with rolled-up sleeves, and an old black waistcoat. "Don't you see? John King was the Blind Man."

"John King?" Melissa said.

"Just listen," he said, and read the entire editorial out loud.

"King of Scare"
The John King Commemorative Edition
Beast Meisters, Weirding Women, and fellow Scare Scapers the world over have mourned with us the loss of our greatest and grimmest King of Scare, the late John King. No

doubt you, like our staff, cried tears of blood when you learned that the once great and gloomy artist and writer had died in a tragic accident on the grounds of his private creepy mansion in the isolated town of Dimvale.

We all remember King's classic covers from issues 275 through to 347 as the glory days of Scare. Indeed, King's ultra-realistic style and unforgiving depictions of gore and ghastliness are what made him the readers' favorite cover artist. In fact, it was you, dear readers, who by sending letters flooding in like locusts in praise of his raw (and bloody) talent forced us to give King his own strip: King's Disturbing Things.

The strip's varied and harried tales of demonic deceit, pestilent plunder, and murderous madness was the raven feather in our creepy cap for six hideous years. Most famous for his tireless research into the lost dark arts, King brought an unwelcome touch of credibility to the horror fantasy realm.

Sadly, all bad things must come to an end, and, as you know, two years ago King lost his sight in an undiagnosed illness. Unable to work, King's black heart was broken. Now, he has left us forever to join his fellow corpses in the underworld.

Please join us on a commiserative, commemorative trip down a memory-haunted lane as we present you with this humble and horrible special collector's edition of some of King's favorite, most fiendish works.

John, we salute your bones and dance reverently on your grave.

The King is dead. Long live the King.
The Editors and Staff. Scare Scape.

PS: Look out for more reruns of King's top terror tales in our regular comic, starting next week.

As soon as Morton finished reading, Melissa snatched the comic from his grasp and squinted in disbelief at the fuzzy picture. At last she placed the comic on the counter. Her hands were trembling.

"Is this a coincidence?" she asked, the tremor in her hands spilling over into her voice.

"It can't be," James said. "It's exactly what Wendy said. He was some kind of artist who went blind."

"But what about the gargoyle?" Melissa said. "Did he have something to do with that?"

"Had to," James said. "I mean, someone who devotes his whole life to writing about dark magic and monsters lived here, and then we find a magic gargoyle, and Morton's monsters, monsters right out of this very comic, come to life. . . . It can't be coincidence."

"This is terrible," Melissa said. "I mean, this King character was a sick man."

"No, he wasn't," Morton protested. "He was really smart."

"Oh, come on, Morton. Grow up!" Melissa snapped. "Tears of blood? Dancing on graves? What kind of a twisted kid are you? It's sick. You're sick!"

"Whoa! Calm down," James said, stepping between Melissa and Morton. "Yelling is not going to get us out of this mess."

"No, but it makes me feel better about being in it," Melissa retorted.

"This is a good thing," Morton said, feeling strangely exhilarated by the idea of not only living in King's house but also somehow getting pulled into his life. "You heard what it said. King did lots of research. Everything he wrote or drew was based on something real. That's why the house looked so familiar to me. King used it for inspiration. I've seen drawings of different parts of this house all over the comic."

"How is that a good thing?" Melissa said.

"Because it means we might find some kind of clue in the comic about how to reverse the wishes."

"I don't know about that," James said. "From what I remember none of the stories end happily."

"That's only because the people in the stories do the wrong thing," Morton explained, eager to convince them.

"Yes, well, we've done the wrong thing," Melissa said. "We've made selfish wishes, so we're probably doomed."

"But we can still look for clues. If King knew anything about the gargoyle, I'm sure he would have put something in one of his comics."

"This isn't one of your stupid stories, Morton," Melissa said coldly. "This is real, and real life doesn't have simple comic book solutions."

Morton clenched his teeth angrily. "Do you have a better idea?"

After a moment's tense silence James spoke up. "Morton has a point," he said. "There might be some clues in there."

"What? I will not read that vile garbage!" Melissa stated firmly.

"Nobody's asking you to," James said. "Morton and I will go through them. How many comics do you have, Morton?"

"Thousands, but only four hundred or so with King strips."

"Four hundred!" James exclaimed.

Morton nodded. "And there are two King strips, Disturbing Things and Night Terrors. Night Terrors didn't start until later, so I think it's about seven hundred stories in total."

James whistled. "That's going to take longer than I thought. Bearing in mind we still have to do homework. Let's see, if we each read three stories a night, that's going to take . . ."

"Months," Melissa said flatly. "If we up it to five stories a night each and I join in, we can do it in seven weeks."

"You're right," James said, after a minute of counting fingers. "But I thought you weren't going to go anywhere near Morton's vile comic."

Melissa pressed her lips together. "It looks like I don't have a choice," she said. "As always, having brothers is going to completely ruin my life."

CHAPTER 6

A DARK DESSERT

An unusual tension hung over the table at suppertime. Morton was eager to begin rereading back issues of *Scare Scape* and, for the first time all day, dared to feel optimistic, but the others seemed somehow glum and reticent, which Dad noticed at once.

"What a cheery lot," he said, dishing out his version of spaghetti and meatballs. "Is everything okay at school?"

"Oh, we're just tired," Melissa said. "We were up so late with Morton's —"

"Card game!" James cut in before Melissa could finish.

"Ah, so now the truth comes out," Dad said. "Which card game is this?"

"The Monster Tarot," Morton said, thinking quickly. "It's really cool."

"Melissa was playing with Morton's monster cards?" Dad said, eyeing them all suspiciously.

Melissa bit her lip and nodded unconvincingly.

"This game wouldn't have anything to do with the broken window in Morton's bedroom, would it?" Dad asked casually.

Everyone exchanged nervous glances. They'd cleaned up most of the mess but had forgotten about the broken window.

"I think it was already broken when we arrived," Morton said, choking on a meatball.

"Or maybe kids are still throwing stones at the house," Melissa said. "Kids always throw stones at abandoned houses."

"Hmm!" Dad said, rubbing his beard. "I'm also trying to figure out what happened to the vacuum cleaner. It was full of some kind of sticky goo. Took me ages to clean it out. Was that something to do with your game?"

This time Morton coughed a rubbery meatball right back out onto his plate.

"Must have been the movers," Melissa said. "I bet they spilled some eggs or something and vacuumed them up. You know how movers are: all muscle and no brain."

"Perhaps," Dad said. "In any case, let's make sure you all get to bed nice and early tonight, shall we?"

"We will," Melissa said earnestly.

A few minutes later Dad put on his tie, grabbed his phonebook-size stack of papers, and went to kiss each of his children on the forehead. Melissa, who thought she was too old to be kissed, turned away at the last minute so that Dad ended up kissing her ear.

"Dad!" she exclaimed, wiping her ear with her sleeve.

"Sorry. Perhaps you'd prefer it if I kissed your feet."

"Gross!" Melissa said.

Dad smiled at Melissa, even though she was looking at him in disgust. "Remember," he said, "best behavior or you get an unctuous babysitter." He waved a finger playfully. "No falling asleep on the couch."

As soon as the car drove away Melissa turned to face James.

"I don't suppose you've figured out what your wish is, have you?" she said harshly.

"No, I haven't," James said defiantly, and Morton noticed that he started rubbing his hands again.

Melissa snorted. "I can't believe you wasted your wish on something and you don't even know what it was."

"Wasted?" James said. "You don't think a giant closet is a waste of a wish?"

"Actually, no, I don't," Melissa said, blowing the hair out of her eyes in the way she did when she was angry, which was most of the time. "Anyway, aren't we supposed to be reading these stupid comics?" she said.

Morton was about to protest and insist once again that they weren't stupid when the doorbell rang.

James answered it. "Are you expecting a pie delivery?" he called out from the porch.

Morton turned to see Robbie standing in the doorway holding a small cardboard box. With everything that had happened he'd completely forgotten that he'd invited him over.

"Sorry I'm late," Robbie said. "Mom insisted on baking a fresh pie. Said a housewarming present had to be warm."

"Real pie!" Melissa said enthusiastically. "As in, pie not made by Dad. How completely awesome. I think there's some ice cream hidden in the basement freezer too," she added, sounding happier than she'd sounded since they'd arrived in Dimvale.

"Come in," Morton said. "This is my sister, Melissa."

"Hi," Robbie said, waving nervously at Melissa.

"I'll get the ice cream," James said.

A few minutes later they were all seated around the table just about to cut into the pie when the doorbell rang again. Everyone turned to see Wendy waving through the screen door. "Hope I'm not interrupting," she said.

"Perfect timing!" Melissa said, practically dragging Wendy into the house. "I was outnumbered three to one."

Wendy was wearing a white T-shirt and jeans. Her hair hung loosely down her back, and she must have been wearing contact lenses because she didn't have her glasses. Morton noticed that James began shuffling nervously in his seat and tucked in his shirt. "Five for pie, then," he said.

Morton remembered that they had a bottle of cream soda in the fridge and poured five glasses and then dished out generous helpings of ice cream. He stopped, however, when he got to the pie. "How do you cut it into five equal pieces?" he asked, scratching his head.

"Oh, that's a geometry puzzle," James said, dragging the pie to his side of the table. "I can solve that. Let me think."

Wendy shuffled in beside James. "You need a compass," she said.

"I don't think so," James said. "I seem to remember there's a way to do it by first —"

"Sorry. You two will just have to get your own pie later," Melissa said, grabbing the knife from James's hand and roughly cutting the pie into six. "We'll fight over the extra piece."

James and Wendy exchanged glances. "I guess not everyone likes geometry," she said, putting her hand on his arm and laughing.

Melissa squinted her eyes threateningly at James, but he was too busy staring at Wendy to notice.

Everyone tucked in happily to the pie, which was delicious. James, Morton, and Melissa in particular ate like hungry animals.

"Does your dad feed you at all?" Wendy asked.

"Oh, he feeds us," Melissa said, wiping ice cream from her chin, "but whether what he feeds us could be called food is up for debate."

"Yeah. It starts out as food," Morton added, "but it's usually just gray goo by the time it gets onto the plate."

"Suffice it to say, this pie is the best thing we've eaten in months," James said, raising his glass of cream soda. "I propose a toast to Robbie's mother."

Everyone lifted their glasses. "To Robbie's mom," they all said, and clinked glasses and giggled. Robbie blushed and smiled so broadly that he looked like a different person altogether. Morton wondered if Robbie had any close friends. He suspected not.

"So this is the Blind Man's house?" Robbie said a few minutes later, as everyone was finishing up their pie. "It's not as creepy as I thought it would be."

"You should have been here last night," Melissa whispered under her breath.

James elbowed Melissa hard, causing a piece of pie to fall off her fork.

"I suppose once you swap all the furniture out, it's just a normal house," Wendy said brightly. "It was the owner that was creepy."

"Was he always creepy, or did he just get strange after he went blind?" James asked.

"Actually, I think he was creepier *before* he went blind," Wendy said. "At night you'd always see him pacing up and down in that round room in the turret, talking to himself or sitting at his desk, working away in the candlelight. After he went blind we never even saw him. The house was always dark, but you knew he was in here, wandering around alone."

"I know something really weird about him," Robbie said, leaning forward and glancing around nervously as if King himself might still be listening.

James, who now seemed to be sitting even closer to Wendy, sighed. "Doesn't anybody know any happy stories about him?" he said.

Robbie and Wendy, who obviously knew more about his reputation than they were letting on, exchanged glances.

"Well, come on. Out with it," Melissa said, somewhat

surprisingly. "I'm sure we'll hear all the creepy stories about him sooner or later."

"Not this story," Robbie said. "This is something that never came up in the papers. It's something only a few people know." Robbie's voice dropped to just above a whisper. "My mom's a cook for the hospital, and she knows the guy who buys all the meat. Now get this, he told her that one time the old man bought five black piglets from him. He said they had to be black and they had to be alive!"

"I don't get it," Melissa said. "What would anyone want black piglets for? Do they taste better than pink piglets? Is there some kind of black-piglet pie recipe or something?"

Morton clutched his head. "Melissa!" he said. "Everybody knows that black pigs are sacrificed in dark rituals."

Melissa rolled her eyes. "Everybody named Morton, maybe."

"You think he was involved in dark magic?" James asked.

Robbie nodded. "I'd heard rumors about it before, but when Mom told me about the pigs, it sort of clinched it."

"What kind of rumors?" Melissa said.

"Well, apparently he collected old books on dark magic. He used to go to auctions and spend huge amounts of money on them."

"Where did he get his money?" Melissa asked.

"He was a successful artist, remember," Wendy said. "And it's not just a rumor about the books. My uncle works at the library, and the Blind Man was always coming in looking for anything to do with dark magic, even *after* he went blind. He said he needed them for his work, but honestly, who ever heard of a job where you need books on dark magic?"

Morton, Melissa, and James exchanged glances. They at least knew the answer to that question.

Robbie pulled in his shoulders and looked around nervously. "He didn't scratch any magic symbols on the floor or anything like that did he?"

"Not that we know of," James said, "but that doesn't mean he didn't. I mean, it's not something you usually see advertised, is it? Four-bedroom house with two baths en suite, and a fine collection of dark magic symbols."

Everyone laughed, especially Wendy.

James laughed even louder at his own joke and was about to say something else when he quite unexpectedly let out a huge belch. It was so loud that Wendy jumped.

"Oooh! Pardon me," James said, covering his mouth with his hand.

Everybody laughed again, except Morton. There was something about the expression on James's face that didn't seem funny.

"It must be the . . ."

Morton thought James was about to say "cream soda," but instead "CRRUUURP!" was all that came out. James took several deep breaths. "I'm sorry. What did your mom put in this pie, Robbie?"

"Don't blame the pie," Wendy said, coming to the pie's defense.

"I'm just kidding," James said. "I don't normally BRRRAAAARRARRRUP!"

This time nobody laughed. This was possibly the loudest belch anybody in the room had ever heard. Melissa too now looked shaken, and her eyes found Morton's from across the table. "That sounded painful," she said.

James went bright red with embarrassment. Wendy was now staring at him with a look of concern on her face.

"Excuse me, I better go to the BRAAARUPthroom! Sorry, again, something BAAARP! funny with the BRAAARP soda!"

James practically ran out of the kitchen, belching three more times before darting upstairs and locking himself in the bathroom.

The four remaining kids sat in shocked silence at the table. Morton had an unpleasant panicky feeling and decided he'd better go and check on James.

"I'll just see if he's okay," he said, and dashed up the stairs after him.

He stood outside the bathroom door and was about to knock when he heard a loud gurgling sound followed by another ear-splitting belch. A moment later a cloud of thick yellow smoke billowed from under the door and an acrid smell bit into his nostrils. Panic shot through Morton's chest like a spear, and he had a sudden urge to bash the door down. If something happened to James . . .

"James! James!" he yelled, pounding wildly on the door.

He heard another groan and felt his own stomach tighten into a ball. An image of James lying unconscious on the bathroom floor popped into his head, and he pounded even harder.

Then, finally, James spoke up. "Just a minute," he said, in a surprisingly calm tone and a moment later he flung open the door and smiled at Morton as if nothing had happened. Morton's fear gave way to embarrassment.

"What just happened?" he said, feeling an incredible sense of relief to see James smiling.

"It's nothing," James said. "Cream soda doesn't agree with me, that's all."

Morton looked searchingly into James's eyes. Yes, he was smiling, but there was something there that didn't feel right. And Morton was sure he could see a faint yellow haze in the bathroom, but the small square window was open and the acrid smell, whatever it was, had vanished.

The two of them returned to the kitchen and James tried to settle back into the conversation, but the mood had been broken and everyone was thinking about getting home.

Morton couldn't help noticing that as James waved good-bye to their guests, he began flexing his fingers and rubbing his hands yet again.

CHAPTER 7

THE CAT BURGLAR

The next week or so felt almost, though not entirely, normal. The biggest change appeared to be in Melissa's mood. She knuckled down earnestly to the comic reading research, often exceeding her quota of five stories a night and even admitting, to Morton's great surprise, that the stories weren't as horrible as she'd expected. "They're quite insightful," she said, "in a ghastly, drowning-in-blood kind of way."

They were all sleeping better too, although Morton thought he'd heard James wandering around after bedtime on more than one occasion. And there had been no sign of the stray monsters. In fact, the only person who laid eyes on any of Morton's monsters was Melissa, who despite James's pleading, insisted on venturing into her magical closet to find new outfits every morning. Nothing could keep her from boldly storming in, baseball bat in hand, to stake her "rightful claim to stylish booty." Some things, she insisted, were worth fighting for.

It wasn't until Friday, almost two weeks after the monsters came alive, that things began to shift again. Melissa appeared at breakfast looking unusually disheveled. Though she wore a dramatic red silk top, tight pin-striped skirt, and expensive-looking pumps, her hair was bedraggled and her face was covered in black streaks.

"I think they're breeding," she said casually.

James spilled his glass of milk, and Morton dropped his spoon under the table.

"What do you mean they're breeding?" James yelped.

"Come on now, James. You know all about the birds and the bees. They're, you know . . ."

James shook his head, as if obstinately refusing to imagine what Melissa was suggesting.

"How do you know?" Morton asked, trying to decipher her exact meaning.

"There's more of them, that's how I know. After they chewed their way out of that old trunk, I'd only ever see one every few days. But now there are swarms of them."

Morton hadn't even considered the possibility that the monsters might reproduce and had a sudden foolish urge to go exploring in Melissa's closet to see for himself. "So how many are there now?" he asked.

"Oh, I don't know. I didn't take a census. Two hundred, at least."

"What?" James exclaimed. "Then why, in the name of sanity, do you still go in there?"

"Oh, don't worry about me. They're frightened of me now. They keep well away."

"Then what's with all the marks on your face?"

"Well, a few of them still don't know who's boss. A Dragon Fly came at me this morning. I wasn't ready for that."

"That still doesn't explain the marks."

"*Dragon* Fly. You know, the breathing-fire kind of dragon."

"Oh. I didn't know Morton had one of those."

"I had two," Morton said.

"Not anymore," Melissa said, smiling proudly.

Dad appeared carrying his mug of tea.

"What an earth happened to your face?" he said at once, looking at Melissa.

"Oh, it's just toast."

"Toast? What were you doing, wrestling with it?"

"You know me, Dad. I like to kill my breakfast and eat it while it's still twitching," Melissa said with a sinister smile.

Morton decided the comics were going to her head.

The real development happened later that morning when James and Morton were walking to school, arguing about whether or not John King was evil.

"Let's look at the facts," James said. "King spent all his time reading about dark magic or writing horror stories. He practiced animal sacrifice and refused to work in daylight. He lived alone in a run-down house and ended up drowning in his own well. It's pretty obvious he was a twisted lunatic."

Morton refused to believe that King was anything other than a genius but realized he didn't have any concrete reasons for thinking that. "But everyone knows King's stories are the best," he said. "And even Melissa admitted that they were insightful."

"Look, Morton, you're an optimist. You always see the best in people, and that's a good thing most of the time, but in this case it's not. King was as cracked as a crater on the moon."

Morton puffed his cheeks and was about to disagree when James stopped suddenly in his tracks.

"Morton," he said, "does anything strike you as odd about the street?"

Morton looked up and saw at once what James was referring to. Every tree and telephone pole for as far as the eye could see had a poster on it. "That's strange," he said. "Is it some kind of festival?"

James walked up to the nearest poster and read it aloud.

LOST. TABITHA. GINGER CAT.
LOVES SARDINES.
PLEASE CALL RACHEL AT 555-2789.

He pulled the poster off, walked up to another tree, and read a second poster.

HAVE YOU SEEN MY BOBBLES?
PERSIAN BLUE.
FRIGHTENED OF TRAFFIC.
GENEROUS REWARD.

Morton crossed the road to find more of the same.

MISSING CAT. ANSWERS TO TIBBITS.
LOST ONE EAR IN FIGHT. PLEASE CALL
555-1750.

Morton began to get that familiar tingling of excited fear that always accompanied a good *Scare Scape* story. James crossed over to join him, now holding several posters in his hand.

"What do you suppose this means?" James asked.

Morton could think of only one explanation. "It has to be the Zombie Twins."

"You think the Zombie Twins are eating the town's cats?" James exclaimed.

"Not eating them," Morton said, surprised by the suggestion. "The Zombie Twins are clever, remember? They control animals' minds and get them to do whatever they want."

"Oh," James said in a dismayed voice. "Why would they want to control cats?"

Morton shrugged. He didn't know. The Zombie Twins always behaved mysteriously in the comic. It was never easy to figure out their motives. He would need to do more research.

As they continued on their way to school they saw more posters. Some were printed with color photos, many were written in pen or permanent marker, one was even hand painted on watercolor paper with a lovely picture of a distinguished-looking black-and-white cat by the name of Count Claw. By the time they reached the school gates James and Morton counted more than forty different posters.

And they weren't the only ones to notice. The whole school yard was buzzing with the news. Several kids had posters to give out and the rest were just chattering excitedly.

"Hey, Morton," Timothy Clarke said, running up to them as they came through the gates. Timmy was in the same grade as Morton, and was also a big *Scare Scape* fan. In fact, he'd asked Morton a lot of questions about how to order merchandise by mail order, and today he wore a new King-Crab Spider T-shirt and was bubbling with excitement. "Guess what? Somebody's stealing cats. It's really cool."

"Cool?" Morton said, confused by Timmy's apparent joy.

"Yeah, it's cool because Finchy . . ." Timmy paused and cast a sudden nervous glance up at James. "I mean, uh, Principal Finch, says the police are coming to ask us all questions after lunch. Which means no classes this afternoon!"

Morton practically choked on his own tongue at the mention of the police but managed to lock his face into a grin. "Oh, that's great," he said, and was relieved when Timmy ran off to continue spreading the gleeful news about canceled classes to the rest of the school.

Morton turned to look at James, who was licking his dry lips nervously.

"Oh no," Morton said gloomily. "What if the police find out about my wish?"

"That's crazy talk," James said, almost as if he was trying to convince himself. "There's no way anyone could figure out that this has anything to do with you. I mean the police are looking for a person, aren't they? They're not looking for, well . . ."

"Zombie Twins," Morton said.

"Exactly. They're not looking for Zombie Twins."

Morton didn't feel very comforted by James's words but decided he better go find Robbie to see if he knew anything more about the situation. As he wandered across the school yard he couldn't help but overhear all the other kids debating the pros and cons of the missing cats. Most of the boys were ecstatic about the possibility of canceled classes, while most of the girls were indignant that the boys could be so insensitive about the suffering of the missing cats.

Strangely Robbie was nowhere to be seen. By the time the bell rang, Morton still hadn't found him. It wasn't until lunchtime that he saw him leaning up against the wall just inside the school yard, folding his arms across his chest in an uncharacteristic manner.

"Robbie, I've been looking for you all morning," Morton said.

"Why?" Robbie said in a sullen, unfriendly voice.

"What's wrong?" Morton asked.

"It's those stupid cats!" Robbie blurted out, his voice cracking slightly.

"Did you lose a cat too?"

"I don't have a cat! I hate cats! It's everybody else who's lost their cats."

"Huh? I don't understand. . . ." Morton then noticed something strange. "What's wrong with your shirt?"

Robbie turned around and showed Morton that his button-down shirt no longer had any buttons.

"Brad and his butt-head buddies cornered me this morning on the way to school. They said I stole the cats."

"That's ridiculous!" Morton said, outraged. "Why would they say something so stupid? Who'd want to steal cats?"

"Well, obviously somebody is stealing them."

"No, nobody's stealing them, it's . . ." Morton managed to stop himself. This would be so much easier if he could just tell Robbie the truth. "Look, it doesn't matter. Who cares what they say?"

"You don't get it do you? They're going to say I stole the cats, and then the police are going to come to my house and start asking questions. And then Mom's going to get all upset again, and, ugh!" Robbie punched the wall hard, scuffing his knuckles on the coarse bricks. "Ouch!" He quickly rubbed his fist with his other hand.

"Now *you're* being stupid," Morton said, trying to snap him out of it. "The police are more likely to suspect a gang of kids, like Brad and his buddies, than a lone kid like you. You can't seriously think they're going to suspect you. I mean that's . . . well, it's silly, isn't it?"

Morton chuckled, hoping to make light of the situation.

"You still don't get it!" Robbie shouted, red-faced. "Of course you think it's *silly* because you live in a big, expensive house, on an expensive street, and your dad is like a scientist. People like you never get in trouble. But me and my mom, it's just the two of us in our tiny house with no money. It's always people like us that steal things. Didn't anybody tell you that?"

Robbie stormed off, leaving Morton speechless and confused. He hadn't expected this at all.

The day didn't improve any from that point onward. The normal functioning of the school was completely upset by the arrival of the police. Classes were not canceled, as the rumors had implied, but they might as well have been. The police set up interview rooms in two of the staff offices and every five minutes one of the hall monitors would come into class and call a student's name. Each student would disappear for about ten minutes or so. Naturally every time someone returned everyone else wanted to know what he or she had said and a squall of whispers filled the room. The teacher would spend the next few minutes getting everyone quieted down only to have the cycle repeat again. It was impossible to get any work done.

Morton's call came in the middle of Mrs. Punjab's math class. A tall hall monitor, with ebony skin and long braids, poked her head in the door, consulting her list.

"Morton Clay," she called out.

Morton felt his mouth go dry. He pushed his chair back slowly and, with trembling legs, followed the girl out of the classroom and down the hall. He was terrified. What would the people of Dimvale do if they found out he had unleashed a host of demonic creatures into their idyllic little town?

The girl led Morton to a frosted glass doorway that said STAFF ONLY. Morton paused at the threshold. He'd never been into the staff area of a school before.

"Come on, they won't bite," the monitor said.

Morton entered a comfortably furnished reception room with several offices leading from it. One of the office doors was open and, to Morton's surprise, the friendly face of Mr. Brown was smiling down at him.

"Young Mister Clay," Mr. Brown said in a playful voice that instantly put Morton at ease. "Come in."

Morton went into the room.

A fierce-looking woman wearing a blue police officer's uniform was sitting behind the desk. Her face was pale and hard, and her hair was pulled back in a tight bun. The room itself looked to be an unused office. The walls were lined with bare bookshelves that were scattered with paper clips and thumb tacks. A couple of ancient, torn posters about the dangers of train tracks and the importance of personal hygiene were the only indications that anyone had ever used the office at all.

The police officer shuffled papers for a moment before acknowledging Morton.

"Morton Clay?" she said at last with a quick professional smile.

Morton nodded.

"Take a seat."

Mr. Brown pulled out a padded chair with wooden arms and gestured for Morton to sit. "Inspector Sharpe is going to ask you a few questions," he explained. "If that's all right with you?"

"Uh, sure," Morton said, his tongue feeling like a lump of leather in his mouth.

"Of course, you're under no obligation to answer any of these questions," Mr. Brown added, "and I'm here to make sure you're comfortable with the whole process."

Morton felt somewhat reassured. It was nice to know that Mr. Brown stood between him and the severe-looking Inspector Sharpe.

"Morton," Inspector Sharpe began, "I'm sure you understand the seriousness of what's happening in Dimvale."

"You mean the disappearing cats?" Morton said.

"Yes. Have you had any pets go missing?"

"No, miss, I mean, uh, Inspector."

"Do you have any pets?"

The image of Melissa's closet crawling with ravenous mythical monsters popped unbidden into Morton's head. He froze for a moment, his mouth open.

"No," he managed at last.

Inspector Sharpe frowned. "You don't seem very certain about that."

Morton wished he'd practiced lying more. "Well, I mean, I used to have, uh, mice, but we lost them in the move."

"Morton and his brother, James, just moved to Dimvale," Mr. Brown explained from the corner of the room. "We know it's never easy starting out in a new town, so we're doing our best to get them settled comfortably, aren't we, Morton?"

Morton forced a smile. He found this a very odd thing to say. As far as he could tell nobody was doing anything to help them settle in, but he decided to nod politely.

"Have you seen anything strange recently?" Inspector Sharpe continued.

"Strange?" Morton said, raising his eyebrows innocently.

"Any people prowling around the neighborhood? Any vehicles you don't recognize? Anything at all that just seems odd?"

Morton could feel beads of sweat forming on his forehead, and he knew that if Sharpe was any good at her job she'd know that he was lying.

"No, I haven't seen anything odd. Everything's very normal. Super normal, I'd say."

The inspector glanced up at Mr. Brown, who was scratching his nose. They didn't believe him.

"It's okay," Mr. Brown said, "no need to get nervous. Nobody thinks you had anything to do with it. Whoever or whatever is doing this —"

"Whatever?" Morton blurted out, failing to mask a note of panic.

"Yes. It's quite possible it's not people doing this," Mr. Brown added.

"Wha . . . What do you mean?" Morton stammered.

"It could be a pack of wolves or hyenas or even a lynx. Only nobody's seen any wolves, so that seems unlikely. We definitely don't think a lone fifth grader is behind all of this."

"What's most worrying to us," Inspector Sharpe added, "is that several of the cats have been reported as taken from inside their homes. Which suggests these are organized thefts. Since they're not just taking cats off the streets, they would have to know in advance who owns one. Has anybody approached you to find out if you have any pets?"

"Only you," Morton said, noting that this was the first completely truthful answer he'd given so far.

Inspector Sharpe sighed heavily and began shuffling papers again. She pulled out a new file and opened it. Morton saw her cast a quick glance at Mr. Brown. Mr. Brown returned an almost imperceptible nod.

"So, Morton, I understand that you're friends with Robert Bolan," Sharpe said.

Morton's stomach lurched like a ship in a storm. "Robbie's got nothing to do with it," he said defensively.

"Nobody is saying he does," Mr. Brown said in a calming voice.

"But that's not true, is it?" Morton said, feeling outraged on Robbie's behalf. "I mean, you're not asking me if I know Timothy Clarke or Phillip Ferguson or that hall monitor who brought me here, are you? No, you're asking about Robbie. Just because he can't afford to buy nice clothes and he doesn't get good grades you assume he's got something to do with it."

"Morton, Morton, calm down," Mr. Brown said, putting his hand on his shoulder. "You're taking this the wrong way. We're trying to help Robbie."

"Robbie has nothing to do with this! I know he doesn't," Morton said firmly.

"How could you know?" Inspector Sharpe said, pouncing on Morton's words.

Morton felt a lump in his throat that was half anger, half fear. This wasn't how things were supposed to go at all. Nothing like this ever happened in *Scare Scape* stories, and Morton had no idea what to do. The only thing he could think of was to get out of the room as quickly as possible.

"You said I don't have to answer any questions if I don't want to," he said. "Well, I'm not going to answer any questions about Robbie."

Inspector Sharpe looked directly at Morton and tapped her pen slowly on the side of her coffee cup.

After what felt like a long time Morton stood up. "So, can I go?"

Mr. Brown put his hand on Morton's shoulder again, only this time there was an air of restraint to the gesture.

"Morton, think about this for a moment. By not answering questions about Robbie you're going to throw suspicion on him."

"I'm not doing anything!" Morton protested.

"Inaction has its consequences. If, as you say, Robbie has nothing to do with this, then you should answer the questions."

"I already said he has nothing to do with it, didn't I?"

"How would you know?" Inspector Sharpe asked again. "How can you be so sure?"

"It's ridiculous. What would Robbie, or anybody, want with a hundred cats?"

"Money, of course," Sharpe explained. "It's happened before in other towns. People will pay reasonable rewards for the return of their cats. The finder's reward is between twenty and a hundred dollars. The pure breeds can go even higher. If you estimate it out to about thirty-five dollars, multiply that by three hundred cats, you have more than ten thousand dollars. It's big business. People love their cats, Morton."

"You're saying that Robbie is running a business kidnapping cats?"

"Not necessarily Robbie. But someone."

"Well, it isn't him. He's my friend, okay? We see each other every day. We talk about stuff. If he was kidnapping cats, believe me, I'd know!"

"Morton," Mr. Brown said softly, "we know Robbie is your friend, and we hope he has nothing to do with this. But you have to understand, the inspector here has to make these inquiries because Robbie does have all the attributes of a potential suspect."

"Potential suspect? What do you mean?"

"Because of his record," Mr. Brown put in.

Morton had a sudden sick feeling in the pit of his stomach. "You're talking about Robbie like he's a criminal."

Mr. Brown and Inspector Sharpe exchanged small frowns.

"I'm sorry, we presumed you knew," Mr. Brown said.

Morton felt as if everything in the room had gone suddenly still. If there had been a clock, he was sure it would have stopped ticking. "What are you talking about?"

"Robbie stole more than a thousand dollars from the school safe. It was money that had been raised for the school library at the summer fair."

"That's not true!" Morton yelled out loud, surprising himself. "It's just a rumor started by Brad and his stupid band."

"Brad Evans?" Mr. Brown said.

"And his buddies. They spread lies about Robbie all the time. He never says anything about it because . . ."

Morton tapered off. Come to think of it, why exactly did Robbie never tell Mr. Brown about the problems he was having with Brad?

"I'm sorry, Morton," Mr. Brown said with a sad expression. "Robbie confessed to stealing the money. He spent six months in a correctional school."

Morton's confusion suddenly gave way to a bitter sense of betrayal. Could he have been wrong about Robbie? Could Robbie have lied to him? Tears welled up in the corners of his eyes, and he clenched his jaw angrily in an attempt to stop them.

"I think we're done here," Mr. Brown said, getting to his feet and opening the door for Morton.

Sharpe nodded silently but kept her deep-blue eyes locked on Morton as he hastened out of the room.

"If you decide you need to talk about anything, you know where I am," Mr. Brown said, escorting Morton back into the hallway.

Morton nodded and paced off back toward his classroom. He was still reeling from what he'd just heard when a tiny blond-haired girl holding a stack of photocopied pages appeared from around the corner and practically walked right into him.

The poor girl's top lip was all puffy, and her eyes were red. She looked like she'd been crying too. Morton wiped his own eyes quickly and put on a fake smile. "Sorry," he said, stepping aside.

"Can you help me find my cat?" the girl said, handing him a small sheet with a picture of a white cat on it. "His name's Squiffy."

"That's a nice name," Morton said, glancing down at a picture of a white long-haired cat. "And what's your name?"

"I'm Willow," the girl said. "That's a kind of tree that grows near water. My mom likes trees. Does your mom like trees?"

Morton felt the pressure of more tears building up behind his eyes. In fact his mother had liked trees, but he had no desire to get into a conversation about that right now.

"Listen, I've got to go, but I'll, uh, I'll keep my eyes open for sure," he said, clearing his throat and trying to pull himself together.

"I've written a poem so you remember what he looks like," Willow said, pointing to the sheet she had just given him. Then, without another word, she let out a tremulous sigh, dabbed a tissue to her nose, and shuffled sadly off in the opposite direction.

Morton looked down at the paper again. There below the picture was a short poem:

> *I love my little Squiffy,*
> *He's very dear to me,*
> *His eyes are green like jelly beans*
> *And his nose is like a little black pea.*
> *His coat is white like fluffy clouds*
> *And he's very easy to see,*
> *So if you spot my Squiffy,*
> *Please bring him home to me.*

Morton's confusion and anger turned to pure numbness. This wasn't fun at all. In fact, it was truly horrible. And as far as he could tell, it was all his fault.

CHAPTER 8

THE ZOMBIE TWINS

Morton didn't see Robbie for the rest of the day, which he was secretly relieved about. He wasn't ready to confront him just yet, although he desperately wanted to talk about the situation with someone. He'd hoped to discuss it with James, but James had rushed up to Morton in the middle of the afternoon to tell him he wouldn't be able to walk home with him because of a "prior engagement" (whatever that meant) and Morton hadn't seen him since. When the day finally ended Morton wandered home alone, kicking moodily at the carpet of fading leaves on the sidewalk.

Just as he was rounding the corner to their driveway, Melissa appeared behind him, and to his surprise she too was alone.

"Where's Wendy?" he asked.

"How should I know? I'm not her keeper."

"Sorry," Morton said. "I just thought —"

"She's gone to the optometrist, if you must know," Melissa snapped.

"So you do know."

"Yes. I lied. Anything else you want to interrogate me about?"

Morton scratched his head, utterly confused by Melissa's behavior but too drained to discuss it any further.

As they stepped onto the back porch, Morton saw a note taped to the door from Dad explaining that he'd gone in to work early and wouldn't be home until breakfast.

Morton handed the note to Melissa.

"Typical," she said. "Notice that he forgot to say anything about supper, once again proving that he doesn't actually care about us."

Morton retrieved the key from under the mat and was unlocking the door when Melissa quite unexpectedly grabbed his arm and sank her nails deep into his flesh.

"Ouch!" he yelped, attempting to pull his arm away. "What the —?"

"Get inside!" Melissa screamed, shoving him roughly through the door.

Morton fell over the step and landed in a heap, bashing his elbow badly. Melissa stumbled in after him and Morton was about to scream bloody murder when he saw why Melissa had shoved him so violently. Hovering on the porch just outside the screen door were two miniature men, about eighteen inches high, with skulls for faces and long leather hooded cloaks. They had no legs or feet and were levitating about six inches off the ground. The Zombie Twins! This alone would have been enough to freeze the blood in Morton's veins, but surrounding them in a menacing formation were four Gristle Grunts — muscular creatures that looked like albino headless dwarfs with unusually strong arms and a single shriveled eye in the middle of their chests — and a pair of Toxic Vapor Worms, which were about a foot long and looked like winged blue snakes with long, curved razor-sharp teeth.

Melissa lunged back in an attempt to slam the door shut behind her, but the creatures were too fast. One of the Gristle Grunts tore right through the metal mesh on the screen door and leaped at the inside door with explosive force. Melissa flew backward into the kitchen, landing in a sprawl beside Morton.

The Zombie Twins drifted silently toward them. Melissa dug her fingernails into Morton's arm again but made no sound. The Twins stopped suddenly, their eyes pulsating with a deep-red light. Morton could hardly believe it. They were behaving just as they did in the comic. This red pulsing light, he knew, meant they were communicating with the creatures they controlled.

Melissa scrambled to her feet and grabbed the nearest thing she could see, which just happened to be Dad's best nonstick frying pan.

Morton braced himself for attack, but to his surprise the entourage of creatures split into two groups. The Twins and the headless albinos lumbered and hovered away, heading for the landing at the bottom of the stairs. Only the Toxic Vapor Worms stayed behind. Morton crawled madly across the kitchen on his hands and knees, getting as far away from the lethal worms as he could.

Melissa either didn't know how deadly these creatures were or else she didn't care — she stepped forward and smacked one of the worms, squashing it flat. A puff of powder-blue smoke came out from under the pan. The worm had seemingly vanished, but the smoke was lingering in the air unnaturally. Then, instead of dissipating, it pulled together in a tight blue cloud and rapidly solidified into a perfectly unharmed worm. Melissa gasped.

"You can't kill them!" Morton warned.

Melissa backed quickly into the corner beside Morton.

"You can't?" she said breathlessly.

Morton shook his head.

"Then what are we supposed to do?"

Morton didn't answer. He was trying to remember how the worms had been defeated in issue 377. They'd tried burning them, pulverizing them, sticking them in the microwave. None of that had worked, but what had they done in the end . . . ?

"Dad's pickled eggs!" Morton called out.

The statement was so incongruous that Melissa dared to take her eyes away from the advancing threat to look directly at him.

"You can't kill them, but you can contain them," he explained pointing to a large, half-empty jar of pickled eggs.

The Toxic Vapor Worm closest to Morton hissed wildly and leaped for him as if it understood his words. Of course Vapor Worms couldn't understand speech but, Morton realized too late, the Zombie Twins could — and they were controlling the worms.

In one swift motion Morton grabbed a carving knife from the draining board and deftly chopped the attacking worm in two. The worm instantly reformed into two smaller identical worms. Unabashed, Morton proceeded to chop each of those into two and the same thing happened again. Now instead of two worms they were surrounded by four smaller worms and one larger one.

"Is that part of your plan?" Melissa said, squeezing more tightly into the corner.

"They have to fit into the jar," Morton said, and then handed her the knife and clambered quickly onto the kitchen counter. He dashed over to the jar of eggs, twisted off the large metal screw top and poured the remaining eggs and vinegar into the sink. Behind him Melissa squealed and lashed out at the larger worm. She hit it so hard with the frying pan that it flew across the room and exploded into blue smoke as it impacted with the wall. The worm reformed more rapidly than before, almost popping back into solid form, and immediately half-jumped, half-flew the full length of the kitchen, hissing savagely at Melissa. The worms then did something that even Morton didn't expect. They leaped at one another and formed into one very large, very frightening Toxic Vapor Worm.

The now waist-high worm propelled itself forward and snapped at Melissa, tearing her dress. Morton could see the toxic venom literally dripping from the creature's fangs.

He clutched the empty jar, not really sure how he was supposed to do this, and jumped down from the kitchen counter. Unfortunately his foot landed on a stray egg and he fell onto his back with a painful thud. To his surprise he found himself staring directly up into James's face. James had stepped through the door seconds before, and standing beside him was Wendy. She was carrying her tennis racquet and the two of them looked like they'd been having a great time until about five seconds ago. Wendy screamed but, to her credit, did not faint at the sight of her first monster. James panicked and looked at Morton as if hoping for instructions.

Morton grabbed the tennis racquet from Wendy and pushed it into James's hands. "Just hit it!" he yelled.

James swallowed nervously, but a loud scream from Melissa seemed to give him the resolve he needed. He gripped the handle of the tennis racquet with both hands, dashed gallantly across the kitchen, and promptly slipped on another pickled egg. He fell forward in typical clumsy fashion, but still attempted to hit the giant worm as he went down. Amazingly the racquet landed right over the worm's head, and the force of James's fall turned the inelegant slip into a surprisingly lethal blow. The fine nylon mesh sliced right through the worm's body, dicing it into long blue french fries that fell limply to the floor and formed into a dozen smaller worms. Seizing his chance, Morton rolled onto his knees and scrambled over to the tiny worms. He scooped them into the jar with the metal lid and then quickly tightened it into place. The worms spat angrily and dashed their heads against the thick glass. They vaporized and reformed in a frenzied attempt to escape. Fortunately their efforts were in vain. The jar held.

Everyone relaxed visibly.

"I thought you were going to the optometrist's," Melissa said, staring accusingly at Wendy.

Wendy didn't respond. By the dazed look on her face Morton was pretty certain she hadn't heard a word Melissa had said.

Melissa switched her gaze to James. "It's not what you think," he said, pulling himself to his feet.

But Melissa didn't have time to probe the situation any further. A sudden thump from upstairs made everyone turn toward the landing.

"There's more of them?" James said.

"Bring a weapon," Melissa said, still clutching the frying pan as she and Morton ran upstairs.

As soon as they reached the landing they noticed that the oak table was lying on its side and the gargoyle was gone. A long scratch ran the length of the hallway, ending at the stair carpet. Morton and Melissa moved carefully up the stairs, followed by James and Wendy, now clinging fearfully to his arm. The scratch started again at the other end of the carpet and led directly into Melissa's room. A loud scraping and banging came from inside.

"What the heck do they want in my room?" Melissa whispered angrily.

Morton shrugged. He honestly had no idea.

"They better not be messing with my closet," she said, raising her voice, and then without further warning burst angrily through the door. Morton felt obliged to follow. To his surprise, two of the Gristle Grunts were holding the gargoyle, one at the head and one at the feet, and the other two had dragged the dresser away from the closet and were now standing in the open doorway. The instant Morton entered the room he felt, rather than heard, an ultrahigh-pitched scream. He looked over to see the Zombie Twins hovering by the open window, their eyes glowing fiercely. The gray sinewy Grunts stopped what they were doing. The two holding the gargoyle dropped it with a loud crash and all four of them lumbered over to stand defensively in front of the Twins.

"Who are these guys?" Melissa said out of the corner of her mouth.

"They're the Gristle Grunts. They're really, really strong."

"How do we stop them?"

Morton scratched his head. "Uh, well, their eyesight is bad, and they get out of breath quickly. They're not very smart either, but that doesn't help much if the Twins are controlling them."

"So, in other words, they're easy to run away from, which doesn't help us at all."

Morton shook his head. "Not really."

"Well, they can't stay in my room," Melissa said. "They're ugly." And to Morton's complete surprise she handed the pan to him and leaped forward, aiming a well-targeted kick right in the center of one of the Gristle Grunt's chest. Morton tried to stop her, but it was too late. The Grunt caught her foot with astonishing ease and twisted it, causing Melissa to yelp in agony and fall helplessly to the floor.

Morton was on the move before he even realized what he was doing. It was as if the frustrations of the day's events were suddenly taking control of his actions. He jumped over Melissa's sprawled body, swinging the round metal pan at the lumbering Grunts. The Gristle Grunts might have been strong and Morton may not have hurt them, but in several fierce blows he sent all four of them rolling across the room like lumpy gray bowling pins. The high-pitched scream pierced the air again, and the Zombie Twins hovered quickly to either side of the open window. Immediately the Gristle Grunts, instead of attacking Melissa and Morton, began to retreat by flinging themselves fearlessly over the window sill right out into the void. A split second later the Zombie Twins too threw themselves down to the garden below.

Morton stood panting, his arms trembling with shock and exhaustion. Melissa pulled herself to her feet, dusted her clothes off, and flicked her hair back from her face as if nothing had happened. "You didn't need to do that," she said. "I had the situation under control."

Morton gaped in disbelief but was too breathless to even attempt to point out that he may have just saved her life.

"Why did they run away without putting up a fight?" James said, peering around the door.

"They're cowards, obviously," Melissa said, still straightening her skirt. "That's one thing I've learned about these monsters: They're all bark and no bite."

"The Zombie Twins aren't cowards," Morton said, though he had to admit he was surprised by their behavior.

Wendy's head appeared beside James's. "Is it safe to come in now?"

"Yeah. They're gone," Melissa said.

Wendy inched cautiously into the room and her eyes fell immediately on the open closet. Her jaw dropped. "Is this some kind of magic?" she said in an airy voice.

James, Morton, and Melissa all exchanged glances. This was not going to be easy to explain.

Half an hour later they were sitting in the kitchen. Wendy clutched a hot cup of mint tea and stared pensively at the Toxic Vapor Worms in the jar on the table as if it were some oversize lava lamp. They'd just finished telling the whole story, and she had yet to say a word.

"The thing I can't understand," she said at last, "is why you would make those wishes."

"Obviously we didn't know we were making real wishes," Melissa said defensively. "And it's not so bad that I wished for a closet, is it? Wouldn't any self-respecting woman wish for the same thing?"

"No!" Wendy said. "There are far more important things than fashion."

"My thought exactly," James said. "The world is a complete mess and her first thought is for vanity."

"But we didn't think it was real," Melissa said again, pleading her case.

Wendy looked away from the Vapor Worms twisting hypnotically in the jar and stared down at her mint tea. "And you really have no idea what you wished for?" she said to James.

James shook his head.

"Well, let's hope it turns out to be something good."

"Yeah, let's hope," James said, his voice suddenly croaky.

Wendy drank the last of her tea and stood up slowly. "I'd better be going," she said. "My parents will be expecting me home soon, and I don't want them to start worrying that something, uh, *odd* is going on."

Melissa jumped to her feet. "But we're still on for homework club tomorrow afternoon, right?" she asked eagerly.

"Actually my optometrist's appointment was rescheduled for tomorrow, which is how come I ended up playing tennis with James, so let's take a rain check," Wendy said with an apologetic smile.

Melissa's face dropped. "Okay. Maybe Sunday, then?"

"Maybe," Wendy said in a very noncommittal way. She gave another forced smile, made a nervous waving gesture to Morton and James, and left in a hurry, running down the driveway without once glancing back.

Melissa walked over to Morton, who was still sitting at the table, and stared at him with fierce eyes.

"What?" Morton said.

"I hate you," she growled. "You and your stupid comics and your grizzly monsters and your ridiculous wishes."

Morton swallowed hard and looked up at Melissa. Normally he would have leaped to his feet and given her a good dose of her own medicine, but after everything that had happened today he was starting to believe that maybe Melissa was right. Maybe she'd been right all along about his obsession with *Scare Scape*.

"Just leave him alone," James said, tugging at Melissa's arm.

But Melissa spun around and turned her hateful eyes on him. "You're just as bad," she said. "It's all secrets and lies with you. Secret wishes that you're too ashamed to admit to, running off with my friends behind my back — you don't even play tennis!"

"I never said I could play, and I've told you a dozen times, I don't know what I wished for!"

"Yes, you do. I can see it in your eyes. The way you rub your hands, that incident with the pie. You think we're idiots, but we see. Even Morton sees. What is it, James? Did you wish to be immortal? Or wait a minute, maybe it's something to do with girls. You never had any luck with girls before and suddenly Wendy's all over you and you're like half her age. . . ."

"You're just jealous!" James shouted, losing his temper.

Something in Morton snapped. He leaped to his feet and stepped between James and Melissa. "Stop it! Stop it! Stop it!" he yelled. "The Zombie Twins just burst in here trying to steal the gargoyle, and all you two can do is fight!"

"You have a better idea?" Melissa hissed. "You want us to read more of your messed-up comics?"

"We've got to figure this out," Morton pleaded. "Why did the Zombie Twins try to steal the gargoyle? And why are they raising an army of cats? And what happened to King? I mean, doesn't anyone else think it's weird that he just fell down a well?"

James started to rub his hands but realized Melissa was watching him and stuffed them in his pockets instead.

Melissa took a deep breath and managed to calm herself down. "The Zombie Twins weren't trying to steal the gargoyle," she said quietly. "They were trying to take it into my closet."

Morton looked up at her and wondered why he hadn't realized that himself. If the Zombie Twins had wanted to steal the gargoyle, they would have marched it straight out the door, but instead they'd carried it up to the closet. "You're right," he said. "But why would they do that?"

Melissa chewed her nails nervously and avoided meeting

anyone's eyes, as if she was feeling guilty about something. "The closet wasn't my idea," she mumbled.

"What do you mean?" James said.

"Isn't it obvious?" Melissa replied.

James and Morton looked back at her blankly.

Melissa took another deep breath and then grabbed her purse from the mudroom. To Morton's complete surprise she pulled out a very wrinkled issue of *Scare Scape* and handed it to him.

"Hey!" Morton said, noting the tears in the cover and the folded-over corners. "Where did you get this?"

"Never mind that now!" Melissa snapped impatiently. "Just read the Disturbing Things story. Maybe *you* can make sense of it."

With that she stomped up the stairs, leaving Morton and James with the comic. Morton flipped to the King story and skimmed quickly through it, while James read over his shoulder.

The story told the unfortunate tale of a poor girl who could never afford decent clothes and was hated by all the other girls at school. Then one night she helped an old lady who had fallen on the side of the road. The old lady granted her a wish and she wished for an infinitely large closet, just as Melissa had.

Morton could hardly believe it. Melissa must have read this story before she made her wish.

He read on eagerly.

The closet was just like Melissa's, vast and filled with amazing clothes. At first the closet solved all of the girl's problems. She became fashionable and popular. Girls started following her around. Boys started asking her on dates. She was pronounced Prom Queen and life was good. But as time wore on she began to prowl ever deeper into the closet. At first she'd only venture inside for a few hours at a time, but hours became days and sometimes she'd be gone for as long as a week. She became so obsessed with the endless fashions available to her that she started to lose touch with her friends. For all of her incredible outfits and her overwhelming glamour, she became reclusive and eccentric. People began to tease her again, saying she was strange. This in turn made her spend even more time in the closet until one day she wandered so far from the entrance that she became utterly lost and was never seen again.

Morton let James pull the comic from his hands. He still didn't know what this meant, or why the Zombie Twins would want to take the gargoyle into the closet, but one thing was very clear: The closet, like the monsters, was a product of King's dark imagination.

"This can't be good," James said.

Morton was forced to agree.

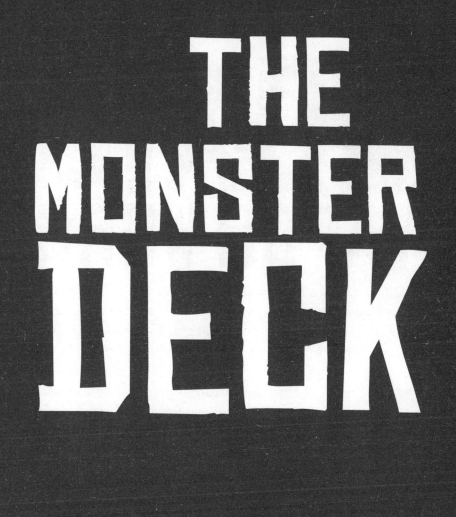

THE
MONSTER
DECK

TOXIC
VAPOR WORM

Small, fast, and venomous, this partially winged serpentine creature is not to be toyed with. Its ability to dissolve instantly into a blue vapor makes it not only capable of passing through air ducts and key holes, but also renders it impervious to physical attack. In fact, it is virtually indestructible. Attempts to diffuse the vapor have met with little success since the Worm can reform itself into smaller replicas even at microscopic sizes. The toxic venom secreted through the fangs of this creature is equal in strength to that of a black mamba. Specimens must be stored in airtight containers and treated with extreme caution.

ACID-SPITTING FROG

Rarely found in populated areas, this seemingly ordinary frog is deadly. Its secret weapon is a constantly replenishing bladder of highly corrosive organic acid. Larger adults of the species can spit a distance of up to fifteen feet, and just one teaspoon of frog acid is sufficient to melt a hole through two inches of plate steel.

The acid-spitting bladder makes for a formidable defense, but is also used for hunting. In normal conditions this carnivorous frog will use the acid to incapacitate only small animals, such as birds or rodents, but remains of bigger mammals have been found in some larger frog colonies.

KAMIKAZE COBRA

This fearsome snake is in fact no relation to the typical cobra. Though it shares that snake's slight flattening of the head and it does have fangs, that's where the similarity ends. Unlike the cobra, which has a venomous bite, this snake's defense mechanism is entirely unique. If the sharp fangs and hissing don't scare away attackers, the Kamikaze Cobra has one final and fatal tactic: It explodes, usually taking the attacker with it. The snake does this by detonating an explosive capsule in its skull.

Skillful snake charmers have been known to successfully behead this creature before it manages to self-destruct, neutralizing the explosive, but there are also many stories of tragic mishaps. This temperamental beast should be avoided at all costs.

FLESH-EATING SLUG

This infamous pest is similar to other slugs, in that it lives in moist soil, often near vegetable gardens or other domestic spaces. Unlike the common slug, however, the Flesh-Eating variety is almost entirely carnivorous. It has small but powerful teeth and will regularly attack mice, moles, and other small land-dwelling creatures. While little more than an annoyance to humans in small quantities, infestations can become dangerous or even deadly. For reasons not fully understood, large numbers of Flesh-Eating Slugs will sometimes adopt a frenzied feeding pattern, causing them to attack larger animals en masse. Feeding frenzies happen only at night, but many family pets have been lost this way, and some human fatalities have been reported.

ELECTRIC KILLER EEL

Though it prefers swampy lakes and stagnant ponds, this slithery vermin is more than capable of moving on land.

Eels usually stick together in swarms of about two dozen and, for the most part, avoid humans. However, beware: A single eel packs a six-thousand-volt shock at two amps when threatened, which is enough electricity to power a small house and stun an elephant.

Thick rubber gloves and boots will offer some protection, but avoidance is always the best defense.

BAT EYE

From a distance this transdimensional creature looks like an ordinary bat, but closer inspection reveals that, in fact, it has no mouth or nose. Its "face" is simply one large eye.

Though it is not dangerous per se, the Bat Eye can be used by unscrupulous individuals as a surveillance tool through the establishment of a low-level psychic bond, which can be strengthened with relatively simple spells. Since the Bat Eye does not appear to eat or reproduce, it must be generated by supernatural methods. Many of these methods are described in detail in The Book of Portals.

HYDRA SNAKE

This venomous four-headed snake is named after the mythical many-headed beast slain by Hercules. Fortunately this snake does not sprout two heads every time one is cut off. It can, however, survive with only one head intact, making it four times harder to kill than a regular snake. It is especially aggressive when guarding its eggs, which it does very well on account of its 360-degree vision. This may be the reason Hydra eggs were once considered to be gifts worthy of a king.

SMOTHER FISH

Sometimes called Paper Wights, these paper-thin creatures flap through the air and pass under doors and through small openings with little trouble. Some strains also have chameleon-like properties and can hide in plain sight on walls, floors, and other flat surfaces.

Though individuals are mostly harmless and feed on smaller insects, they have been known to travel in shoals of up to a hundred. Such numbers enable them to smother larger prey, which they then slowly digest, usually over a period of months.

Fortunately Smother Fish are easily disposed of with a good sharp pair of scissors.

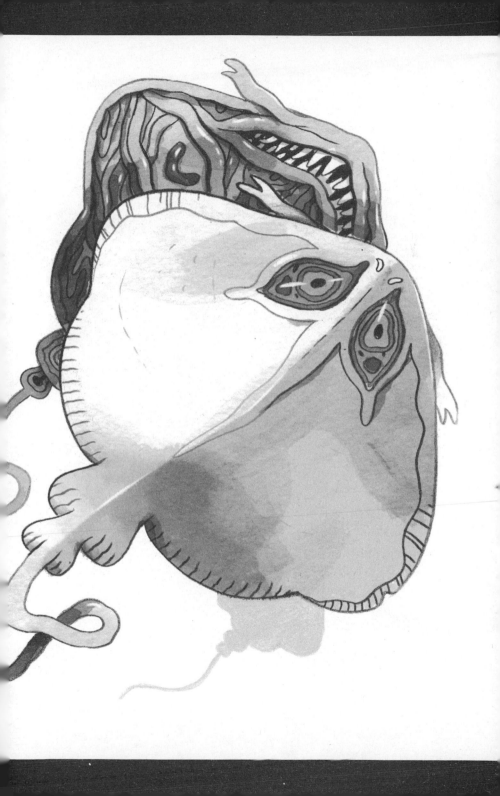

VISIBLE FANG

The defining characteristic of this rare creature is its reclusive nature. It avoids being seen by taking advantage of its translucent body and confining itself to shadowy places. Despite its diamond-hard fang, from which it gets its name, it has never been known to attack conscious prey, instead first using some as yet unverified hypnotic technique to place its victims in a trance. Though it will eat anything, it is believed that it prefers dense muscular organs, particularly the heart.

It is also said that the Fang avoids crowds, seeking out houses where people live in solitude. This is almost certainly true, though some debate continues about why the Fang adopts this habit. Some claim it is a purely defensive strategy, while others suggest that the hypnotic powers of the Fang are more effective on vulnerable and lonely souls.

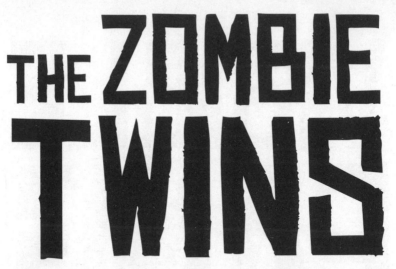

THE ZOMBIE TWINS

Not to be confused with zombies, the small but powerful Twins are named for their ability to gain psychic control over other beasts, living or dead. The Twins' influence over living creatures is limited to animals with lesser intelligence, but they are capable of controlling the cadavers of any creature, including those of recently deceased humans.

It is believed that the Twins are more powerful when in proximity to each other, enabling them to create some kind of psychic feedback loop.

Despite having no physical strength or defenses, their extraordinary intelligence and strategic brilliance, combined with their ability to raise armies at will, makes them a foe of truly formidable proportions. What is not clear is what motivates the Twins. They have been known to battle both for and against otherworld interdimensional powers. Leading theories suggest that the Twins originate from their own dimension and it is therefore impossible to interpret their actions on the "mortal plane."

GRISTLE GRUNT

Small, sinewy, walking walls of muscle. What you see is what you get with this myopic creature. It has no head, most likely because it has very little brain. Its preferred weapon is a club, and its preferred hangout is a very damp, smelly cave.

Grunts live only in rocky, mountainous regions and hunt in packs of about five, tracking down larger game such as goats, deer, and stray humans. They do not, however, eat raw meat, instead roasting their food over an open flame. Many experts believe that only the female Grunts are intelligent enough to actually light fires, and though it is almost impossible to tell male and female Grunts apart, several independent reports support this theory.

FLESH BULB

Often found hanging in caves, this tennis-ball-size creature has a unique attack technique in which its opalescent skin flashes so brightly that it can cause temporary blindness. The Bulb then quickly attaches itself with its four leglike tentacles to its prey and feeds through the mouth on its underbelly.

The Flesh Bulb is a large parasite and, like ticks or other blood-sucking parasites, once it is attached it is almost impossible to remove. Acetone or lighter fluid has shown the best results. Though the Flesh Bulbs do not intentionally kill the host, they are occasionally found in large swarms and human fatalities have been reported.

INK
BLIGHT

Extremely rare, almost nothing is known of this strange, creeping, oily entity. It looks like slow-moving black tar and consumes everything with which it comes into contact, thus no effective studies can be done. In fact, it is uncertain whether the Blight is even an organism at all. Some experts believe it is a manifestation of dimensional collapse, and that any apparent mobility is dictated by random fluctuations in some unknown ether. Contact with the Blight has proven fatal in all known incidents, and there is absolutely no known remedy for occurrences. Any areas infected must be evacuated until the Blight naturally subsides, which usually takes one to two weeks.

KING-CRAB
SPIDER

This giant arachnid has a bony crablike carapace that makes it impervious to most predators. Adults can weigh as much as four pounds. It has strong venom, which, while not lethal in small doses, will render most people unconscious for several hours.

Though it does spin an incredibly tough web, it does not use the web for capturing its prey, merely for storing and immobilizing it. Like many larger spiders, it hunts by hiding in holes and leaping directly onto its intended victim, which it then neutralizes with its venom.

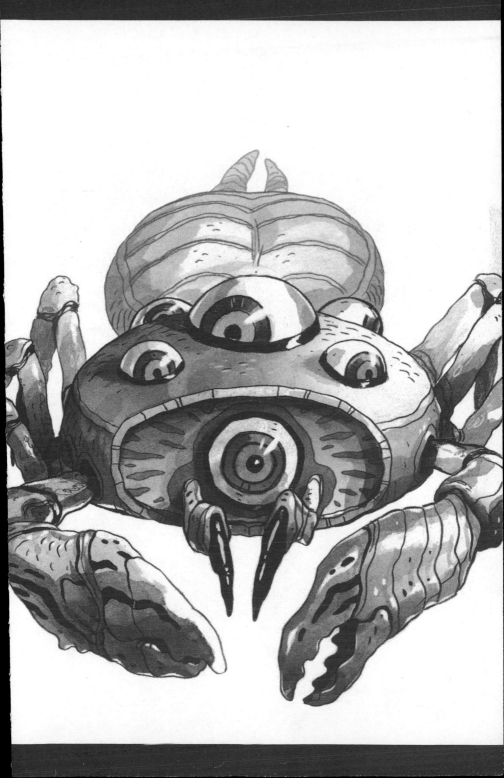

GREATER SPOTTED
WARGLE
[RHYMES WITH GARGLE]
SNARF

Few creatures boast the raw power of the Snarf. Up to fifteen feet long, with an impenetrable bony carapace and a double ring of razor-sharp, metal-ripping teeth, this behemoth is tough enough to tackle a tank . . . and win. Like its smaller cousin, the Lesser Spotted Snarf, the Wargle can paralyze its victims by secreting a fear-inducing pheromone from glands distributed all over its body.

This nocturnal creature has perfect night vision, and its sense of smell is ten times more acute than that of a bloodhound. Few humans can survive an encounter with a Snarf, and the unfortunate ones who do discover that exposure to the Snarf's poison-tipped barbs causes a slow, painful transformation into a hybrid human-Snarf creature.

Legend has it that the Snarf draws its demonic power from the brimstone in its stomach, which it gets by drinking from the boiling rivers of Hades.

FLESH-EATING COCKROACH

These creatures are almost identical to the familiar domestic pests, but with two significant distinctions: They are at least five times the size of an average cockroach, and they are completely carnivorous.

The only good news about these pests is that they are rare, and reports seem to indicate that they are naturally repelled by clean, bright environments, preferring derelict homes and slums.

However, if you do get an infestation, be prepared to move out in a hurry. Each roach eats twice its body weight every day, and females reproduce at a fearsome rate, capable of laying several pods in a month. Each pod in turn is capable of holding more than one hundred eggs.

TEN-EYED
SALAMANDER

This seemingly harmless creature is, in fact, one of the deadliest pests in the arcana. Despite its name, the Ten-Eyed Salamander can have any number of eyes, ranging from six to twenty. It is commonly accepted that the extra eyes are a by-product of its extremely advanced regenerative abilities for, like all salamanders, this creature is capable of regrowing lost limbs. Unlike regular salamanders, this one can regenerate limbs in a matter of seconds. Some have even been observed to regrow large portions of their bodies.

In addition to their resilient regenerative abilities, these Salamanders have highly toxic skin, which can cause instant paralysis, and are exclusively carnivorous. They also have an unsettling habit of jettisoning their poison-saturated tails when under extreme stress. The tails continue to move, usually twitching and jumping violently, distracting or paralyzing would-be attackers while the salamander itself escapes — or strikes.

SHARK HOUND

Sometimes referred to as a Land Shark, this savage creature is a four-legged nightmare, bringing the ocean's worst terror to dry land. It can outrun a human with ease, and its ferocious teeth make it a match for most other wild creatures.

Though it has a highly acute sense of smell, its one weakness is its vision. It has a blind spot both directly in front of and directly behind it.

Legend has it that the Shark Hound hunts only on the full moon, but in fact this is a myth, no doubt propagated because it hunts exclusively at night, depending as it does on scent rather than sight.

DRAGON FLY

This large flying insect is one of the few true fire breathers. Despite being little bigger than a hummingbird, it can belch out a shaft of flame six to eight feet in length and generate temperatures of up to 700 degrees.

Though fire breathing is a highly effective defense, it may serve another purpose. Some experts believe that Dragon Fly eggs can hatch only after exposure to high temperatures and that the insects build small nests from twigs and incinerate them to catalyze germination. No studies have been able to verify this.

TWO-HEADED MUTANT RODENT

This unique strain of wild rodent has two heads and hence twice the ferocity of the meanest sewer rat. It will eat anything, from old rope to old bones, and it is *always* hungry. Like many plague beasts, the rodents have rapidly growing populations, which, in the right environment, can double in size each week. They are also impervious to traditional pest control techniques. Most traps don't seem to work and poisons have no effect on the Rodent's seemingly indestructible digestive system.

It is also rumored that these creatures are more intelligent than average rats, which might explain why traditional trapping techniques are ineffective.

GALOSH

Often called the foot soldier of the underworld, this humanoid creature is not of earthly origin. However, history documents many incidents involving this being and there is no doubt it is a powerful and formidable foe. It is obedient and fearless and very strong.

Its thick leathery skin forms a tough natural armor, and like many other-dimensional beasts it cannot be killed by normal methods. It is commonly accepted lore that the only certain way to stop a Galosh is to hack it to a thousand pieces, which is almost certainly true since the Galosh is not actually alive in any natural sense of the word.

SWAG SPRITE

Though completely harmless, these small marsupial creatures are aggravating and infuriating. Capable of appearing and disappearing at will, they seem to spend all of their time stealing small items that they stuff into the pouch on their backs. They are also known to occasionally replace stolen objects with other items, presumably stolen from some other location. No reasonable explanation has been proposed for this behavior. Swag Sprites seldom stay in one place for long, but folk remedies claim that burning a potpourri of bergamot oil will discourage their appearance.

CHAPTER 9
THE NIGHT PROWLER

By the time Morton dragged himself out of bed on Sunday morning, it was almost noon. He had spent an entire day reading comics and then most of a restless night lying awake thinking. Everything was going wrong. Melissa seemed to hate him more than ever, James was growing secretive and distant, and so far, reading *Scare Scape* hadn't helped with any of their unanswered questions.

And then there was the trouble with Robbie, which for some reason upset Morton more than everything else.

When he finally made it downstairs the house was empty. He found Dad in the backyard, raking and mowing the overgrown lawn with the help of the now-repaired mower. Dad had hardly made any progress at all since Morton's first failed attempt, though that didn't seem to have dampened his spirits.

"What do you think?" he said proudly, leaning his rake up against a tree and turning to face Morton.

"It looks great," Morton said, trying to sound enthusiastic. "Do you need any help?"

Dad looked in surprise at Morton. "Not reading your comics today?"

Morton shrugged and looked down at his feet.

"Oh, growing out of them are you?"

"I dunno. Maybe," Morton said.

"Well, what about going to see your friend Robbie?"

Morton shook his head. "Things aren't going so well with Robbie."

"Oh dear. What's wrong?"

"It turns out he's not the person I thought he was."

"Meaning what, exactly?" Dad asked.

"I found out that last year he stole a lot of money and they sent him away to a correctional school. That's why everybody else avoids him, because they know he's a thief."

"That's very unfortunate," Dad said. "Did he tell you why he stole the money?"

"Does it matter?"

"Of course it does."

"He lied to me," Morton said, the pain surfacing in his voice. "He told me he never stole anything in his life."

Dad took off his gardening gloves and perched himself on the side of the wheelbarrow. "You can't always take things at face value," he said. "It seems to me that you should at least give Robbie the chance to explain himself."

"Why?"

"Because it sounds like you're missing something. I told you about Copernicus, right?"

"Dad!" Morton groaned. "Why does everything have to be about astronomy? We're talking about people, not planets."

"Copernicus was a person, wasn't he?"

"Yes, Dad. He was the person who figured out that the Earth is not the center of the solar system," Morton recited mechanically. "You've told me like a hundred times, but what's that got to do with Robbie?"

"It teaches us an important lesson about life. One we should never forget."

"The fact that Earth goes around the sun and not the other way around is an important lesson?"

"No, that's a discovery. The lesson is that what appeared to be true turned out to be completely false. It seemed so obvious that the sun went around the Earth that for thousands of years nobody even questioned it. But if you dig a little deeper, investigate some of the smaller clues, like the movements of the other planets, or the cycle of the stars, you'll find that the truth is exactly the opposite of the obvious."

"You mean, you think Robbie might not be a thief?"

"I mean the obvious solution is not always the true one. And truth likes to hide, so you should never judge anything based on a few facts. Why do you think I turned to astrophysics? Believe me, it's much easier trying to understand the behavior of a star that's three billion miles away than it is to understand why James and Melissa fight all the time."

"Oh, you've noticed, huh?" Morton said.

"I notice a lot of things," Dad said, ruffling Morton's hair, "but I can't explain all of them. So, do you want to help do some raking, or are we going to have more astronomy lessons?"

Morton grabbed hold of a rake. "Raking!" he said.

The rest of the afternoon passed quickly and Morton found puttering around in the garden with Dad a welcome distraction. It wasn't until Melissa and James returned just before supper that Morton's worries seeped back to the surface. Melissa hadn't spoken to either of them since revealing the source of her wish, and James was far from his usual upbeat self. Morton got the sense that he was brooding over something. Dad noticed the mood too and decided to buy pizza in an attempt to cheer everybody up. Unfortunately it didn't work. Melissa sat picking at her plate, glowering at James, and James, who looked ill even before the meal, wolfed down three slices of Hawaiian pizza and then suddenly raced upstairs to lock himself in the bathroom again.

"What's wrong with James?" Dad asked with a look of genuine concern.

"Stomach flu," Morton said before Melissa could speak. "It's been going around. Everyone at school has it." Melissa gave Morton a questioning look and Morton shook his head, hoping she wouldn't say anything.

"I should go see if he's okay," Dad said.

"No!" Morton said abruptly, grabbing Dad's arm before he could leave the table. "I mean, it's probably very infectious.

And I'm sure he'd rather be alone until he's finished, you know, barfing his guts out."

Dad settled back down. "You're probably right. Best to let nature take its course."

It was a full twenty minutes before James finally came back downstairs. Morton noticed at once that James's skin was so pale it had a silvery gray sheen, and he couldn't be sure, but the whites of his eyes seemed to have a greenish tinge.

"Goodness, James," Dad gasped. "You look like the walking dead. Is it true you have this stomach flu?"

James glanced briefly at Morton, and Morton nodded to him behind Dad's back.

"Yes," James said. "That must be it. But I feel much better now."

"Well, you don't look any better. You should drink some milk of magnesia and go straight to bed."

"I think I'll pass on the milk of magnesia, but I will go to bed," James said. "I'm really sorry."

"Sorry?" Dad said. "Why on earth would you be sorry? It's not your fault you're ill."

James shrugged and smiled weakly before going back upstairs to his room. Morton couldn't help noticing that he'd been looking at Melissa when he'd said sorry.

After supper Morton wanted to talk to Melissa about King's closet story, but she insisted she had important homework and went straight to her room after washing the dishes. Morton decided to press on with the comic reading research alone. He could hardly believe that only a few short weeks before, nothing could have made him happier than curling up under his blankets and reading *Scare Scape*. Now it felt like a chore. All he really wanted was to find a story about a gargoyle that granted wishes or a story where Zombie Twins herded cats. He wanted to find something, anything, that could help them understand what was happening in Dimvale. But there was nothing, and Morton couldn't help feeling somehow betrayed. The comic had always helped him before. It had always seemed to have answers. Now it seemed determined to remain silent.

It was very late when he finally turned off his light. A dense blackness filled the room, and sleep crept slowly up on him. He began to dream that a large centipede-like monster with a double ring of lamprey-like teeth was juggling cats in a circus. Then the cats and the monster vanished in a cloud of yellow smoke and John King appeared in their place, his face dimly illuminated by the light of a single, hovering candle. Then, unexpectedly, John King grabbed the darkness around him as if it were a black curtain and literally tore it apart. A swarm of monsters spewed out of the tear, growling and hissing and baring their teeth.

Morton awoke with a start and reached immediately for his reading light. It took him a moment to realize that he'd just had his first nightmare and the terror that was still gripping him was not real but the echoes of his dream. He suddenly wished he was still sharing a room with James, but knew that wouldn't really make much difference. James was so distant and secretive these days that Morton felt he hardly knew him.

He had just rolled over in an attempt to get back to sleep when he heard the sound of the screen door opening downstairs. He sat up at once, his senses on high alert. Dad was not working tonight, so he wouldn't be going anywhere, and it was far too late for it to be anyone else. Morton slipped quietly out of bed and opened the door to his balcony. He stepped into the dewy night air and peered down over the back porch. A silhouette emerged from the door below and dashed into the shadows of the tree-lined driveway. Morton recognized the dark shape as James immediately, and his heart began to thud nervously in his chest. Why would James be going out at this time of night? He knew at once that he had to find out.

Morton pulled on his slippers and dashed downstairs as quietly as he could. Just as he stepped onto the back porch, he saw James reach the end of the driveway, turn left, and walk determinedly down the street. Being careful not to be seen, Morton followed him into the night.

James seemed to know exactly where he was going. He'd half-run, half-walk along one street, get to the corner, pause for a brief second, and then dash off again. Morton had a hard time keeping up with him without being seen. Before long James had made his way to a lane passing between two rows of houses. Morton had to pinch his nose as soon as he rounded the corner because a strong smell of rotting food emanated from a green Dumpster halfway down the lane. To his surprise James made directly for the Dumpster. Morton tucked himself out of sight behind a rickety wooden fence and peered through the slats. Inexplicably James climbed right into the Dumpster and began rifling around, looking for something. He seemed to sniff at the garbage bags and then chose one and threw it down to the gravel road. Morton squinted to see more clearly in the dark, but all he could see was the outline of James jumping down and crouching over the shiny black bag. He stayed hunched over in that position for what seemed like a very long time, and Morton had just decided to come out of hiding and simply ask James what he was doing, when a car suddenly turned onto the lane. The bright headlights surprised James as much as they did Morton, and James snapped his head up in shock. The driver of the car obviously didn't see James because he passed by without slowing, throwing the lane into darkness again. But Morton saw. In the brief flash of light he saw something he'd never forget. Something more confusing and terrifying than everything else that had gone before. James was eating a slab of slime-covered steak writhing with white maggots. Morton almost threw up at the sight of it.

He ran back to the house in confused panic. Part of him had wanted to stay and talk to James, to ask him what was happening, but another part of him was afraid. And yet, how could he be afraid of James? James was his brother and had always been his closest friend. He loved

James. Morton's confusion mounted, and he knew that if he didn't talk to someone about what he'd just seen, he'd explode. He also knew that the only person in the world he could talk to was Melissa, who, under normal circumstances, was also the last person in the world he'd go to.

When he got back to the house he was surprised and a little relieved to see a shaft of yellow light spilling out from under Melissa's bedroom door. Could she too still be awake, or had she just fallen asleep with the light on? Morton decided to chance it. He pushed the door open and peeked inside. But Melissa wasn't there. Her bedding was thrown back in a rough pile, but her bed was empty. Then Morton noticed that the closet door was slightly ajar and the dresser that normally held it shut had been pushed to one side. Morton's heart skipped a beat. Had something happened to Melissa? He examined the room more closely. There was no sign of a struggle; no bits of squashed, monstery things on the floor; no overturned furniture. No blood. He moved silently into the room, his senses on full alert.

He was halfway to the closet when he noticed Melissa's diary lying open on her desk. Melissa never, ever left the diary open. She always locked it and kept the key carefully hidden. This was not a good sign. Did something emerge from the closet and drag her in? Morton moved closer to the diary. He knew it was very wrong to pry into the deepest most personal thoughts of another person but, he told himself, maybe it would give him a clue as to her whereabouts. He began reading the elegant black print.

September 23

Another nightmare. Can hardly sleep anymore. Perhaps if I write them down, they'll stop, or at least they'll have less of a hold on me. Tonight I dreamed I woke up in darkness and walked out onto the yard. A giant pit had opened up like an ugly black mouth right in the middle of Dad's perfect lawn. I moved closer to the pit. I put my toes right on the edge and peered down. I didn't want to. I was screaming inside with fear, but I had to know what was down there. Guttural voices seemed to call from the blackness. No words, no language I knew, and yet, I understood. They were telling me to jump. Jump and everything would be right, they were saying. Everything would be just as it had been before. My heart pounded so hard it felt like a wild animal trapped in my chest, desperate to escape. Could it be true? Could I go back? The pit was so dark. So terrifyingly dark. "It's only one step," the voices urged. One step. I bit my lip until it hurt. I felt tears running down my cheek. I jumped. Icy wind rushed around me, so cold it felt like pieces of glass slashing through my clothes, tearing at my legs and arms. At first I thought the voices were moaning, whimpering in the darkness, until I realized it was me. I was crying, not screaming with fear, but crying like a pitiful lost baby. I don't ever remember feeling so alone. And then, when I thought the blackness would consume me forever, I landed. I crumpled into

soft ground, unhurt. When I stood up I saw I was on Dad's perfect lawn, exactly where I started, except the pit had gone. But somehow I knew. This was not where I started. It just looked the same. Something was horribly wrong with this place.

Morton heard a sudden hissing grunt from inside the closet and snapped the diary closed, his heart hammering with fear. Melissa's nightmares, it seemed, were much worse than his.

Morton tiptoed over to the closet and dared to peer in. He saw nothing but an empty landscape of somewhat tattered clothing. It looked like his monsters had been chewing at the garments nearest to the door, perhaps in a desperate attempt to find something edible.

"Melissa?" Morton whispered.

There was no answer. He ventured farther into the brightly lit aisles. The everlasting lights on the ceiling made everything seem somehow flat and unreal, as if he were walking into a picture in a magazine. Morton wondered absently where the electricity to keep those thousands of lights blazing came from. Hopefully it wouldn't show up on Dad's electricity bill.

"Melissa!" he called again, more loudly this time.

A skittering noise behind him made him whirl around, but there were no monsters in sight. The echoes of Melissa's nightmare, mixed in with the image of James eating a maggot-infested steak still flitting about in his brain, did nothing to calm his nerves. He began to wonder if he was imagining things but then heard the scampering of tiny claws and a faint gurgling once more. He followed the sound only to find a moment later it was behind him, as if whatever it was had doubled back. He whirled again, and again saw nothing. The skittering moved off into another aisle. Morton followed, from one aisle to another until he realized, too late, that he'd lost track of the exit. He stood on his tiptoes, attempting to see over the top of the clothing racks, but couldn't get any sense of direction. From where he stood it looked as though the closet just went on forever.

The skittering noise moved closer again. This time it seemed to be coming directly toward him. He looked all around, infuriated. It was only at the last moment that a vague, glassy shape revealed itself directly before him. He realized at once what had been hunting him. It was the Visible Fang, the transparent creature that resembled a large walking jelly. Only now it didn't have cheap paper stickers stuck to its belly to represent its inner organs, like it did when it was just a toy. Morton could clearly see the creature's heart, stomach, and lungs pulsing and beating in its translucent body. As soon as the Fang realized it had been seen, it hopped out of sight again. This time the skittering noise began racing in circles, and Morton knew that it was preparing to pounce. He looked quickly around him for a weapon but saw only pants and shirts. His heart began to beat wildly. The creature didn't have toxic venom, like the Vapor Worms, but it did have a diamond-hard fang that could rip a person's flesh open like a wet paper bag.

He was just about to flee in any random direction when Melissa appeared from nowhere, running like an athlete. She brandished a long silver sword before her and homed directly in on the barely visible creature. In one surprisingly graceful move she skewered it right through its belly. It let out an earsplitting shriek and then simply popped, like a sackful of watery jelly, leaving nothing but a slimy clear pool on the carpeted floor.

Morton had never been so happy to see Melissa in all his life.

"You shouldn't come in here," she said flatly. "They've gone almost two weeks without food. They're getting a lot more savage."

"Where did you get that sword?" Morton asked, amazed by her heroic appearance.

"It was way down the back, with the medieval armor."

"Medieval armor?"

"Yeah. As far as I can tell the farther away from the door you get, the farther back in time the fashions go. I haven't made it back to the Stone Age, but I'm sure it's there."

"That's freaky."

"Yeah, it's also freaky that my baby brother is wandering around in my closet at two in the morning. What exactly are you doing here?"

Morton suddenly wanted to ask Melissa the same question. He could almost understand her dashing in every morning to grab a new outfit, but why exactly was she in here now when she should have been sleeping? Was she becoming seduced by the closet like the girl in King's story? Morton made a mental note to keep an eye on her.

"I needed to talk to you," he said.

"Talk? Couldn't it wait until morning?"

"It's James. He's . . . well, he's doing strange things."

"Tell me something I don't know."

"This is serious," Morton pleaded. "I think it might have something to do with his wish."

Morton suddenly had Melissa's full attention. "Okay, I'm listening," she said.

Morton described how he'd followed James and seen him eating food from the Dumpster. Melissa listened in silence, and by the time he was finished she looked sickly and pale.

"What kind of a wish makes you eat garbage?" she said.

"I don't know," Morton said. "I'm worried that he might be suffering some kind of possession or something like that."

"Why would he wish for that?"

Morton scratched his head. He'd been asking himself that question. "Remember what happened before the blue light? You two had a big fight and then he went up to his room in a bad mood, and he said he didn't make a wish, but obviously he did, only he didn't make a conscious wish. Maybe because he was angry. Dark magic feeds off anger."

Tears welled up suddenly in Melissa's eyes. Morton hadn't expected this response at all. He had half expected her to find some cruel satisfaction over James's situation.

"This is stupid!" she said angrily. "This sort of thing doesn't happen in real life. It's even worse than the stories in your comic. They at least make sense in the end. I feel like we're trapped inside of one of King's sick jokes."

Morton was beginning to feel he might agree with Melissa. This situation was complicated and muddled, where the stories in *Scare Scape* were always straightforward with a simple ending.

"What are we going to do about James?" he asked.

Melissa grabbed a nearby T-shirt and wiped her face dry, pulling herself together.

"Don't confront him alone," she said. "Like you say, he may be possessed. He may even be dangerous."

Morton felt a horrible sick feeling creeping over him again. The thought of James being possessed by something evil was more than he could bear.

"We'll talk to him after school tomorrow," Melissa went on. "When we're all together."

Morton nodded in agreement and then followed Melissa through the labyrinths of the closet back to her room. As he did so he had an overwhelming urge to hold on tight to Melissa's hand, but decided this was not the time to indulge in fear. If he was going to get through this, he was going to have to be strong — stronger than he'd ever been in his life.

CHAPTER 10
THE LIVING DAD

Both Morton and Melissa watched James very closely at breakfast the next morning. To Morton's surprise he seemed unusually perky. He breezed into the room holding a brand-new basketball, his eyes gleaming brightly.

Dad looked up at him. "Glad to see you're fully recovered," he said. "Fancy some breakfast?"

"I have basketball practice, so I gotta go," James said.

"Basketball practice?" Dad said, voicing Morton's own surprise. "Since when were you on the team?"

"Just joined," James said, grabbing his schoolbag.

Morton knew this had to be a lie. James couldn't even catch a ball, let alone get on the basketball team.

"Aren't you going to eat something before you go?" Dad called.

"Can't eat before practice," James called back.

"Wait just a minute!" Dad said, stopping James at the screen door.

Something in Dad's voice made Morton and Melissa look up in alarm.

"Come here," Dad said.

James hesitantly went and stood beside Dad, who pulled him up against his chest and put the palm of his hand on his head. James came right up to Dad's chin.

"Last time I looked you were right down here," he said, pointing to his lower chest. "I think you grew in the night."

Melissa dropped her fork loudly onto her plate and Morton almost choked on his cereal.

James looked down at his legs. "I'm sure you just shrank, Dad," he said, and ran for the door, this time making a successful exit.

Morton looked over to Melissa, but Melissa avoided his gaze. She jumped to her feet and left the room.

Half an hour later Morton trudged off to school feeling utterly alone. He began to wish he had a friend he could confide in and started to feel very guilty about the fact that he'd been lying to Robbie almost since they met. It would be so easy if he could tell him the truth — confess that this whole confusing mess with the missing cats was his fault. But then, if Robbie really was a thief, that might not be such a good idea. Either way Morton wanted to talk to him and made up his mind to seek him out as soon as he got to school.

But Robbie arrived late. He slumped into class, a full twenty minutes after the bell, looking sleep deprived and ruffled. Mrs. Houston, the geography teacher, sighed heavily and stopped talking until he was seated, clearly annoyed by the interruption.

Morton tried to catch Robbie's eye, but Robbie just stared zombie-like at his desk for the rest of the period.

After class Morton waited for him in the hallway.

"Hey, Robbie," he called as soon as he appeared.

Robbie glanced up at him but kept walking. Morton persisted and followed him.

"That Sharpe woman sure dragged me over the coals on Friday," Morton said.

"Yeah, well, now you'll know better than to hang out with me, won't you," Robbie said coldly.

"No, I didn't mean it like that. I meant . . ." Morton faltered. What did he mean? "I just wondered if they said anything to you."

Robbie stopped at his locker and threw the metal door open angrily.

"No, they didn't say anything."

"Oh, good, because —"

But Robbie hadn't finished talking.

"They searched the whole house though. Came knocking on the door late at night and insisted on poking their noses into everything. Mom was really upset."

A ball of guilt tugged heavily in Morton's stomach. "I . . . I'm sorry," he stammered. "I didn't realize the police would actually search your house."

"Yeah, well, they did," Robbie said bitterly.

Robbie pulled his sneakers and his gym bag from his locker and slammed the door as angrily as he'd opened it, and stormed off. Feeling suddenly desperate, Morton called out, "I know you don't have anything to do with the missing cats."

Robbie kept walking, so Morton ran up and stood in front of him, blocking his way.

"I know it wasn't you because I know who did it."

This time he had Robbie's attention. Robbie stared right into Morton's eyes as if trying to read his thoughts.

"If you know, then why didn't you tell Inspector Sharpe?" Robbie said, suspiciously.

Morton puffed his cheeks. He didn't quite know how to answer that question. "Look, it's complicated, and I want to explain it to you, but not here."

"Let me get this straight," Robbie said. "You know who took the cats, but you let me take the blame?"

"No, it's not like that at all," Morton said, flustered. But now that he thought about it, that was exactly how it was. He did know who had taken the cats, and yet he'd said nothing.

"If you'll give me a chance to explain," Morton said.

Robbie pressed his lips together and shook his head. "No. Don't tell me," he said bitterly. "I've got enough of my own trouble already. I don't need any of yours."

Robbie pushed past Morton and walked away without looking back. Morton was about to call after him one more time when Mr. Darcy, the gym teacher, strode by along the hall.

"Come on, Morton," he said brusquely. "Everyone else is just about ready to start, and you're not even changed yet."

"Yes, sir," Morton said, and raced back to his locker to retrieve his gym clothes.

When he got into the changing room everyone was yelling noisily as usual, opening and slamming lockers, throwing socks, and generally being rowdy. He was just beginning to change when a familiar, aggressive voice rose above the din.

"Hey, jailbird! My sister's cat is still missing. Ready to fess up?" It was Brad. Morton turned to see that he'd cornered Robbie on his way out to the field.

Robbie attempted to ignore Brad and walk past him, but Brad shoved him back against the hard tiled wall.

"Why would I want your sister's stupid cat?" Robbie said defiantly.

The noise in the changing room died down as everyone turned to watch. Morton felt the guilty lump in his stomach swelling until it was almost painful.

"That's the question I've been asking all along. Why do you want all those cats? I heard you were eating them."

Robbie attempted to push past Brad again, but Brad blocked his way for the second time.

"I mean, I knew you were poor, but I had no idea you were that desperate."

"Leave him alone, you tone-deaf jerk!"

Morton had said the words even before he realized he was going to speak. A peal of laughter ran through the changing room. Brad was momentarily shocked, but he quickly regained his composure and a malevolent grin spread over his face.

"I always knew you two were in it together," he said, and then without warning he shot forward and snatched Morton's bag right from his hands. "Let's see if you've got any cats in here, shall we?" He was about to spill the contents of the bag all over the floor when Mr. Darcy loomed behind him.

"I hope you weren't about to do something that would put you in detention, Evans," Mr. Darcy said with a hint of glee in his voice.

Brad froze in midaction and gritted his teeth angrily.

"Somebody stole my sister's cat," he grunted.

"Really?" Mr. Darcy said. "And you think Morton is hiding it in his bag?"

"No," Brad said.

"No, what?"

"No, sir."

Mr. Darcy smiled thinly and pulled the bag from Brad and gave it back to Morton. "Come on," he said clapping his hands sharply. "Everybody, stop staring. If you're not out on the field in two minutes, you'll get a hundred laps."

For the rest of the day Morton hoped to get another chance to talk to Robbie, but Robbie seemed more determined than ever to avoid him. He kept his distance during gym and at one point, between English and math, he even turned and walked in the opposite direction when Morton tried to approach him.

Morton made up his mind that this situation couldn't go on. For better or worse he was going to corner Robbie after last period, which was history with Mr. Brown. Unfortunately when the end of the day finally came, and Morton was about to leave class, Mr. Brown caught his eye and beckoned him over with a clear gesture. "Morton, a quick word," he said.

Morton cursed under his breath, knowing full well that Robbie would waste no time hanging around and that this "quick word" was going to prevent him from sorting out the mess.

He gathered his books and sauntered over to Mr. Brown's desk.

"I wanted to apologize again for being so indelicate about Robbie," Mr. Brown said. "I know you've become friends and the truth is, he's probably not a bad kid. He just made a mistake, you know. Anyone can make mistakes."

Mr. Brown stared at Morton as if awaiting some kind of response. When he didn't get one, he continued: "Surely you've made mistakes before, Morton?"

"Yes, sir. I have."

"Of course you have. We all have. The important thing is that you don't feel alone. I mean, we're here to help you. If you've made a mistake, it can be undone."

Morton still didn't know how to respond. Just what was Mr. Brown driving at?

"Sir, if it's about the cats, I honestly didn't have anything to do with it."

Mr. Brown laughed heartily. "No, no. Of course it's not that. I'm just speaking in general terms. It's important that you know if you, or your friend Robbie, are in trouble you can come to me."

"Yes, sir."

"Good." Mr. Brown smiled at Morton and patted him on the head. "Chin up!"

"Thank you, sir," Morton said, and left the room wondering just what Mr. Brown was talking about.

When he arrived on Hemlock Hill about twenty minutes later he was completely surprised to see Robbie sitting on the low wall that ran in front of his house. He was staring resolutely at a crack in the sidewalk and didn't seem to notice Morton approaching.

"Robbie?" Morton said, trying to sound casual but feeling certain he was about to receive another barrage of abuse.

Robbie looked up. His brow was furrowed and his eyelids were heavy, making him look equal parts tired, angry, and confused.

"You're mixed up in something bad, aren't you?" he said without making eye contact.

The frankness of Robbie's statement took Morton by surprise. "Yes," he said flatly, "I am." It felt good to tell the truth for once.

"Do you want to talk about it?" Robbie said, staring again at the crack in the sidewalk.

"I wouldn't know where to begin," Morton said honestly. "And even then I doubt you'd believe me."

"Try me," Robbie said.

Morton let out a big sigh and dropped his heavy book bag to the sidewalk. It would feel good to come clean, to tell Robbie everything. But could he trust him?

"Mr. Brown told me about the money you stole," Morton stated.

Robbie sniffed. "That figures. Brown loves telling people about me. Likes to gloat about how he got me to confess."

"He's not like that," Morton said. "He just thought I should know since we're hanging out. And I think he's right, don't you? I think I have a right to know the truth."

"Yeah, well, Brown doesn't know the truth. He wouldn't know it if it kicked him in the butt."

"It's true you stole the money, isn't it?" Morton said.

Robbie raised his voice. "I told you before, I never stole anything, ever!"

"But you just said you confessed."

"I did," he said in his gravelly voice. "But I didn't steal anything."

Morton was confused. "You confessed to stealing and then got sent to correctional school, but you didn't steal anything?"

"It's complicated," Robbie said.

Morton started to feel irate. Did Robbie honestly expect him to believe that he would confess to a crime he hadn't committed?

"Look," Morton said. "No offense, but the last thing I need right now is a game of riddles, so either you —"

"My dad's not dead," Robbie cut in. "I misled you about that, but everything else I told you is true."

Morton's jaw froze in an open position.

"I always used to lie about Dad," Robbie went on. "I used to say he was an explorer who got lost in the jungle, or that he died at sea rescuing a sinking ship, or he was a secret agent and got kidnapped, because I couldn't bear the thought of anyone knowing the truth."

Morton stared at Robbie incredulously, unable to think of anything to say.

"The truth," Robbie went on, "is that my dad is a drunk and a crook."

"Oh," Morton began, but he still didn't know how to react. Wasn't it better to have a living dad, no matter how disappointing he might be, than to have a dead dad?

"I know what you're thinking," Robbie said. "You're thinking any dad is better than no dad, but you're wrong. You think that because your dad is a great guy. You can't even imagine what it's like to live with a drunken dad."

"I suppose not," Morton admitted. "But what does this have to do with you confessing to stealing the library money?"

"Mom threw my dad out of the house when I was a baby because he was good for nothing, and for as long as I can remember it's just been the two of us. But then, one day, just over a year ago, I came home from school and there was this sweaty man stinking of beer and cigarettes sitting in the middle of our living room watching our TV. 'Hello, son,' he says, 'I'm your pop.' You can imagine how shocked I was."

Morton nodded. In truth it sounded so completely bizarre that he couldn't really imagine it at all.

"Things went from bad to worse pretty quick. He started stealing Mom's money, and he'd just eat and drink and shout, and this time he had no intention of leaving. The house was always a mess. The place was packed to the ceiling with beer cans. One day the school was raising funds for the library, so I took all of his empty beer cans to the recycling depot and got almost a hundred bucks for them and donated it to the fund. Mom had been asking him to clean up for weeks, but he never did anything around the house. Anyway, he got really angry when he found out what I'd done and said it was his money. He got so mad about it that he broke into the library on curriculum night and took the money. All of it! He was so drunk when he got home that night that he bragged to me about what he'd done."

"Wait a minute," Morton said, "you're telling me your dad took the money and you confessed?"

"Yes."

"But why?"

"I'm a minor," Robbie said. "If I confess to the crime, then I don't get a criminal record. Dad was already a convicted crook. He would have gotten two years in prison."

"Exactly!" Morton said. "You would have been rid of him for two years. What's wrong with that?"

"It's not long enough, that's what's wrong!" Robbie exclaimed. "I wanted him gone forever, so I made a deal. I said I'd take the blame for stealing the money if he left home and never came back. I figured he was too much of a coward to take the blame, and I was right. He left. My plan worked."

Morton didn't know what to say. He was at once utterly impressed by Robbie and deeply saddened that anyone should ever have to make such a terrible sacrifice.

"I can't believe your dad would let you do that," Morton said.

Robbie shrugged dismissively. "It doesn't matter. Nobody's life is perfect. I mean, everyone has their problems, right?"

Morton nodded in agreement. Now that he thought about it, they both had their share of problems, but to Morton's surprise he found himself thinking suddenly that his problems were not nearly as bad as Robbie's.

"So, you think you can trust me enough to tell me about the cats?" Robbie asked.

Morton nodded. "I think you better come in. It will be easier if I show you."

As they walked up the driveway Morton spotted Dad sitting alone on the porch swing wearing his pajamas and drinking a cup of tea. In their old house Dad started his days like this whenever the weather was warm, except he didn't used to do it alone. Morton felt a sudden chill, as if the sun had gone down prematurely.

"Hey, Dad," Morton said, clearing his throat. "This is my friend Robbie."

Dad looked up, startled, and a moment of confusion swept over his face, as if he'd forgotten where he was. "Oh, goodness yes, Robbie," he said at last, his usual smile returning. "So glad to meet you. Morton tells me your mother cooks a delicious plum pie."

Robbie shrugged. "I guess."

"Well, thank her from me for the housewarming gift. Even though I didn't get to eat any of it, my children haven't stopped talking about it for days, so I can quite honestly say it brought some real warmth into our new home."

"Oh, uh, thanks," Robbie said, squirming uncomfortably.

"I was just going to show Robbie the new lawn," Morton said, and he dragged him away quickly.

"Why is your dad still in his pajamas?" Robbie whispered as they continued down the path.

"He works nights, remember, at the observatory. Our evening is his morning."

"Oh, right," Robbie said. "I forgot about that."

A moment later the two of them stood facing the backyard. It was now completely transformed. The lawn was raked and mowed, although still not quite up to Dad's standards. The flower beds were weeded and ready for the spring bulbs to appear next season, and at the very bottom of the yard the old well had been cleared of growth.

Morton led Robbie to the place where he'd unearthed the gargoyle and steeled himself to recount his story.

"This is all going to sound crazy," Morton warned, "so don't say anything until I've finished."

Robbie shrugged in an "if you say so" kind of way.

"It turns out the Blind Man was an artist called John King who used to draw stories for *Scare Scape*."

Robbie opened his mouth to speak, but Morton shushed him. "Wait! Hold your questions or I'll never finish," he said. "Just before school started I was helping Dad clear the lawn when I found this weird stone gargoyle almost completely buried in the ground. It had three fingers on it and a rhyme that said by breaking a finger off you get a wish. We don't know where the gargoyle came from, or why it was buried here, but John King must have had something to do with it. And the thing is, well, Melissa, James, and I each made a wish and they came true . . . kind of."

Morton could tell Robbie wanted to ask more questions but was forcing himself to remain silent.

Morton then led Robbie across the sagging porch, through the kitchen, and up into Melissa's room. He was quite sure Melissa would be out, but knocked just in case. As he suspected, her room was empty. He led Robbie over to the closet, pushed the dresser aside, and gripped the round ceramic doorknob.

"This is the freaky bit. Melissa wished for an infinitely large closet, and I wished my monster toys were more realistic, which brought them to life. We had to hide the monsters in here. Now, don't faint on me."

Morton yanked the closet door back dramatically. Robbie

gasped, somewhat predictably, but thankfully did not pass out. In fact, after the initial reaction, Robbie seemed to take it in stride. Morton took him a short distance into the closet, where a swarm of Ten-Eyed Salamanders was tearing nastily at what looked to be the carcass of a Gristle Grunt. Morton noted that there were way more Salamanders than he had ever owned, meaning that Melissa's observations about the creatures breeding were obviously correct.

Robbie inched closer to the ravenous beasts. The nearest ones turned their heads and made wet, glutinous hissing noises.

"Better not get too close," Morton warned. "They're hungry."

Robbie stood staring, transfixed by the savage scene before him. After a couple of minutes Morton tugged him on the arm and dragged him out of the closet. He slammed the door firmly behind him.

"I can't believe it," Robbie said. "I mean, I saw it with my own eyes, but I can't believe it."

"I know the feeling," Morton said. "I still keep hoping to wake up and find out that it's all a dream. Or, to be more precise, a nightmare."

"So how do the missing cats fit in with all of this?" Robbie said, looking very puzzled.

"It's the Zombie Twins," Morton explained. "They usually control monsters but since there aren't many monsters around, we figure they've settled for cats."

"Why do they want the cats?"

"We don't know," Morton admitted. "There's a lot we don't know. In fact, now you know as much as we do."

Robbie squinted shrewdly at Morton. "Wait a minute. You said there were three wishes. You've only mentioned two. What was James's wish?"

Morton sighed. The last thing in the world he wanted to do was describe the horrible scene he'd witnessed the night before, but he'd made up his mind to come clean with Robbie and told him the entire story.

"We don't really know what his wish is, but it's something bad," he said finally. Robbie's jaw dropped open and he sat speechless on the chair beside Melissa's writing desk.

"You want to see the gargoyle?" Morton asked after a minute of embarrassing silence.

"Sure," Robbie said, appearing to snap out of his dazed state.

Morton led him to the small alcove at the bottom of the stairs and flicked the spotlights on.

"That's freaky!" Robbie said, leaning in closer to the blackened stone artifact. He read the poem out loud several times and rubbed his fingers over the stumps on the gargoyle's outstretched hand. "It doesn't look very magical."

"Well, what looks magical?" Morton said. "It's always like that in the stories isn't it? An old oil lamp, a lost ring, a monkey's paw, a mummified big toe that smells of cheese."

Robbie chuckled. "What are you going to do?" he asked.

Morton shook his head. "We have to find a way to reverse the wishes before . . ."

"Before what?"

Morton was just considering how to answer that question when James burst into the hallway panting and sweating as if he had just run all the way home from school.

"Morton, we need to talk," he said.

"Sure, what is it?" Morton said.

"No, I mean, we need to talk *alone*," James replied, eyeing Robbie.

"It's okay, he knows," Morton said.

James's face twisted in confusion.

"I told him everything. About the gargoyle, Melissa's closet, my wish . . ." Morton stopped himself before mentioning James's wish.

"But . . . but we said we weren't going to mention it to anyone," James growled, trying not to raise his voice.

"Well, I got fed up with lying," Morton said defensively. "And Robbie's involved just like the rest of us."

James sighed heavily. "I suppose you're right. Welcome to the madhouse, Robbie."

Robbie gave a thin smile.

"So, what's the panic about this time?" Morton asked.

A frantic expression crossed James's face again. "You know that Simon Bean kid from sixth grade? Well, he saw the Zombie Twins, and he's telling everyone about it. By morning every kid in school will know that creatures from *Scare Scape* are stealing cats."

CHAPTER 11

A PORTRAIT OF KING

A few minutes after James had made his revelation about Simon Bean, the boys shut themselves in the downstairs study and James told the whole story just as he'd heard it. Apparently, sometime before midnight, Simon awoke to the sound of his cat yowling and spitting like a crazed animal. He went downstairs to see it clawing at the door as if it were desperate to get out. Still half asleep, Simon opened the door, and the cat shot off like a bullet. Only then did he realize he probably should have kept his cat inside, so he ran out after it. That's when he saw a small hooded figure with a white skeletal face and glowing red eyes hovering in the shadows. Simon bravely chased the cat (or so he claimed), but both cat and creature vanished into the darkness before he could catch them.

"Simon doesn't read *Scare Scape*," Morton said. "Maybe he won't realize it was one of the Zombie Twins."

"He will," Robbie said flatly. "Simon hangs out with Timothy Clarke. They might not figure it out right away, but it won't take long, I guarantee it."

"It still won't lead anybody to us," Morton said, trying to sound optimistic. "I mean, we didn't invent the Zombie Twins."

"No," James said, "but we're living in the house of the guy who did. How long do you think it will take Inspector Sharpe to figure that out?"

Morton's heart sank. Robbie and James were right. Whichever way you sliced it, this was bad news.

When Melissa got home a while later, the boys revealed to her that Robbie was now in on the secret. She seemed irritated and probably would have given them an earful but for the fact that Dad came in and invited Robbie to supper before she had a chance. This time Robbie accepted, despite clear warnings from James and Morton about the dangers of Dad's cooking. He served a stodgy meal of mashed potatoes oddly decorated with sausages and grated cheese, insisting it was a real recipe. Morton couldn't help noticing that James ate the sausages but didn't touch the potato. Robbie was the only one who politely ate everything on his plate.

"Are you sure you're all right?" Dad asked James later, as he was clearing the table. "You haven't touched the potatoes."

"Oh, uh, well, I'm not a big fan of potatoes," James said.

"Since when?" Dad said, with a very perplexed look on his face. "Mashed potatoes have been your favorite food since you were eight months old. Your mother and I called you the Mash Monster until you were three."

Morton tensed and found himself glaring involuntarily at James. He sensed that Melissa was doing the same.

James began stammering nervously, "Oh, yeah, I, uh, hum . . ."

"Oh my gosh, look at the time!" Melissa cut in. "Here, Dad, let me do the dishes, you're going to be late."

Fortunately Melissa's tactic seemed to have the desired effect. Dad looked at his watch and frowned in the way he did when his mind was suddenly fixated on his work. "Well, the sun is sinking," he said, "and I'm not going to refuse your offer to do the dishes, since it happens so rarely."

As soon as Dad's car pulled out of the driveway Melissa stomped back into the kitchen and turned an accusing stare to James. "So, not eating mashed potatoes anymore, are we?"

Morton glanced at Robbie. "Please, don't bicker in front of our friends," he said.

"Well, now that Robbie's in on the secret," Melissa said, "he's practically family, so he'll just have to get used to the way we communicate, won't he? And this has gone on long enough. James is going to tell us just exactly why he's been going out at three in the morning these last few nights."

"Melissa!" Morton exclaimed. "Now is not the time!"

"Now is the perfect time," Melissa persisted.

"I, I was getting some air, that's all," James said, lying very badly.

"Getting some rotten meat, is how I heard it."

James went suddenly pale and began rubbing his hands nervously. Morton had never seen him look so uncomfortable, but before James had time to respond a light knock came from the door.

"I'm not interrupting, am I?"

It was Wendy. Melissa turned away from James and opened the screen door, looking at her in surprise. "Wendy," she said. "I haven't seen you for days and I thought . . ."

"What? That I was avoiding you?" she said.

"Well . . ."

Wendy smiled. She had a pile of newspapers tucked under her arm. "I'm sorry about that. I have to admit I've been in shock for a couple of days but . . ." She stopped midsentence when she spotted Robbie.

"It's okay," Melissa said. "Robbie knows."

"Oh! Well, the more the merrier," she said.

Wendy then spun around to look at James. "Any news about your wish?" she asked nervously. James looked at Melissa imploringly.

Melissa paused, mulling the situation over, then shook her head. "No, nothing yet," she said. James sighed, and Morton was surprised to discover that he shared in his sense of relief. He was no more ready to confront this issue than James was.

"I've been trying to think of some way to help," Wendy went on. "So I started doing some research on John King. You remember I told you my uncle works at the library? Well, he helped me find all these newspaper and magazine articles."

Morton practically ran to grab the pile of papers from under Wendy's arm.

"That's a great idea!" he said.

Wendy shrugged. "It's the least I could do."

"That's very thoughtful of you," Melissa said.

Morton dropped the pile of papers on the table and began poring over them eagerly. "Did you find out anything useful?" he asked.

"Well I thought we should read them together. I mean, you have a better idea about what kind of clues we're looking for."

"More reading," James said heavily.

"Yes, but this might be better," Morton said, glancing at the first newspaper. "This is fact, not fiction."

"My how the world turns," Melissa said. "Now Morton thinks newspapers are more interesting than comics."

Five minutes later they were all seated around the table drinking frothy hot chocolate prepared by Melissa and reading their way through the generous pile of papers.

Most of the articles were disappointingly short and, as the pile diminished, Morton's initial optimism began to fade. They did, however, begin to develop a much more detailed picture of John King. His first job as a teenager had been working for an auction house restoring damaged antique books. According to one interview it was this job that sparked his passion for the occult and inspired him to apply his artistic gifts to drawing macabre pictures and eventually comics. But early in his artistic career, his young wife, referred to only as Mrs. King, passed away unexpectedly. This loss made him focus even more acutely on his art. The rest, his rise to infamy in the underground horror comic scene and his unfortunate death, were all as reported in the somewhat twisted obituary they'd already read in *Scare Scape*. The only additional tidbit they gleaned from the official obituary in the *Dimvale Star* was that John King was not his real name. He'd been christened John Smith by "the world's least imaginative parents."

Morton pushed the last paper in his pile to one side. He hadn't noticed until now that the sun had set and deep-blue shadows were creeping across the room.

"It doesn't say anything about how he went blind," he said, disappointment crowding in on him again. "It just says he did and leaves it at that."

"Oh! There is an interview here about his blindness," Wendy said, picking up a color supplement. "Remember I told you he always worked by candlelight?"

"Yeah, up in that round room that Dad's using as his study," James said.

"Well, this is the last interview he gave before his death. After refusing to talk about it for his whole life, he finally explained why he'd only worked at night by candlelight."

Wendy paused dramatically and cleared her throat. A stillness seemed to ripple out from the kitchen. Everyone put their papers down. Morton became suddenly aware that the house was utterly silent, as if it too were ready to listen to the last printed words of its previous owner.

Wendy began to read:

A Portrait of John King
Eccentric Hermit or Cloistered Prophet?
by Warren Fletcher

It is a Friday afternoon in July, and I have been granted the once-in-a-lifetime chance to interview the legendary horror comic writer and illustrator John King. As I approach my destination in the oppressive heat of the midsummer sun, I cannot fail to notice the showcase of majestic houses that adorn this Victorian street. I see at once why John King chose this town as his home. These clapboard-and-shingle houses are relics of a vanished age. I'm told Dimvale has several old churches, two very creepy graveyards, and a suitably turbid history that hints of hangings and witch burnings. Just as landscape painters retire to coastal homes or mountain retreats, so this horror writer has found a place filled with picturesque echoes of ghostly voices.

In this respect King's house is perfect: old, slightly crooked, and boasting a dramatic circular turret where King created all his work, incredibly, by candlelight.

"It's all about the turret," he explains to me once we're sitting in his fabled circular studio. "I didn't really bother much with the rest of the house. I slept here, worked here, did all my research here. Now, of course, all I can do is sit here and think. I spend too much time thinking."

Since King is notorious for cutting interviews short and avoiding the press, I decide to jump straight to the question that propelled me halfway across the country.

"Mr. King, I understand that your blindness was brought on as a direct result of many years of working in poor light. Apparently this condition was common in the days before electricity and many writers and artists suffered from it, Thomas Hardy and Michelangelo among them. We can, all of us, revere these artists who sacrificed so much to bring the world their works in an age before Edison and the lightbulb, but in your case it seems unnecessary, almost self-inflicted. You refused to follow your doctor's advice with the tragic result that you can now no longer enjoy the two greatest passions of your life: reading and drawing. My question is simply: Why? Why work exclusively at night by candlelight, even to the ruin of your career?"

For a moment I wonder if I have lost my chance of an interview. Mr. King stands up in silence, fumbles for his white cane and paces the room, tripping slightly on a fold in the rug. I cannot tell if the clumsiness of his actions is due to anger or inexperience in his sightless world. When he finally speaks I am surprised to find his tone polite.

"Firstly, Mr. Fletcher, please call me John. King is

neither my name, nor my nature. It was forced upon me by publishers who understand business, for which I have no stomach. Secondly, you must know I have refused to talk publicly about my work habits."

This is the response I have expected. I already have my strategy in hand. It's a risky one, but I feel certain that it is the only one that can possibly work. It's a strategy seldom used: complete honesty.

"John, you must know that your publisher has encouraged speculation that you could only draw at night because you are possessed by a beast from the underworld."

He waves his hand dismissively. "The underworld, they say? Why not the overworld? Or simply, the world?"

I point out that *Scare Scape* has promoted the idea that he is demonically inspired because it boosts sales. Yet I believe his stories are filled with moral guidance and hidden wisdom.

"To allow this rumor to persist is to invite a dismissal of your work," I say. "You surely cannot want that?"

John King places his cane directly in front of him and leans toward me. He stares in roughly my direction, but misses slightly, making me feel strangely disembodied.

"Very well. For your records, young man, I will tell you. Though you may not find the truth much different from the rumors."

I make no sound and dare not move from my spot. I have come here to listen.

"A flame is an organic thing," he begins. "It is not alive, as such, but it is very nearly alive. It has moods and it responds to the environment, just as we do. On a hot night, the candle flame will be tall and reach up beyond itself, swelling optimistically into the darkness. When it is cold, and chill winds creep around the cracks in the windows, it is small and flickers timidly, never able to take a firm hold, barely able to create light at all. So very human, don't you think?"

I nod and realize he cannot see me. He goes on nevertheless.

"But there is another way in which a flame is like us. If you gaze into the heart of a candle flame, you will find it black, devoid of any light at all. Just as the yellow flame emerges from this void, so too do we emerge from nothingness. In fact, the whole, unimaginably complex galaxy around us emerged from the same nothingness — the original void, if you like."

John reaches carefully now for the bookshelf behind him. His fingers skim lightly over the innumerable titles until they pause on one. He traces the spine and nods to himself. It is a fat, leather-bound sketchbook. He holds it out in my general direction, and I stand up to take it from his hands. I sit again and let it fall open on my knee. It is filled with pencil drawings of candles. Hundreds of pages of candles, each utterly unique and each a work of art in its own right.

"All creatures are born from this darkness, and to darkness they shall return. So it is with ideas. Ideas are creatures in our minds just as creatures are ideas in the universe, coming and going, flickering in and out of existence in exactly the same way.

"When I became aware that I was an idea who had ideas, I adopted the candlelight as a way of focusing my mind on that single curious realization. When I gazed into the dark heart of a flame, ideas popped into my head from a place I can never understand. The candle helped me see what I cannot see, to know what can never be known. Sadly, I became dependent on the practice. It became a crutch, if you will, or a thread to guide me through the labyrinth of my own mind. In time I came to realize that I could no more draw in the daylight than I could walk through walls.

"I believe in the void, Mr. Fletcher. If that is an evil from which my creative spirit draws its power, then so be it, the rumors are true. I worship darkness. Let the world judge me for that."

"There's a little more," Wendy said, placing the pages in the middle of the table. "But that's the most interesting part."

"That's one creepy guy," Robbie said.

"Ugh!" Melissa said. "To think he spent all those years in Dad's study, practicing his weird dark magic."

Despite everything Morton still felt annoyed by Melissa's attitude. "It doesn't say he practiced dark magic," he protested. "He just got his inspiration from candlelight. That's not dark magic."

"Uh, hello!" Melissa said mockingly. "It doesn't get much darker."

"Let's just agree to say that he was eccentric," James said, waving his hands in a calming gesture.

Morton puffed in frustration and picked up the magazine from the center of the table. He stared at the glossy photo of King. Why did everyone insist that King was either crazy or evil? Morton remained determined not to believe that was the case but realized it was getting harder to convince himself of that with each passing day.

In the photo, King was seated crookedly on a plain wooden chair in the middle of the famed circular room. Morton recognized the shelves as the same ones that still lined Dad's study, except that in the picture they were crammed with books from floor to ceiling. Dad had always said that anyone, no matter who they were, would get smart if they read enough books. And King obviously had read a lot of books.

"I wonder what happened to all his books," Morton mused. "There's hundreds of them here. Even Dad doesn't have that many."

"I guess they sold them because he was bankrupt," Wendy said. "I remember them emptying the whole house into a big moving truck after he died."

Morton felt a little saddened by the thought of King's vast book collection being split up and auctioned off to various bookstores and flea markets. Going blind must have been very difficult for someone with a passion for books. And King had clearly been passionate. Not only were all the shelves packed tightly, but precarious piles of books were scattered over the floor like termite hills. Many of the books were immensely large and ornately decorated. One book had a big black jewel set in the front and another appeared to have tree bark for a cover. Morton noticed one book was as large as a footstool.

It was funny to think that their dad was now using the very same office that King had once inhabited. The book-cluttered room looked so different and yet it was the same. All except for the books and . . .

Morton felt the hairs on his arms suddenly stand on end.

"I think I found something!" he screeched, jumping out of his seat.

Everyone leaned over to look at the photo.

"What is it?" Robbie said, getting up and walking around to Morton's side of the table.

"It's the one place in the house we haven't seen," Morton said.

"Dad's study?" James said, confused. "We've been in there dozens of times."

Morton shook his head. "I should have guessed. I saw bats up there the week we arrived. Look, it's staring us right in the face."

Morton pointed at a place on the photo directly behind John King's head. At last everyone else saw what he saw. There on the ceiling was a large wooden hatch with a decorative brass handle.

"An attic!" Wendy exclaimed.

"Yes!" Morton said. "The turret has its own attic. It's not connected to the main attic at all."

"But that trapdoor isn't there now," Melissa said.

"It has to be," Morton insisted.

Melissa was the first to bolt out of the room and bound up the stairs. Everyone followed, and within seconds they were all staring up at the ceiling in Dad's study. The hatch, which was plainly visible in the photo, simply was not there. The ceiling, like a few other rooms in the house, was covered in decorative tin tiles. Everyone seemed momentarily deflated, but Morton had a clear plan of action. He held up the magazine and walked around the room until he was standing roughly where Warren Fletcher had snapped the photo some years earlier. He dragged a chair to the center of the room and pushed Robbie into a pose similar to John King's. Then by carefully comparing the room to the photo and counting the tiles on the ceiling, he got Melissa to stand directly beneath the place where the hatch should be.

They all joined Melissa and peered up. Suddenly they could see it. If it hadn't been for the overall disrepair of the house, it would have stood out a mile. As it was, it was a barely noticeable quirk in a house full of oddities. A large square of nine tiles was much dirtier than the others, with scratch marks running right across them and, most telling of all, four small screw holes marked the corners.

"A secret hatch," James said. "What old house would be complete without one?"

"Now what?" Wendy asked.

"We get a flashlight and a screwdriver," Morton said, dashing back downstairs, and a few minutes later he returned with a stepladder balanced on his shoulder, a screwdriver in his left hand, and a small flashlight between his teeth.

Robbie rushed to help with the ladder and set it up below the panel.

"Well, who wants to go first?" Melissa said, a hint of trepidation in her voice.

Everyone looked up at the hatch but nobody stepped forward.

"Do we have to go in tonight?" James said. "I mean, wouldn't it be better to wait until daylight?"

"It has to be now," Melissa said.

"Then let's draw straws," James said.

"No, I'll do it. I'm not afraid," Morton said, although in truth he was.

Melissa grabbed hold of the flashlight. "Okay, I'll be right behind you," she said in a surprisingly comforting voice.

Morton stepped up to the ladder, took several deep breaths like a high diver preparing for the plunge, and forced his feet to climb.

CHAPTER 12

KING'S CLOISTER

The ceiling panel dropped away, revealing a dark ebony hatch with a large brass ring bearing a ghoulish face. The eyeless sockets of the tarnished face made Morton feel as if blind John King himself were glaring down at him. Nonetheless, he brushed a thin layer of dust from his shoulders and gripped the ring with both hands. It rotated easily, emitting a satisfying metallic thunk. He glanced down at the other four, who were all staring up anxiously.

He wanted to say something funny or clever, like, "Say good-bye to Kansas," or "Let's play Scrabble instead," but everyone else looked so pale and serious that he decided to say nothing.

He folded the hatch all the way back and, without giving fear a chance to take hold of him, he hoisted himself into the inky blackness. He noticed a strong musty smell that for some reason reminded him of a church. "I am afraid of nothing," he whispered, and groped his way clear of the hatch on his hands and knees, aware only of the texture of the worn rounded planks that made up the floor.

A blue-white light slashed randomly around the room as Melissa climbed in behind him holding the flashlight. Robbie climbed in next, followed by James, and last, Wendy.

They huddled together behind Melissa, who cast out the tiny flashlight beam like a narrow sword ahead of them. The darkness was so complete that it was difficult to build a picture of the room. Morton saw glimpses of stone pillars and what looked like an ornate wooden lectern set against a hazy clutter of cobwebs and grime.

"I think we need a bigger light," Wendy said.

"There must be a light switch in here somewhere," Melissa said.

"I doubt it," James said. "We're talking about the candle king, remember."

James was right. Morton shuffled carefully over to the nearest stone pillar to discover it was a large, elaborate candleholder. A dust-covered box of plain household matches rested on a wide lip halfway down the pillar. He lit the first candle, which pushed a welcome globe of warm light into the gloom. He then worked his way around the darkness, lighting each candle in turn, each revealing a little more of the room, until the fifth and final candle was lit. Only then did he turn to take in the view.

It was like standing inside a giant witch's hat. The conical roof spiraled up from the floor like an intricate rib cage of wooden rafters and struts that converged at the central peak high above.

Directly beneath the peak, in the dead center of the room, stood an ornate stone font, carved with hissing serpents and grinning, toothless faces — unnervingly reminiscent of the gargoyle. The five stone candlesticks stood equally spaced around it in a circle, and in front of each candle was a skeletal carcass still partially covered in mummified parchment-like skin. Each carcass had a large metal spike protruding from its back. At first Morton thought they might have been chickens or rabbits, but he quickly remembered Robbie's tale and realized what they were.

"Are those what I think they are?" Melissa asked, in a nauseated voice.

"The black piglets," Robbie said, crouching down to look more closely at one.

"That is the most disgusting thing I've ever seen."

"And a waste of good bacon," James put in, with his usual dry tone.

Nobody laughed.

Morton moved to the center of the circle. A thick sandy grime lay over everything. He crouched down and brushed an area of the floor with his hand. There were some kind of markings on the wooden boards.

"What's that?" Wendy said, leaning over him to get a better look. Morton was pretty sure he knew but said nothing. He crawled quickly around on his hands and knees, brushing dust aside to reveal what he'd hoped not to find. Someone had painted a geometrically accurate spiral in purple ink that started at the font and wound outward to the circle of candles. Morton felt something curl up inside him. This *was* dark magic. No doubt about it.

"What is it?" James asked, moving in beside Wendy.

"I've seen this in one of King's stories," Morton said shakily. "The spiral is like the road that leads down to the underworld. You walk along the spiral, chanting spells, until you reach the center, where you summon beings from . . . someplace else."

"So," Melissa said haughtily, "still think King was a benign genius?"

Morton swallowed and looked shiftily at the room, trying to hide his disappointment. There was no way to avoid the facts. Morton had secretly hoped for a hidden library, or a sealed office — something that would show King in a new light. But this was the exact opposite. This was the most deeply diabolical place he'd ever seen. There was nothing to redeem King at all. And the rest of the attic was almost bare. A few empty shelves, a pile of cluttered oddments and an antique trunk with two drawers in the bottom were the only other furnishings.

Wendy was crouching beside the trunk, looking in one of the drawers.

"Hey, look, more newspapers," she said, pulling out a small bundle of yellowed papers. "They're English. From England, I mean."

She carried one of the papers close to the light of a nearby candle and read aloud. "The Welsh Chronicle. According to the date it's two years old."

"What's on the cover?" James asked.

"Nothing important, just politics. Oh, wait a minute, I've found something!"

Everyone huddled around Wendy so they could see. There was a large black-and-white photo of a chillingly familiar gargoyle, with all three fingers intact.

"Why is there a picture of that in a Welsh newspaper?" Robbie mused.

Wendy shrugged and began to read.

Police are baffled by a recent theft at a small museum on the outskirts of the picturesque city of Aberystwyth on the Welsh coast. An elaborate break-in was staged sometime between midnight and four a.m. last night, but only one obscure item was taken. The large gargoyle, of uncertain origin, was not considered to be among the museum's more valuable pieces but obviously appealed to one eccentric collector. "It's a crazed hippie, I shouldn't wonder," explained Miss Penrose, the museum's curator. "The odd little creature was carved out of Preseli Bluestone, which is the only reason I can think anybody would want it." Miss Penrose explained that the famous Preseli Bluestone, which is found only in the Welsh mountains, was used to erect the inner ring of Stonehenge in 2000 BC. This

connection would be enough, she thinks, to attract any number of fanatics to the object. It is thought that the statue itself was carved less than a hundred years ago by a modern sect of an ancient cult that believes the Bluestone holds magical powers.

Despite the mystery, Miss Penrose didn't seem too upset by the loss. She concluded the interview with this statement:

"To be perfectly frank, I'll not miss the ugly little fellow at all. No doubt whoever took it will be dancing around it in his underpants come this summer solstice performing some crackpot ritual. Honestly, you'd think people had something better to do with their time."

"I'd say we know who did it," Wendy said. "But King couldn't have stolen the gargoyle himself. He was already blind by that time."

"Maybe he wasn't blind after all," Robbie said. "Maybe he was just pretending to be blind."

"If he wasn't blind, then how come he fell down the well?" Melissa said.

"You know," James said, "I keep thinking about that. There's a three-foot-high wall around the well. Even if you were blind, how would you fall down it?"

Wendy tapped her finger to her lips in a pensive manner. "I don't know. That Fletcher, the man who interviewed him, said he was still a bit clumsy. I mean, he wasn't an experienced blind person."

"I'm clumsy," James said, "but I don't think even I could manage to fall down that well."

"You have a point," Wendy said.

"What if he wasn't blind *and* he didn't fall down the well?" Robbie said ominously.

"What are you suggesting?" James asked.

"He's suggesting that King is still alive," Morton said. "Am I right?"

Robbie nodded. "They never found his body. What if he faked his death and his blindness? That way he could have traveled to England . . ."

"Wales," Wendy corrected.

"Whatever, he could have stolen the gargoyle and brought it back here."

"If King went to all the trouble to steal the gargoyle, then he must have known it was magic," Morton said, feeling certain they were still missing something vitally important. "And if he knew it was magic, then why bury it and fake his own death?"

"Crazy people don't need reasons," Melissa cut in.

Morton still didn't buy it. King might have been evil after all, but he was too brilliant to be merely crazy.

He wandered over to the font to take a closer look. Curiously it was filled with ashes, as if someone had lit a small fire in there. Half buried in the dark cinders was a lumpy black object. At first he thought it was a dead bat, but as he moved closer he realized it was the charred remains of what was once a leather-bound book.

"Hey!" Morton said, holding up the blackened fragment in his hand.

"What is it?" James asked, walking over to get a good look.

Morton carefully peeled open the brittle remnant. There was almost nothing left at all, just a few charred pages with mostly unreadable snippets of handwritten text. Only one page had anything legible, and that was meaningless. It merely said:

"... *spreads, like ink on blotting paper, or fire in a forest* ..."

"I don't know," Morton said. "A diary, maybe?"

"Blind men can't write diaries," Melissa said dismissively.

"Whatever it was," Robbie said, "King must have been trying to hide it. Otherwise, why burn it?"

Melissa began to chew angrily at her nails. "This is stupid. We haven't learned a thing!"

"That's not true," Wendy said. "We know where the gargoyle came from, and we know it had something to do with ancient magic."

"Yes, but none of that is going to help us get rid of Morton's monsters."

Morton dropped the charred fragment back into the font. Melissa was right. If anything, the discovery of the attic had only raised more questions. Was King still alive? If so, where was he? And why did he fake his own death? Was it even true that he was blind? Why did he burn his diary, if that's what it was? And, most perplexing of all, why did he bury a magical gargoyle in a shallow grave at the bottom of the garden after going to all the trouble to steal it from a Welsh museum?

"Well, I better get going," Wendy said. "I don't want my parents to start asking questions."

"I've had enough of this place anyway," Melissa agreed.

The girls left first, and Morton, James, and Robbie resealed the hatch. As soon as they were finished James went straight to bed and locked himself in his room, no doubt to avoid Melissa confronting him further about his wish.

"I can't believe King was evil," Morton said to Robbie as he walked him to the end of the driveway. "My dad says things aren't always what they seem. You know, like the way the sun looks as though it goes around the Earth, but really it's exactly the opposite."

Robbie pointed to the almost full moon that was just rising behind the bare branches of the trees. "Yeah, but sometimes things are *exactly* what they seem."

Morton realized that Robbie was right. The moon revolved around the Earth, just as it appeared to, and King was probably just a crazed lunatic who practiced dark magic. Unfortunately they'd already fallen into his web, and no matter how much they struggled, there didn't seem to be any way to break free.

CHAPTER 13
AN INCIDENT WITH AN ANGRY MUSICIAN

Morton lay awake feeling utterly hopeless. After everything that had happened, learning that King really did practice dark magic was the most difficult thing for him to swallow. He had been wrong about King, and he had been wrong about *Scare Scape*. And yet, even as Morton gave in to that idea, his mind kept struggling. He couldn't shake the feeling that he was missing something, some tiny detail . . .

The sound of the screen door opening downstairs interrupted his thoughts. It must have been long after midnight and no doubt James was stealing out into the streets again. This time Morton had no desire to follow him. The thought of James prowling down back alleys, feasting in garbage cans, and sniffing out appetizing morsels of decomposing food made his stomach twist in knots. He wondered again what kind of wish would make James need to eat rotting meat. Melissa had been right to try to confront him.

Melissa, it turned out, was right about a lot of things.

The next morning Morton decided to talk to James on the way to school, but unfortunately James had headed out early, pretending to have basketball practice again. Morton wolfed down his breakfast and ran after him, hoping to reach him before classes started, but as soon as he entered the school gates Robbie grabbed him by the arm and pulled him aside.

"Don't look now," he said, "but I think Brad and his cronies are out to get me again."

Morton looked over and saw Brad and his two band friends huddled in a circle casting sinister looks in their direction. Robbie tugged him around.

"I said, don't look."

"What's going on?" Morton asked.

"Apparently Inspector Sharpe searched his house last night looking for cats."

"So?" Morton said. "What's that got to do with you?"

Robbie sighed heavily. "Remember I told you the police came to my house?"

Morton nodded.

"Well, they started asking me questions and, well, Brad's name came up."

"What do you mean, 'Brad's name came up'?"

"You know, about how he's always bullying me and trying to pin things on me."

"You ratted out Brad?" Morton exclaimed.

"No!" Robbie protested. "It wasn't like that! They kept pushing me to say something, as if I was supposed to know who was behind it all, and I remembered how you'd said it was much more likely to be a gang of kids, like Brad and his buddies, so I think that's what I said."

Morton slapped his forehead with his hand. "Oh no! Why would you say that?"

Robbie frowned angrily. "Like any of this is my fault! Let's not forget who wished for those monsters to come alive in the first place."

"I didn't mean it that way," Morton said apologetically. "It's just . . . things are bad enough without Brad on our backs."

As Morton was saying this, shouting broke out among the band members. He and Robbie looked over to see that a fourth boy, also wearing a Wall of Noise shirt, was raising his voice. Morton had seen this fourth boy talking with them before, but for some reason he didn't usually hang around with them.

"That's Nolan Shaw," Robbie said. "He's the keyboard player, and as far as I know he's the one who writes all their songs, if you can call them songs."

"I thought it was Brad's band," Morton said.

"That's because Brad acts like it's his band, but Nolan's the real brains behind the thing. I think he just invited Brad because he looks like an angry goat and has a voice like a box of broken glass."

Nolan, who was quite a bit smaller than the fearsomely large Brad, suddenly pushed Brad hard on the shoulder, breaking the circle open, and stormed away from the group. With clenched fists Brad turned to watch him go. For a moment, Morton was sure Brad would run after him and thump him on the head, but he just turned back and began to conspire with his two remaining friends.

"What do you suppose that was all about?" Morton asked.

Robbie swallowed hard. "I don't know, but I can tell you one thing: I've never seen Brad looking so angry."

"Maybe we should tell Mr. Brown," Morton said, beginning to feel desperate.

"Brown!" Robbie said, in a surprisingly vehement tone. "Why would you go to him?"

"Because he said he would help with this sort of thing."

"I don't trust that guy," Robbie growled angrily.

"Why not?" Morton said, caught off guard by Robbie's response. "He's been really nice to me."

"Yeah, he seems that way, but he's all talk. When I confessed about stealing the money, he said that I was brave for coming forward and that he'd put a good word in for me, but he never showed up at the court hearing. And there was no statement on my record from him. I never heard from him again until I came back here."

"Well, maybe you should give him a second chance," Morton said. "Everyone deserves a second chance, right?"

"What's that supposed to mean?" Robbie said defensively.

"Nothing," Morton said, growing ever more confused by Robbie's hostile tone. "It means we should give Mr. Brown a second chance, that's all."

"Look, you do what you like," Robbie said, "just don't mention my name. I don't want anything to do with him."

And then Robbie stormed off across the yard and ran in through the main doors of the school.

Robbie avoided Morton for the rest of the day. Morton decided it would probably be best to give him some space and spent morning recess and lunchtime in the library.

Just after lunch Morton was retrieving books from his locker, on his way to geography, when somebody snuck up behind him.

"Hey, kid!"

For a horrible moment Morton thought Brad had cornered him, but he turned instead to see Nolan Shaw, the band's reticent leader.

"You're Morton, right?" Nolan said, glancing cautiously up and down the hall.

Morton nodded.

"Listen, did Robbie tell that inspector woman that Brad's been stealing the cats?"

"No," Morton said. "It wasn't like that at all."

"You sure?"

Morton began to feel angry. "Listen, I don't care what you guys think," he said. "I've got bigger things to worry about."

"You're missing my point," Nolan said. "I believe you. I don't think Robbie's that stupid. The problem is, Brad figures everyone's as dumb as he is."

"Why won't he just leave Robbie alone?" Morton said.

"Yeah, well, he's after both of you now. Thinks you're in it together."

Morton groaned. "We are not stealing cats!"

"That's what I told him. I figure there's got to be something bigger going on here, what with the police all over the place and that little kid's weird story about the skull-faced man. Brad doesn't care though. He just wants to get mad at someone, preferably Robbie and his friends."

"I figured."

"Anyway, my point is, I told him to leave you both alone or leave the band. He said what happened outside the band was his business, so I threw him out. Glad to be rid of him to tell you the truth. It's all going to his head, and he never shows up to rehearsals anymore. But the thing is, my throwing him out of the band is probably only going to make him madder. The way his mind works, he'll blame you guys for that too."

"Great!" Morton said sourly.

"I just thought you should know. He's not very rational at the best of times, and the police really spooked him yesterday. My advice: Steer clear of him."

"Thanks for the tip," Morton said, although he'd already made up his mind to do that.

Nolan grunted in a friendly sort of way and swayed off down the hall.

Morton felt even more nervous now. If Brad really was as angry as he looked, there was no telling what he might do. Robbie might even get hurt.

By the end of the day Morton was so worked up that, despite his disagreement with Robbie, he decided to pay an unscheduled visit to Mr. Brown. As soon as the bell rang he made his way to Brown's office, taking care to inspect all the hallways before going down them. He even went so far as to avoid going past his own locker, because that would be the obvious place for Brad to find him.

Following the map that Brown had given him on the first day, Morton finally found the frosted glass doorway with STAFF ONLY printed on it in black letters. He hadn't realized Brown's office was the same room where Sharpe had interviewed him.

Morton knocked timidly. Nobody answered. He knocked again, a bit more boldly this time. There was still no answer, and Morton began to have second thoughts. Maybe Robbie had been right. Maybe Mr. Brown wasn't the best person to confide in. In fact, maybe it was just plain cowardly to get a teacher involved at all. He had just about talked himself out of the whole plan when the door swung open. Mr. Brown was eating a sandwich and the strong smell of onions and mustard wafted out of the room.

"Morton! To what do I owe the pleasure?"

"I wondered if I could talk to you," Morton said.

"Certainly. Come in, come in."

Morton, still carrying several books and his heavy schoolbag, shuffled in to the empty room. There was nobody else around. Mr. Brown closed the door firmly.

"Don't you have an office of your own?" Morton asked.

"Yes, this is it," Brown said, sitting back down behind his desk.

Morton looked around. The room was as cold and bare as before. Mr. Brown noticed the look on Morton's face.

"Oh, I know, I know. You'd think after two years I would have found time to move in properly, but they just work me to death here."

"You've only been here two years?" Morton asked.

"Yes, I'm a relative newcomer to Dimvale, just like you. You don't mind if I finish my lunch do you?" Mr. Brown took another bite of his sandwich.

"Lunch?" Morton said. "It's almost suppertime."

"Like I said, they keep me so busy I don't even have time to eat."

Morton looked around the room again. There was only one book on the shelves and it was the history textbook they used in class. Somehow it didn't seem right, a teacher with no books in his office.

"Don't you have any books, sir?" he asked.

"Oh, mountains of them," Mr. Brown said. "Boxes and boxes. Too many to fit in here. You know me, a real history nut. Anything ancient or old or historical, I can't resist it."

Morton had a curious thought. If Mr. Brown had so many books, and he was a history buff, then maybe, just maybe, he might know something about ancient magic. "Do you have any books on ancient magic?" he said.

Mr. Brown, who had just taken a sizable bite of his sandwich, took a sudden sharp intake of breath. He then froze and the color drained from his face until it was a pale blue. For a moment Morton thought he looked the way people do in murder mystery movies when they've just been stabbed in the back by an unseen killer. His eyes grew wider and redder, and Morton was certain he was about to keel over onto the desk, dead. Fortunately this didn't happen. Instead, he began thumping his own chest violently. A second later he broke into an explosive, choking cough and a small red projectile shot out of his mouth, landing on the desk directly in front of Morton.

Mr. Brown stood up and continued to cough for a few more moments. His face went from deathly white to dark purple, which Morton thought was probably a good sign. The projectile, it turned out, was a small cherry tomato.

"Are you all right, sir?" Morton said, feeling bewildered.

"I do beg your pardon," Mr. Brown said at long last, clutching a napkin to his face. "That will teach me to eat and work at the same time."

Morton found himself unable to take his eyes from the slightly ruptured cherry tomato on the desk. Mr. Brown followed his gaze and spotted the object that had, moments before, barricaded his windpipe.

"Oh, goodness," Mr. Brown said, and quickly whisked up the tomato in his napkin and threw it in the wastebasket. "Again, very sorry."

Mr. Brown coughed a few more times and then, discarding the remainder of his sandwich, settled back into his chair. "Now, what was it you were asking?"

"Magic, sir. Do you know anything about ancient magic?"

"What a curious question."

"It's for a geography project."

"Oh, Mrs. Houston's class. I see." Mr. Brown nodded thoughtfully. "Well, I hate to disappoint you, but I really don't know about that sort of thing. Not my area of expertise. Now, ask me about Napoleon, and I'll keep you here until the middle of next week."

"It has to be ancient magic, sir."

Mr. Brown shrugged. "Sorry, I really can't help you." He glanced at the watch on his wrist and jumped up. "Well, I must be getting on. Sorry to rush you . . ."

"But, sir, that's not why I came, I just . . ."

"Sorry," Brown said in a hasty voice, "I just remembered I have a dentist's appointment. If there's something else, maybe we can discuss it tomorrow? Not too urgent, is it?"

Mr. Brown rushed to the door and held it open in an almost hostile manner.

"I guess it can wait," Morton said, gathering his books and bag hastily.

"Tomorrow it is, then," Mr. Brown said curtly.

Morton limped out of the door, trying not to drop anything.

"Thank you," he said, although he didn't feel he should be thanking Mr. Brown for anything. Mr. Brown smiled and gave a small wave before practically slamming the door on his back.

Morton was still puzzled as he left the school grounds. Every other time he'd spoken with Mr. Brown, the teacher had bent over backward to let Morton know he'd be there to help him, and yet now, when he really needed help, Brown claimed to be too busy to hear him out. Maybe he was just embarrassed about the whole choking-on-the-tomato incident. But he'd seemed normal until he'd mentioned ancient magic. Could Brown know something about the strange events going on in Dimvale? This possibility was just beginning to take root in Morton's mind when he rounded the corner to cut across a small park and saw something that made his heart sink.

Brad and his two dedicated followers, Dave Michaels and Sid Jones, had Robbie facedown on the ground with his arm twisted behind him. Sid was holding Robbie's arm and pressing his knee into the middle of his back. Dave, meanwhile, sat lazily off to one side on a large hockey bag, his pale acne-ridden face grinning and nodding eagerly. The moment they spotted Morton, Dave and Brad raced toward him, and before he knew what was happening he too was flat on his stomach with his face pressed hard in the grass.

"Let Robbie go!" Morton shouted. "He didn't do anything."

"Don't waste your breath," Brad said, grabbing Morton's hair and pushing his head down. "I know you're in this together."

Morton twisted his neck around in an attempt to make eye contact with Brad. To his own surprise he wasn't even slightly afraid. He was just angry. "Robbie's got nothing to do with it!" he yelled.

"Listen, I don't care what you do for a bit of money on the side," Brad said, increasing the pressure on Morton's face, "but telling Sharpe it was me that stole the cats, that was a big mistake, especially since my record isn't exactly clean to begin with."

"We didn't do anything," Morton said fiercely.

"Everybody knows this thing started right after you arrived in town and got together with Robbie. Robbie's not smart enough to do it alone. I don't know if it's supposed to be a joke or if you're making money, and I don't care, because as of right now you're going to admit to what you did, or I'll break Robbie's arm and your nose, and that's just for starters."

Morton couldn't believe what he was hearing. Brad genuinely believed that he and Robbie were behind the cat-nappings.

"You think Sharpe is going to believe you're innocent if you beat us up?" he said, hoping to make him see reason.

"But we're not beating you up," Brad said. "We're all in a rehearsal right now with our new band, aren't we boys? And we've got each other as witnesses."

"Yeah, well, what about me?" a voice said from behind Brad. Morton had never been so happy in his life to hear James's voice. Brad jumped to his feet and stood facing James. Morton was still pinned down by Dave, but he managed to twist onto his side to see what was happening.

"Let them go or I'll call the police," James said. Morton

could hear the nervous tremor in James's voice, and no doubt Brad could too, but he couldn't help thinking that there was something unusual about the way James was holding himself. He was taller than he used to be, that was part of it, but there was something else too — something a little menacing in his stance.

Brad raised his sizable fist in the air and stepped closer to James. "I'm not scared of you."

James stepped backward. "You can beat me up if you want, Brad, but I'm not going anywhere until you let Robbie and my brother go."

Morton felt simultaneous waves of pride and fear rush through him. James always did the right thing, but he was a terrible fighter, and if it came to blows, there was no doubt he'd lose hands down.

"Run!" Morton yelled. "Go get help."

"Yeah, you heard him," Brad said. "Run, you little coward."

"I'm not going anywhere until you let them go," James repeated calmly.

"Oh, now I get it," Brad said. "*You're* the mastermind behind the whole plan. I thought it was a bit too complicated for these two."

"Well, if I am the mastermind, then you should let them go and have it out with me."

"Don't tell me what to do. I'm in charge here!" Brad shouted, pushing James on the shoulder.

James stumbled backward, but instead of reacting to the shove he did something very odd. He began to sniff in the air.

"You're afraid of me aren't you?" he said.

Brad seemed as surprised by the question as Morton was. "What are you talking about? I'm not afraid of anyone."

"Yes, you are," James said, now taking a step toward Brad. "I can smell it."

Morton felt a sudden chill run down his spine. He'd never seen James behave this way before. He usually managed to talk his way out of fights by reasoning with people. He must surely know that this kind of talk would get Brad more riled up than before.

"I don't smell," Brad said, unexpectedly taking a step away from James.

"Yes, you do," James said, now in a hauntingly hypnotic voice. "You reek of fear. And you know what the problem with fear is? People who are afraid always make stupid mistakes."

Brad took two full steps backward this time and swallowed hard.

"You don't scare me!" Brad said, but his eyes betrayed the truth. Morton could see that he really was afraid. But why?

James held out his hands in a gesture of truce. "We don't have to fight," he said. "You'll only lose if we fight, so why don't you just let Morton and Robbie go and we can talk about it."

Now Morton began to think that James was playing a very clever bluff. It was a bit out of character for him, but maybe he realized that Brad would only respond to threats. Brad seemed momentarily cowed and looked around at Sid and Dave as if asking their advice. Both of them made grim faces and shook their heads. No doubt this spurred Brad on, because at that instant he broke into an abrupt fit of rage and kicked James hard in the gut. James wasn't ready for the savage attack and doubled over like a crushed pop can. Morton cried out, feeling his pain, but stopped when he saw what happened next. James suddenly belched out an impossibly large cloud of acrid yellow smoke. Morton coughed as the fumes from the yellow haze drifted over him.

"What the heck?" Sid said.

The yellow gas wafted into Brad's face, and he too began to cough. "What's this? Some kind of joke?"

James pulled himself back into a standing position and leered at Brad. Morton had thought he was done for, but James looked angrier and more powerful than Morton had ever seen him. "You'd better run now," he said sinisterly, "because I just lost my patience."

Brad blanched for a moment and seemed to waver until Sid and Dave started laughing behind him. Brad joined in the laughter then, obviously thinking the whole thing was an elaborate prank. Without warning he threw a punch right at James's face. James reacted with lightning speed and raised his arms up to block the blow. Brad's fist struck James's forearm with full force and then, inexplicably, Brad dropped to the ground and curled into a ball, screaming and clutching his fist.

"Arrrgh!" he cried. "He cut me!" Blood began to run down Brad's arm like red ink, dripping from his elbow and staining his white shirt.

The grins vanished instantly from Sid's and Dave's faces, and the two jumped to their feet, releasing Morton and Robbie. They glanced at James, staggered back a few paces, and then turned and hurtled across the park in a panic. Brad looked at the bleeding gash on his hand with a sickly expression.

"I'm sorry," James said, seemingly equally shocked by what had just happened. He stepped forward and offered his hand, but Brad shuffled backward like a crab.

"Keep away from me!" he cried, and then, wrapping his bleeding fist in his shirt, he leaped to his feet and followed Sid and Dave across the park as fast as his stocky legs could carry him.

Robbie and Morton jumped up and dusted themselves off. James stood motionless, gazing off into the distance.

"Are you okay?" Morton asked, but James didn't answer. He fell to his knees and spewed out another giant cloud of yellow smoke.

CHAPTER 14
THE WARGLE [RHYMES WITH GARGLE] SNARF

The first thing Morton noticed when he grabbed James's arm was that his skin was almost too hot to touch.

"James! What's happened to you?"

James pulled himself groggily to an upright position. The strength that he'd shown just a few moments earlier had drained from his eyes, and he looked suddenly fragile and weak. He attempted to smile. "Sorry, got carried away."

He clutched at his stomach and moaned painfully again. "You better get me home," he croaked.

Morton looked over at Robbie, who was hanging back at a safe distance.

"Can you grab his other arm?" he asked. At first Robbie didn't move, but he eventually nodded and stepped forward to grab James.

"Be careful," James said.

"Does it hurt?" Morton asked.

"No. I don't want you to cut yourselves," James explained, rolling back one of his sleeves to reveal a row of razor-sharp spines running the full length of his arm and ending just above his wrist. So that was what had cut Brad's hand.

"What *is* that?" Robbie said, failing to mask the fear in his voice.

"I was hoping Morton could tell me," James said, shrugging innocently. "They started growing a couple of weeks ago. I have them down my back too. I thought I might have caught some kind of disease from one of the monsters."

Morton looked closer at the spines. They didn't look familiar, but then again, his experience with mystical diseases was confined to comic book illustrations.

"Come on," he said. "We'll figure it out later."

James managed to stand, but his legs were shaking badly. Robbie and Morton did their best to support him, but several times on the way home he doubled over again and belched yellow acidic smog.

When they finally arrived at the foot of the driveway, Melissa and Wendy were approaching from the other direction. The girls immediately noticed that something was wrong and ran toward them.

"What happened?" Melissa asked, her face going pale.

"We'll tell you later," Morton said. "First we need you to distract Dad while we get James to his room."

Melissa nodded solemnly and sprinted off ahead of them.

Moments later they crept quietly up the stairs, successfully managing to get James to his room without Dad seeing him. James pulled off his jacket and slumped on his bed, panting heavily, sweat running down his face.

Melissa and Wendy came in behind them and closed the door.

"This is your wish, isn't it?" Melissa said in an accusing tone.

"I don't know," James said weakly. "I think I might have caught some kind of disease from one of Morton's monsters."

Morton looked again at the hard bony spines on James's arms. In *Scare Scape* there were lots of stories about strange diseases and curses, but few that gave you spines.

"It could be a Cactusite," he said hesitantly.

"Sounds fun," James said. "What is it?"

"It's a really dangerous cactus plant that gives off spores. If you inhale them, they grow in your bloodstream and eventually baby cactuses start sprouting on your skin. Have you developed a phobia of water?"

"No."

"Do you feel the need to be in constant sunlight?"

"No."

"Any yearnings for the desert?"

"Definitely not."

"Hmm! Probably not that, then. Do you have any other symptoms?"

James gasped suddenly, and his eyes rolled up into the top of his head. For a moment Morton thought his brother was going to pass out, but then he opened his eyes again and spoke. "The smoke, the spines. My sense of smell is a lot stronger. I can see in the dark better, and I crave rotting food, especially meat."

This didn't make any sense. The only thing Morton could think of was a giant centipede-like creature called a Wargle Snarf, which had poison spines. But Morton had never owned a Snarf toy. In fact, the Snarf rarely appeared in *Scare Scape* and had been on the cover only once. . . .

A truly horrible realization crashed into Morton's brain. Suddenly the room was spinning, and he felt as though he were suffocating. "Where's that comic?" he gasped. "The one with the girl that looks like Melissa on the front."

"A girl like me?" Melissa said questioningly.

James looked guiltily around the room and then pointed to his dresser. The comic was sitting crumpled under piles of homework. Normally a crumpled comic would have made Morton screech in protest, but that was the last thing on his mind right now. He looked at the cover. A large centipede-like creature with a vast mouth and two rings of razor-sharp teeth was about to devour a skinny girl. Just as Morton had feared, this creature was the Snarf.

Morton's stomach twisted in horror. "You wished to be a Wargle Snarf," he said in a tone of utter disbelief.

"A whattle what?" Melissa said.

"It's one of the deadliest monsters in *Scare Scape*," Morton replied.

Melissa let out a dismissive laugh. "That can't be right. Why would he wish to be that?"

Morton couldn't bring himself to explain it. Instead, he handed the comic to Melissa. As soon as she glanced at the cover her jaw dropped. The look on her face told Morton that she too had figured it out.

Just before the strange blue light appeared, she and James had been having a horrible fight. James had stormed angrily up to his room with the stone finger in his pocket. Obviously he'd been looking at the image of the girl in mortal danger — the girl who looked just like his sister — and, whether consciously or unconsciously, he'd wished to be the monster in the picture so that he could take his revenge.

Melissa dropped the comic and glared at James. "How could you?" she hissed in a cold, hateful voice.

James was shaking his head from side to side as if still unable to believe the truth. "I didn't . . . I mean . . . I was angry and I . . . I might have thought about it for a moment."

"Thought about killing me, you mean?"

"It wasn't like that!" James shouted, so forcefully that another puff of yellow smoke erupted from his mouth.

"Can we please not fight about it," Morton said firmly. "I mean, the gargoyle is dark magic. It doesn't grant you what you want. I didn't wish for my toys to come alive, and Melissa only wished for a big closet, not an infinite one. And obviously nobody really wants to be a Wargle Snarf."

"Morton's right," Wendy said in a calming tone. "It doesn't matter how we got into this. The important thing is to figure out how to get out of it, which means figuring out how to make James well again."

Morton was thankful to Wendy for being a voice of reason. His head was throbbing, and it was hard to focus. James was transforming into a Snarf before his very eyes, and despite what Morton had just said about dark magic, all he could think about was how it was all his fault. If he hadn't been so obsessed with *Scare Scape*, he would never have bought all those stupid plastic monster toys, and James would never have been looking at that comic. Instead, they probably would have wished for sensible things, normal things like health or happiness. But now, because of him, here they were living in a town crawling with monsters, and his brother was only half human.

"Maybe we should take him to the hospital," Robbie said.

"No!" James said firmly. "I can't go there!"

"It probably wouldn't do any good anyway," Melissa said. "I mean, how do you stop someone from turning into a walking meat grinder?"

"Well, we have to do something," Wendy said. "Morton, you know all about these monsters. Don't you have any ideas?"

Morton rubbed his face and tried to clear his head. Feeling guilty wasn't going to help anybody. "I'll be right back," he said, and dashed down the hall to his bedroom. Sitting in the top drawer of his bedside table was one of his most prized possessions. It was a set of cards printed in faded ink to resemble an ancient deck of tarot cards, but instead of the traditional figures, like Death and the Hanged Man, the cards featured some of the most popular monsters that had appeared in *Scare Scape*. It was called the Monster Tarot, and it had cost him a lot of money. He pulled out the pack and began to riffle through it. After a moment of going back and forth he finally slid out the card he was looking for. The frightening creature illustrated on the front had a bony-ridged back with sickle-like barbs running along its entire length. He squinted at the card to read the small print at the bottom.

The Greater Spotted Wargle (rhymes with gargle) Snarf.

He flipped the card over and read the reverse.

Few creatures boast the raw power of the Snarf. Up to fifteen feet long, with an impenetrable bony carapace and a double ring of razor-sharp, metal-ripping teeth, this behemoth is tough enough to tackle a tank . . . and win. Like its smaller cousin, the Lesser Spotted Snarf, the Wargle can paralyze its victims by secreting a fear-inducing pheromone from glands distributed all over its body.

This nocturnal creature has perfect night vision, and its sense of smell is ten times more acute than that of a bloodhound. Few humans can survive an encounter with a Snarf, and the unfortunate ones who do discover that exposure to the Snarf's poison-tipped barbs causes a slow, painful transformation into a hybrid human-Snarf creature.

Legend has it that the Snarf draws its demonic power from the brimstone in its stomach, which it gets by drinking from the boiling rivers of Hades.

Brimstone! That was the clue Morton was hoping for. He dashed back down the hall, clutching the cards in his hands.

"Coal!" he said as he burst into the room. "James has to eat coal."

The others looked at him with rapt attention as he quickly read the back of the card to them.

"The coal counteracts the brimstone," he explained. "And without the brimstone the Snarf has no power, so James will be able to resist the transformation."

"How do you know this?" Wendy asked.

"It was in one of King's stories. I'd forgotten about it until now, but it's about a man who escapes from a Snarf and then begins to turn into one. He eats coal to slow down the transformation."

"Slow it down, or stop it?" James asked.

"Uh, it doesn't stop it altogether," Morton admitted. "But it will buy us some time."

"What happened to the man in the story?" James asked.

Morton looked down at his feet. He couldn't bring himself to tell him that the man had finally transformed into a Snarf and eaten his entire family, but then, it seemed his lack of answer was enough. Nobody asked him a second time.

"Where do we get coal?" Wendy said urgently.

"I can get you some," Robbie said. "They sell it at the corner store for barbecues."

Morton looked up at Robbie appreciatively. Despite everything, he was still willing to stick by them. "Thanks," Morton said, "for all your help."

Robbie just shrugged. "What are friends for?"

"I know, but . . ."

"Don't even think about it. I'll be back in a few minutes," Robbie said, going for the door, "but then I better go. My mom's going to be worried about me."

James rolled over and let out another painful-sounding belch of yellow smog. This time it filled the room, and they all began to cough. Wendy ran to open the window.

"I need food," James said. "Food stops the belching."

"By food you mean rotting meat," Melissa said.

James nodded guiltily. Morton couldn't even begin to imagine how James must be feeling.

"I'll go get you some food," Melissa said, thoroughly surprising Morton.

"No, I can go," Morton said. "I know the best places to look."

"We'll go together, then," Melissa said. "I don't want you skulking down back alleys alone. Wendy, you'll have to stay with James and keep an eye on him. Lock the door, and I'll tell Dad we've all been invited to your house for supper. Hopefully he'll be gone by the time we get back."

Thirty minutes later Morton and Melissa arrived at the spot where Morton had first seen James scrounging for food. The sun was just setting and cold blue shadows were creeping down the narrow lane, filling Morton with a sense of desolation. Melissa shivered and pulled her arms tightly around her.

"Let's hurry," she said. "I don't want to be here after dark."

A thick, vinegary odor greeted their nostrils, and a swarm of flies buzzed around the Dumpster like an angry gray mist. Morton clambered up onto the pile of garbage bags, which squelched beneath his feet like giant foul-smelling black marshmallows.

"I am definitely going to throw up," Melissa said, climbing up after him.

Morton tried not to think about it and tore open the first bag.

"Okay, what are we looking for?" she said, producing a large plastic container.

"Meat," Morton said. "The older the better."

"This wouldn't have happened if I'd had sisters," Melissa sighed.

Morton ignored the comment and began to tear open more garbage bags. The smell was almost too much to bear. When he thought about poor James having to eat this food to fend off his gaseous attacks, the now overwhelming weight of guilt began to crush down on him again. This was by far the worst thing that could have happened. He angrily tore open another garbage bag, but as he did so he slipped on a soupy substance beneath his feet and slid down between the gaps in the bags. Before he knew what was happening, he was up to his waist in garbage. He struggled to climb out, but his hands slithered over the slimy bags and he realized he was completely stuck.

Quite suddenly his face was wet with hot, angry tears. It took him a moment to realize he was crying. He hadn't cried in so long that he'd forgotten what it felt like. In fact, he'd pretty much convinced himself he was no longer capable of crying. But now that the floodgates were opened, he felt as if he'd never be able to stop. His chest heaved and his hands trembled as giant sobs wracked his body. This was the end, he thought. James would turn into a monster and join the Zombie Twins, and he'd be left utterly alone in the world, trapped forever in a mound of decomposing slime.

That's when someone put their hands under his elbows, dragged him back to the spongy surface, and pulled him into a tight hug. It was Melissa. Morton had momentarily forgotten that she was even there. But realizing that it was her only made him more confused. Melissa never hugged him, ever. But even as he thought this, he had a sudden flash of memory of a time when they were much younger and Melissa had carried him about the house and pushed him around in his stroller. There had been a time when she *always* hugged him, and Morton realized that he'd missed that feeling so much. Even sitting here in the stench of old soup and chicken bones, Melissa's protective arms around him made him feel safe in a way that he hadn't felt in a very long time. Morton gave into it and continued to sob. He sobbed until he felt as if his entire chest were empty and there was nothing left inside, but Melissa continued to hold on to him. At one point he realized that she too was crying, silently, rocking him back and forth, and the two of them sat there until the sun had dropped completely below the horizon and real darkness swallowed the sky.

"I'm so stupid!" Morton said at last, feeling utterly forlorn and hollow. "It's all my fault. I feel like burning my stupid comics."

Melissa wiped her own eyes. "It's nothing to do with your comics, Morton. If this is anyone's fault, it's mine."

This was the last thing he'd expected Melissa to say.

"You only wished for a closet. How does that make any of this your fault?"

"James was angry when he made that wish, and I made him angry, so it's my fault. I'll never forgive myself for what I said to him."

Morton cast his mind back to that fateful day. Melissa had goaded James about being a mummy's boy for as long as Morton could remember. He knew it had just become a habit and had been a slip of the tongue, nothing more.

"I know you didn't mean it," Morton said.

"I did and I didn't," Melissa said. "I was always so jealous of James because I thought he was Mum's favorite. I see now Mum didn't have favorites. She just made sure we all got what we needed, and James needed her more than we did. I realize that now. She always told us you were the toughest one, you know."

Morton looked up at Melissa in complete surprise. "Mum said that about me?"

Melissa nodded. " 'Don't worry about Morton,' she used to say. 'He's got the courage of a lion and the wisdom of an owl. He's tougher than the rest of us put together. You'll see.' "

Morton could hardly believe what he was hearing. He didn't feel tough. He'd never felt tough.

"But that's not true," Morton said. "I just spent the last nine months reading *Scare Scape* trying to avoid everything. That's not being tough at all."

"You might not see it yet, but Mum was right," Melissa said. "That's why James and I are banking on you to get us out of this mess."

"Me?" Morton said, even more shocked than before. "Why me?"

"I'd have thought that was obvious. You're a natural at all of this. You're not afraid of the dark or the monsters, you never panic and, well, you know this stuff like the back of your hand."

"But James is the smart one," Morton said. "I'm just —"

"Oh, James is just like Dad. He can solve any complex math problem, but don't ask him to hang a shelf or, heaven forbid, change the batteries in the smoke alarm. No, James is the wrong kind of smart. If anyone can get us out of this, it's you."

Morton swallowed hard and wiped the last of the tears from his face. It had never for one moment occurred to him that James and Melissa were looking to him to find a way out of this mess, and he almost wished Melissa hadn't told him. He wasn't at all sure he could live up to their expectations.

Melissa stood up and pulled Morton back to his feet. "Don't worry," she said, looking him directly in the eye. "I know Mum was right about you, even if you don't. Now come on, let's get this food back to James before he eats Wendy's liver."

CHAPTER 15

OUT OF THE BAG

Morton should have guessed something was wrong when James came down to breakfast the next morning wearing sunglasses.

"Cool, don't you think?" he said, bounding up onto a chair and doing an odd little dance.

"The word *cool* does not spring to mind," Melissa said. "Are you sure you're feeling okay?"

"Never better," James replied. "I slept so well last night I feel like a whole new person."

"Is that because of the charcoal?" Melissa asked, casting a sideways glance at Morton.

Morton nodded. When they had returned to the house the previous night to give James the scavenged food, James had already eaten an entire bag of barbecue coals and was in much better spirits. The coal was definitely helping, but Morton now wondered if it was possible to have too much of a good thing.

"It's amazing," James said. "I feel . . . I feel like I could leap to the top of the house."

"Please don't," Melissa groaned. "It might attract attention."

James jumped off the chair and began eating cereal straight from the box. "Well, no, not literally. But I do feel like . . . I feel like singing. You know, I actually have a pretty good singing voice."

Melissa and Morton gaped blankly at each other.

Fortunately Dad bustled in with a pan of scrambled eggs before James had a chance to demonstrate.

"James, take those ridiculous sunglasses off," he said.

"Sorry, Pops. It's the new me," James said with a mock swagger.

"The new you, is it?" Dad said. "I don't know; growing like a string bean, losing your appetite for mashed potatoes, and now making wayward fashion choices. I think I preferred the old you."

"The world turns, the sun burns," James said incongruously.

"Are you sure you're all right?" Dad asked, moving closer to him. "You know, you don't seem to have ever recovered from that stomach flu. And your skin looks paler than ever."

James waved his hands dismissively. "Dad, take a chill pill," he said. "I'm just fine."

Dad sighed, shook his head, and began serving the eggs, although Morton could almost hear the gears turning in his brain and wondered how much longer they could keep him in the dark.

Half an hour later, as Melissa and the boys parted company at the end of the driveway, Melissa leaned in close to Morton and whispered in his ear. "Maybe we should cut down on the coal next time," she said. "It's making him weird."

Morton nodded in agreement.

For the rest of the day James continued to wear his sunglasses. Morton approached him at lunchtime and suggested that he take them off, pointing out that the other kids might think it strange. James insisted that he was starting a new trend and said Morton was too young to understand.

By afternoon recess Morton was starting to get really worried. He met up with Robbie at the lockers in the main hallway and told him about James's increasingly odd behavior. "There's something wrong with him," he said.

"You mean, something more than the fact that he's turning into a Snarf?" Robbie asked, genuinely confused.

"Well, maybe not," Morton went on, "but he won't take those sunglasses off."

Robbie scratched his ear, clearly not understanding.

"The Snarf is nocturnal," Morton explained. "It can see in total darkness, but bright light blinds it. I think daylight hurts James's eyes now."

"But I thought the coal would slow things down," Robbie said.

"So did I," Morton sighed. "Something's not right."

"Morton! Morton!" Timothy Clarke yelled, appearing suddenly at the end of the hallway pushing his way through the crowd. The urgency in Timmy's voice made Morton's mind leap immediately to James. Had something happened already?

"What is it?" Morton gasped as Timmy approached.

Timmy was out of breath and stood panting for a moment. "It's, it's . . ."

"What?" Morton snapped, grabbing Timmy's shoulders in panic.

Timmy looked up, momentarily confused, and then handed him a large canvas bag. "It's my *Scare Scape* toys," he said. "I finally got them in the mail. I ordered them from the back pages of the comic, just like you told me to."

Morton sighed with relief. He'd completely forgotten that he had shown Timmy how to order his own toys and even helped him fill out the form.

"They're totally cool!" Timmy was saying. "Take a look."

Morton opened the bag and pulled out each of the toys in turn. There was a large purple Hydra Snake, two King-Crab Spiders, and several Two-Headed Mutant Rodents. It was strange to see them in their primitive plastic form again now that he'd had so many face-to-face encounters with the real things.

"Oh, that's great," Morton said, pretending to be enthusiastic, but in fact still recovering from the rush of fear that had consumed him.

"So, when can I come over?" Timmy said, still bouncing with enthusiasm.

"Huh?"

"You said you'd invite me over to see your collection when mine arrived, remember?"

Morton grimaced. He'd forgotten that too. But how was he going to break it to him that he didn't exactly have a collection anymore?

"You know what," he said, "Dad's renovating, so I had to pack them away."

Timmy's face dropped. "Oh. I really wanted to see your Zombie Twins. They're like super rare collector's items now. Maybe you could bring them to school?"

Morton held the bag out to give it back to Timmy and was wondering if he could order some new Zombie Twins to get Timmy off his back when the bag began wriggling in his hands. Timmy, who had just reached up to take it from him, froze in midaction. His eyes widened incredulously, and he looked back and forth between the bag and Morton. The bag jerked suddenly in Morton's hand, and he dropped it to the polished tile floor where it quickly started to swell. Timmy stumbled fearfully away. With incredible speed the bag swelled to twice its size and the stitched seams split open and, almost before Morton could draw a breath, several snarling creatures burst free of the now completely shredded canvas.

Morton gasped, and somewhere behind him several kids started screaming. Robbie's eyes widened until they looked like they might fall right out of his head.

The monsters paused, looking hungrily around at the densely packed corridor of now terrified but fascinated students.

Fortunately Morton managed to recover from the shock before the creatures had time to act. He whipped off his jacket, threw it over one of the King-Crab Spiders, and tied the sleeves together. Robbie followed suit and attempted to do the same thing with the other Spider, but one of the Mutant Rodents raced forward and sank both sets of its teeth into his ankle. Robbie let out a scream. Suddenly James appeared from the crowd, still wearing his sunglasses, and snatched a baseball bat from the hands of a nearby seventh grader. In one swift motion, he squashed the Two-Headed Mutant Rodent. Its two heads squealed in a final chorus of high-pitched agony. Robbie fell to the floor clutching his injured ankle.

Morton meanwhile realized that the Hydra Snake was slithering down the hall, heading directly for a small blond-haired girl who stood paralyzed with fear, staring at the impossible sight before her.

"Willow!" Morton cried. But Willow didn't even seem to hear him.

He broke into a run. Robbie started yelling, but Morton could hear nothing over the pulsing of blood in his own ears. The snake was practically on top of Willow now, less than a foot away. Morton threw himself toward the snake and slid on his belly, managing to snatch the creature by its tail a mere millisecond before it sank its venomous fangs into the still-paralyzed Willow. Four hissing heads turned immediately on him, but he threw the snake hard up at the wall where it landed, dazed, on top of the row of lockers.

Morton then realized what Robbie was yelling about. The first King-Crab Spider had somehow wriggled free of the jacket, and he and James were now desperately swatting at two Spiders in an attempt to keep them at bay. Morton sprinted back and kicked one of the Spiders, sending it spiraling twenty feet down the hall. The spider hit the floor, bounced, rolled, and then quickly got back to its feet. The group of kids cowering at the far end of the hall screamed and scattered like frightened ants. At the same time, the Hydra Snake recovered from Morton's attack and began hissing at a clutch of children huddled below, while the remaining Two-Headed Mutant Rodents were still busily snapping at ankles all over the hall. Morton's heart sank to his stomach at the sight of the chaos spreading like wildfire all around him.

But then something unexpected happened. An intense, high-pitched whistle filled the crowded corridor. Every single student clutched their ears painfully.

Suddenly, eyes glowing like red-hot embers, hoods pulled up around their bony white faces, the Zombie Twins floated in through an open window. Yet another outbreak of screams pealed through the school. Simon Bean broke away from somewhere in the crowd of terrified children and began pointing in excitement.

"That's them! Look! They're the ones who stole my cat!"

"The Zombie Twins," a dazed and bemused Timmy Clarke murmured, emerging from his locker where he had apparently been hiding the whole time.

The Hydra Snake slithered along the top of the lockers as if answering a call from the Twins and threw itself out of the window. Immediately afterward both King-Crab Spiders turned, ran along the corridor, skittered up the wall, and crawled out through the same narrow opening, accompanied by the surviving Mutant Rodents. A moment later the Zombie Twins drifted back through the window and dropped out of sight.

An eerie, shocked silence filled the corridor.

Morton made his way over to the still motionless Willow. "Are you all right?" he asked, panting.

Willow nodded.

An instant later the entire school flooded in around them, jabbering excitedly.

"You saved her life," one tall girl said admiringly.

"Those Zombie Twins were cool," Timmy was saying.

"That's Morton," a first grader whispered in awe. "His brother beat up Brad."

It was then that Morton noticed Brad in the crowd. He had a large white bandage around his right hand that would have made him appear comical had it not been for the murderous expression on his face. He stared silently with cold, unblinking eyes, while everyone else chattered in nervous excitement around him.

Morton was beginning to feel dizzy when the sound of clicking heels echoed down the hall. Principal Finch and several other teachers were running toward the huddle of students. Mr. Brown limped along behind them.

"Just what exactly is going on here?" Finch demanded.

Morton realized with a sense of panic that everyone was standing facing James, Robbie, and himself. Finch pushed through the crowd and stepped toward them. "Well, explain yourselves," he said, looking directly at James.

"Sir?" James said innocently.

"Take those ridiculous sunglasses off when talking to me, Clay," he snapped.

James didn't move at first, but Finch stared him down until he had no choice. He drew them slowly away from his face. Practically every kid in the school let out a loud gasp. The whites of James's eyes were a vivid green — almost, Morton thought, the shade of mint ice cream.

James squinted painfully. So Morton had been right. Daylight hurt his eyes.

A look of confused suspicion crossed Finch's face.

"What the devil . . . ?" he began, but quite suddenly Mr. Brown appeared from behind James and placed a hand on his shoulder.

"James has a rare form of jaundice," he explained, returning the glasses to his face. "He's not to remove his glasses. I have a doctor's note in my office if you wish to see it."

"When did this happen?" Finch snapped suspiciously.

"Actually, he's had it for several weeks, but the symptoms only flare up from time to time," Brown said evenly. "No doubt the stress of recent events is a contributing factor."

Finch did not seem convinced, but neither did he pursue the issue. "In any case, how do you explain all of this?" he said, gesturing to the chaos in the hallway.

The boys stood mutely. They couldn't really have explained it even if they'd wanted to.

"I think this might shed some light on the matter," came a voice from behind Morton.

Morton turned to see Mr. Noble, the biology teacher, peering over his spectacles at the limp remains of a squashed rat. "This rat seems to have two heads."

Mrs. Wallis, the art teacher, clapped her hand to her mouth and let out a muffled yelp, and the other teachers all began to mutter among themselves.

"It must be some kind of mutant strain," Noble went on with an excited glint in his eye. "This could be the scientific discovery of a lifetime!"

Principal Finch did not share in Mr. Noble's optimism. "More like the health hazard of the century," he said bitterly. "Are you sure it's real?"

Mr. Noble frowned. "It looks pretty real to me."

Principal Finch turned to face the boys and began snapping his fingers nervously at his sides.

"Okay, you three. To my office! We're going to get to the bottom of this right now. The rest of you, back to class! This is a school, not a circus."

The teachers quickly began rounding up the other pupils. Morton caught sight of Mr. Brown amid the crowd. Quite mysteriously he raised his finger to his lips. Before Morton even had time to think about it, an angry-looking Finch whisked them off down the stairs, and he and the others half-ran, half-walked as they tried to keep up with him. Morton was feeling more confused than ever. Why had Mr. Brown stepped in to help James? He suddenly remembered Brown's odd behavior when he had visited him in his office. He'd wondered then if Brown had known more than he was letting on. Now it seemed certain that he knew something.

After a couple of minutes of speeding along narrow passages they finally arrived at Finch's secluded office.

Finch flung open the door and quite rudely pushed them all into the room. "Wait here," he said. "And absolutely no talking." Then he shut the door and locked it from the outside. The boys stared at one another in shock.

"He can't lock us in here!" Robbie said in an outraged whisper.

"Maybe he's calling our parents," James said. "That's usually what happens when kids bring monsters to school, isn't it?"

Nobody laughed.

"He's still not allowed to lock us up," Robbie said bitterly. "What just happened anyway? How did Timmy's monster toys come alive?"

Morton had been asking himself the same question.

"I think the wishes are getting stronger," he said. "It's as if I only have to touch toys to make them come alive now."

"The Midas touch," James said, pulling a bag of barbecue coals from his schoolbag. "We'd make a great double act. I'll belch out rings of yellow smoke and you can —"

"Will you be serious!" Morton snapped, feeling unusually irritated by James's charcoal-induced banter. "The wishes are getting stronger, you're getting sicker, and I don't know if you noticed, but Mr. Brown just outright lied for no reason that I can understand."

"He knows something," Robbie said.

Morton had already come to the same conclusion and told them both about the time he'd asked Brown about magic. "He might be able to help us," Morton said, when he'd finished the story.

Robbie shook his head adamantly. "I already told you, I don't trust that guy."

"Me neither," James said. "Anyway, it's too early to get anyone else involved."

"Too early!" Morton exclaimed. "It's been weeks! We've re-read all the stories, we've found King's secret attic, we know where the gargoyle came from, and we're still not one step closer to reversing the wishes."

"We are," James insisted. "I know we are. We have all the clues, we just haven't put them together yet."

"But you're getting worse!"

"Just a few more days," James pleaded. "Something's going to give, I can feel it."

"We might not have a few more days," Morton said, struggling to suppress the rising panic within.

At that moment Finch's voice echoed in the lobby outside, clearly in a heated discussion with someone else, and the boys fell silent. Morton strained to listen, but he couldn't make out what Finch was saying. A minute later, the door clicked open. To Morton's horror, Inspector Sharpe breezed into the room looking calmly officious. She was followed by Finch.

Sharpe settled herself in a chair at the corner of Finch's desk and began pulling papers out of her briefcase, while Finch threw himself into his own soft leather seat.

Sharpe flexed her cheek muscles into her usual facsimile of a smile, but she didn't speak for several seconds.

"Things are getting a little complicated in Dimvale," she said at last, "and this most recent spate of incidents is even more alarming than the rest." Sharpe held up the dead rat, now stiff with rigor mortis, and swung it before her as if looking at it for the first time. "Two-headed rats?" she said. "I'm sure this sort of thing happens in nature once in a while, but what are the odds of finding one in school do you suppose? And if you believe what the other children are saying, there was also a four-headed snake and two giant spiders in the hallway. Do you believe what the other children are saying?"

Morton knew it was pointless to deny it. He looked at the others, and they all nodded in unison. "We saw them with our own eyes, Inspector," he said.

"Now, you have to admit that's more than a bit strange," Sharpe said, "especially if you combine it with the inexplicable disappearance of every single cat in Dimvale."

Morton realized she was watching for reactions. He attempted to hold on to an innocent expression but swallowed hard, all too aware that the bobbing of his Adam's apple might as well have been a confession of guilt.

"We honestly don't know anything about . . ." Morton began, but Finch didn't let him finish.

"He's lying," he spluttered, suddenly wobbling in his chair like an over-wound clockwork toy. "Any fool can see he's lying! Don't think I haven't noticed the pattern, Morton Clay. It all started happening the day you and your brother set foot in my school. For years nothing, and then you come along, get together with this hoodlum Robbie, and the next thing I know we've got missing cats, reports of small footless men, and mutant rats and snakes frightening the life out of my pupils!"

The boys exchanged fearful glances. Finch looked beyond angry. The corners of his mouth were wet with spittle and his eyes bulged like hard-boiled eggs.

"You don't think we had anything to do with what happened today?" James protested.

Finch hammered the desk with his fist and leaned forward so that his face was a mere inch from James's. "Of course we do!" he bellowed. "Why else do you think you're here?"

James jumped so violently he almost toppled over. Sharpe raised her arm and pushed Finch firmly back into an upright sitting position. He quickly regained his composure, clamping his mouth shut and folding his arms. "Just — get on with it," he hissed angrily.

Get on with what? Morton thought.

Inspector Sharpe began rummaging in the leather briefcase.

"You're not supposed to question us without our parents here," Robbie said belligerently.

Sharpe wasn't even pretending to smile now. Her face was set, as expressionless and unreadable as a wooden puppet.

"You're absolutely right," she said, placing a large manila envelope on the desk. "I can't make you answer questions, but I can give you information. Information that may be important for your well-being. James's medical records have just been sent to me from his previous doctor." She tapped the envelope before her. "There's no mention of jaundice, or any odd eye condition. In fact, the doctor has never even heard of such a thing. Of course, this doesn't make you a cat-napper, nor does it tell me anything about today's odd events. But here's what it does tell me: It tells me you are liars."

Sharpe's last comment hit home like a wasp sting, all the more so because it was true.

Principal Finch snorted and was about to speak up when Sharpe shot him a warning glance. She wasn't finished yet.

"It would be best if you just told me," she continued, in an almost hypnotically soft voice. "We all know there has to be a simple explanation."

"We don't know anything," Robbie said.

"Robbie's right," James said. "We don't know anything."

Sharpe folded her hands calmly on the desk in front of her. "Have you ever been in a prison cell, James? It's not very nice. Even tough kids cry the first time."

"You're bluffing," Robbie said. "You can't lock us up without charging us, and we haven't committed any crimes."

Sharpe twitched slightly, but no hint of emotion escaped from behind the bars of her cast-iron face.

"Don't underestimate me," she said. "I can be kind. I play by the book most of the time. But when things get out of hand, when little girls get attacked by dangerous animals, I'll do what I have to do to protect the innocent people who live in my town."

Morton had a sudden urge to leap up and run from the room. Instead, he gripped tightly on to the arms of his chair as if to hold himself in place.

"Let's say, for example, that I accept that you do have a rare disease," Sharpe said to James. "Well, in that case, you pose a serious health risk. The next thing you know you'll be locked up in a medical facility, not allowed to come into contact with anyone. They'll poke you and prod you and stick you so full of needles you'll start to feel like a pincushion."

"You can't do that!" James yelled, suddenly shocked out of his blithe mood. "It's not a disease, it's . . ." James tried to stop himself but it was too late.

"It's what?" Sharpe said, pouncing eagerly on his slipped confession. "What exactly do you have?"

James pressed his lips together and looked apologetically at Morton and Robbie.

Morton almost wanted to cry. James had suffered enough. He couldn't let him go through any more torture, especially when none of it had really been his fault. This was his moment to be strong, he thought. It was time for him to step forward and confess. He'd take all the blame. After all, he deserved it.

And he would have done it too. He would have told Sharpe about the gargoyle and the wishes. He would have told her about the closet and the Zombie Twins. He would have told her about John King and the secret attic above Dad's office. He would have told her everything if Mr. Brown hadn't burst in through the door at that exact moment.

"Boys, don't say another word!" he commanded.

Finch jumped to his feet at once. "What the blazes do you think you're doing?" he said irately.

"I'm protecting their rights," Mr. Brown said firmly. "You're coercing them into making statements they might regret. You know perfectly well you have no right to question them without a parent or guardian present unless you're willing to press charges." Mr. Brown tugged Morton and the others to their feet. "Come on. We're leaving."

"You can't do that!" Finch protested.

"Yes, I can," Brown said, looking directly at Sharpe, "and Inspector Sharpe knows it. Acting as the boys' counsel, I'm insisting that they answer no more questions until you press charges or produce a warrant for their arrest."

Finch puffed angrily and threw his arms up in outraged disbelief as Brown led the boys out of the room.

A moment later they found themselves on the other side of Finch's door.

"Walk quickly," Mr. Brown said to the three of them.

"But, sir," Morton said, following him down the hall, "where are we going?"

"I know everything," Mr. Brown said. "I know how to reverse the wishes, and I'm here to help."

CHAPTER 16

A MURKY TALE

Brown hobbled in a half-run, half-skip along the hall, his cane tapping out a rapid rhythm. Morton and the others had to break into a canter to keep up with him.

"But, sir," Morton repeated.

"Don't say anything yet," he replied. "I'll explain soon enough."

Morton nodded as he, Robbie, and James followed Brown to the parking lot. Brown opened the back door of his black sedan and motioned for them to get in. They paused.

"Where are you taking us?" James asked, eyeing the backseat suspiciously.

"Home, of course," Brown said.

"Home?"

"Listen to me, boys, there's something you have to know. The wishes can only be reversed on the full moon, and that's tonight. Can you really wait another month?"

Morton had already made up his mind about that. He wasn't sure if they could even wait another hour, but the idea of climbing into Brown's car went against all his instincts.

"The most important thing right now," Brown went on, "is to get you safely home where Sharpe can't come asking questions without a warrant, which she won't be able to get until tomorrow at the earliest. By then we'll have reversed the wishes and everything will be back to normal."

"How?" James said, sounding suddenly hopeful. "How can you reverse the wishes?"

"I'll explain on the way."

"Okay, I'm in!" James said, and jumped into the backseat without waiting for the others. Morton moved to follow him, but Robbie put his hand on his arm.

"Are you sure about this?" he said.

"No," Morton said, "but James is running out of options."

Morton climbed in beside James, and Robbie reluctantly followed them.

Brown didn't even wait for them to get their seat belts on before speeding away. "I haven't been completely honest with you," he said, glancing cautiously in his mirror as he began to weave his way along the backstreets, "but then again, you haven't been completely honest with me, have you?"

"No, sir," Morton admitted.

Mr. Brown laughed through his nose. "You can call me Rodney if you like."

For some reason the idea of calling Mr. Brown "Rodney" didn't appeal to Morton at all.

"How do you know about the wishes?" Morton asked, eager to move the conversation forward.

Mr. Brown puffed his cheeks. "I should have said something sooner, before things got out of hand. But you've been very secretive. You see, I used to know John King, and I knew he dabbled in dark magic. Although, to be honest, I never really believed it was real. I thought he was just a crazy old man desperate to get his sight back."

"Is that why you acted, uh, *weird*, when I asked you about magic?" Morton asked.

"I admit, I was pretty shocked. You see, that's how it all started. About two years ago King approached me, just as you did, asking about mystics and ancient magical ceremonies. I was surprised when you came out with the same question."

"King came to see you?" Morton asked in surprise.

"Yes. Somehow he'd gotten hold of this gargoyle, and he insisted it could grant three wishes. Except it wasn't that simple. The gargoyle in itself isn't magic. It's just a vessel. That's how he described it. You have to activate the magic with some kind of dark ceremony — a ceremony that can only be performed on the night of the full moon, of course. King asked me if I knew anything about this mystical stuff." Brown shook his head and sighed with a look of shame. "The problem was, I did. I'd come across this book in an auction that was all about ancient magic — you know, animal sacrifice, mystic rituals, sun worship, that sort of thing. It wasn't very expensive, and I had no idea when I bought the book that it was the only one in existence. It was handwritten, copied from much older texts, which had also been copied from other, even older texts. It didn't even have a title. King had a name for it though. He called it The Book of Portals. Sure enough it had an illustration of the gargoyle in it, with a detailed description of how to perform a dark ceremony that would summon magical powers from another dimension.

"Of course I didn't believe in any of that. Why would I? But King kept on asking. It wasn't just that he wanted the book, mind you. It turned out it took two people to perform the activation ceremony, so he couldn't do it alone. I tried to humor him at first, but he started harassing me at work. Then he promised me I could have two of the wishes to myself. He wanted only one wish: to get his sight back. I still didn't believe in magic, not really, but he was so convincing. Two wishes, I thought. I could do a lot with that. Get rid of this bum leg, for one thing. So I agreed to help him. The way I saw it, it was a bit like buying a lottery ticket. You never really expect to win. In fact, you know it's almost impossible to win. But yet you still go ahead and buy the ticket don't you?" Brown steered the car onto Hemlock Hill. "I should never have agreed."

"What happened?" Morton asked, unsure he wanted to know the answer.

Brown parked at the foot of the driveway and turned to look up at the turret that had once been King's studio. He shook his head yet again. "I joined him on the night of the full moon, up there in the attic. Up until then it had been just a silly idea, a way to humor an old man, but when I climbed into King's attic it became suddenly very real. He had everything ready for the ceremony. The black pigs were in a bag hanging from the rafters, squealing. A spiral was neatly painted on the floor. And the gargoyle sat in that stone font in the middle of the room with some kind of incense burning beneath it, filling the air with smoke. I panicked. I told him I couldn't go through with it. He'd expected me to say that, of course. He might have been crazy, but he wasn't stupid. Before I knew it he'd kicked the hatch closed and snapped a padlock over it. Then he revealed the truth of his plan. He wasn't going to share any of the wishes with me. He didn't need me to recite lines, or light candles. That's not why he'd asked me to help him. The truth was that for the magic to work he needed a human sacrifice. He laughed when he told me. Laughed because I had been so predictable. Everybody's the same, he said. They'll risk everything for the promise of power. But that's not how it was. I didn't want power. I wouldn't have minded getting full use of my leg back, but mostly I was just curious. Curiosity should be the eighth deadly sin. It almost killed me that night.

"King attacked me with a large curved dagger — like a scimitar but smaller. The fact that he was blind didn't seem to matter. He started lashing at the air savagely, and because of my leg I couldn't move without making a noise.

Every time I tried to slip away, he homed in on me, slashing and swinging that horrific blade. I knew if I was going to survive I needed the key, so I plucked up the courage to attack him. I don't really remember what happened except that there was a struggle and the key fell out of his pocket. Somehow, I honestly don't remember how, I managed to get the hatch open and get out of there with my life. I didn't look back. I never saw King again."

The three boys had barely breathed while Brown told his story. Once it ended, they all suddenly gasped as if surfacing from a long dive.

"What do you mean, you never saw him again?" Robbie asked. "Didn't you call the police?"

"I probably should have," Brown replied. "But King died later that night, and I didn't want to get involved. I should have come forward, I know I should have, but I figured he was dead. What more could the police have done?"

"What happened after you left?" Robbie asked.

Brown shook his head. "I don't know. I drove straight home and locked the door. I always presumed King had been stumbling around his garden, still looking for me, when he tripped and fell down the well. It made sense at the time. He was crazed with anger."

Morton felt an odd mixture of disappointment and denial. It seemed absolutely certain that King was a murderous mad man after all. But there were parts of the puzzle missing. "That still doesn't explain why he buried the gargoyle," Morton said.

"Buried it?" Brown said, shooting a curious look at Morton. "King buried the gargoyle?"

Morton nodded. "Just a few feet from the well. I found it when I was mowing the lawn just after we moved in. Dad said the frost must have pushed it up, so it couldn't have been buried very deep. I thought it might have been done in a hurry."

Brown rubbed his chin and seemed to drift off into thought. "Of course," he said quietly.

"Of course what?" Morton prodded.

Brown turned to face the boys directly. "If King performed the ceremony and then fell down the well, wouldn't his death have been the equivalent of a sacrifice?"

"I don't follow."

"Ever since I first suspected that something unnatural was going on," Brown explained, "I began to wonder. First, where the gargoyle had vanished to, and second, how the wishes could have been activated without a human sacrifice. This answers both questions. If King fell down the well, then maybe the other-dimensional powers, or whatever they are, accepted that as a sacrifice."

"It still doesn't explain why he buried the gargoyle though," Morton said, holding out hope for a better explanation.

"He was crazy," Brown said dismissively. "Trying to understand a crazy man is like trying to build a house out of sand. Best not waste your energy."

"So you think he's dead, then?" James asked.

"Of course. Why wouldn't I?" Brown shot back.

The boys exchanged glances. "We don't know," Morton said honestly. "But the Zombie Twins tried to steal the gargoyle. They're obviously on some kind of mission. We wondered if they might be working for King."

Brown's eyes darted nervously around him. "Then we had better be extra cautious," he said. "We should perform the ceremony in King's attic. If we keep it locked, we'll be safe in there. Can you carry the gargoyle up to get it ready?"

The boys nodded.

"I'll take care of the rest," Brown said. "But we don't have much time. The ceremony will only work while the moon is in the sky."

"How do you know all this?" Morton asked.

"King's book describes how to reverse the wishes in great detail," Brown said reassuringly. "Don't worry. I'll be back with it as soon as the sun goes down, and we'll make this all go away."

The boys clambered out of the car and Brown crunched it into gear. "Oh yes, and you'll need all three fingers," he said, through the driver's side window. "Do you still have them?"

James and Morton nodded.

"Good. That's the most important thing."

The boys watched in silence as Brown drove away.

"I guess you were right about him," Robbie said. "We should have told him sooner."

Morton nodded but didn't say anything. Something about Brown's explanation wasn't quite right.

Not long afterward Melissa and Wendy ambled gloomily down the driveway. The boys, who had been waiting on the porch, pounced on them at once and told them all about the day's events. When the story was finished, Melissa became unusually silent. She stood for a long time peeling loose flakes of paint from the side of the house.

"Let me get this straight," she said at last. "Your creepy history teacher is coming here tonight to help us reverse the wishes?"

"That's a funny way of putting it, but yes," James said.

"I don't know," Melissa said wearily. "Are you sure we can trust this guy? Why didn't he say something sooner?"

"For the same reason I didn't tell you about my wish or you didn't tell us where your wish came from. Because it's all so weird and spooky that nobody wants to talk about it. Anyway, we really don't have much choice, do we? It's tonight or . . ."

"I know," Melissa said. "You're a nine-foot flesh-eating centipede by the end of the week. I get it, I just don't like it."

Morton remained silent, but somewhere inside he didn't like it either.

Later that evening, Dad invited Wendy and Robbie to supper and tried not to show his disappointment when nobody seemed to be hungry. "Is it exam week?" he said.

"I don't think I've ever seen such a miserable bunch of children."

"We're sorry, Mr. Clay," Wendy said. "It must be the change in weather."

"I suppose I could pretend to believe that," Dad said. "After all, it is almost Halloween. Actually, I'm surprised Morton hasn't started decorating already. Usually the house is covered in fake cobwebs and plastic skeletons by now."

Morton feigned a smile. "I'll be sure to put them up soon," he said, although nothing could be further from his mind.

"I should hope so. You know, one of the reasons I chose this house was because I knew you would love it."

"I thought it was because it was cheap," Melissa said.

"That too," Dad confessed with a sheepish grin.

It was almost completely dark by the time Dad left for work, and as Morton watched him drive away he noticed that the full moon was already hovering over the rooftops . and the swarm of bats was flapping around the turret again.

"I can't believe it's going to be over tonight," Melissa said as they stepped back into the kitchen.

"I know," James said, stuffing a fistful of coals into his mouth eagerly. "It's so amazing. It almost makes you want to sing," and James opened his mouth but instead of singing a small yellow cloud of smoke billowed out.

Melissa snatched the bag of coals from James's hands.

"Will you stop eating those things!" she said irritably. "They're making you weird."

"They are?" James said naively. Nobody answered, but Wendy gave him a small nod and a sympathetic smile.

"Oops!" James said, putting his hand to his mouth and giggling. "Well, I think I'll go get some food to tide me over."

"What, *now*?" Melissa exclaimed.

"No time like the present," James said, strolling out onto the porch.

"James! We have to get things ready. We need to get the gargoyle into King's attic and . . ."

"I'm leaving!" James growled, suddenly not sounding like James at all.

Morton felt his whole body tense up. Everybody fell into sudden silence.

"I think you should stay here," Wendy said after a long pause.

"And I think you should mind your own business," James said, removing his glasses and staring threateningly at her.

Wendy let out a small scream and even Robbie gasped. Morton felt a pulse of pure horror run through his veins. James's eyes had changed again. The whites were now a vivid green, laced with deep-purple veins surrounding an enormous octagonal pupil. The wishes really were getting stronger. It was only then that Morton realized why. "It's the full moon," he said. "I should have realized sooner.

247

Ancient magic often follows the cycles of the moon. James, if we don't reverse the wishes, you're going to turn *tonight*."

"Like I care," James said, and he turned back to the night and sniffed at the air, letting out a low tiger-like growl.

"Monsters," Melissa grunted angrily. "They're all the same." Then, to Morton's amazement, she produced a length of chain and a large pair of cast-iron manacles seemingly from nowhere. With surprising speed and agility she shot forward and clasped the manacles onto James's wrists, looped the chain around his ankles, and tugged tightly on the other end, toppling him to the floor face-first.

"Ouch!" he protested, sounding suddenly like James again. "What are you *doing*?"

"It's for your own good," Melissa said.

"Where did you get those?" Wendy asked, shocked by the sudden attack.

"I found them in the closet with all the medieval clothing," Melissa said. "There's everything in there: swords, maces, crossbows. Not exactly my definition of accessories, but to each his own."

James rolled onto his back and looked up at Melissa. "I'm sorry," he said. "I got a bit carried away there. But I feel fine now. Take them off and I'll behave myself, honest." James made a pleading look, but somehow, with those grotesque green eyes, it was impossible to trust him.

"Right," Melissa said, completely ignoring James and looking at Wendy and Robbie. "It looks like we've got our hands full, so you two should probably head home before this gets any uglier."

"Home?" Wendy and Robbie exclaimed, glancing at each other in surprise.

"We can't go home now," Wendy went on. "Not when James is . . . well, not quite himself."

"I'm not actually giving you a choice," Melissa said firmly. "This could get dangerous, and I'm not prepared to get anybody else involved."

"But we're already involved," Robbie said in an unusually adamant tone. "And I don't know about Wendy, but I'm not about to walk out of here and leave my friends to fend for themselves when they're up against the wall. So, we can stand here and waste time arguing about it or we can just get on with what needs to be done, but either way, I'm not leaving."

"Ditto," Wendy said, putting her hands on her hips in a defiant gesture.

Melissa puffed her cheeks and glanced over to Morton as if seeking his advice.

Morton could understand Melissa's point of view. They'd already caused more than enough upset, and the idea of any harm coming to Robbie or Wendy was unthinkable. But, judging by the looks on their faces, he could also see that any arguments would be futile.

"I suppose we could use the help," Morton said. "I mean, we have a lot to get ready."

Melissa opened her mouth as if to protest one more time, but Wendy cut her off quickly.

"Good, that's settled. I was thinking we should go into Melissa's closet and get some of those swords, for self-defense, just in case things do get 'uglier.'"

"Of course," Morton said. "That's a great idea."

"I'm not just a pretty face," Wendy said.

"I suppose I would feel better with a sword in my hands," Melissa admitted.

"We better get started right away," Robbie said, glancing at his watch. "The moon sets in five hours."

"He's right." Morton nodded. "But be careful in there. The wishes are getting stronger, and we don't want you disappearing forever like the girl in King's story."

"Believe me, that's not going to happen," Melissa said. "Not all the monsters in *Scare Scape* could stop me tonight." And she and Wendy headed out of the room.

"We should get that gargoyle into the attic," Morton said, already feeling drained and exhausted.

Robbie looked at Morton and must have seen the strain on his face. "Don't worry," he said. "How does that saying go? 'It's always darkest before the dawn.'"

Morton made a thin smile. He was secretly overjoyed that Robbie was here to help, but he knew that something sinister was about to unwind, and despite Robbie's supportive words he didn't feel optimistic at all. No matter how hard he tried, he couldn't convince himself that they would in fact live long enough to see the dawn.

CHAPTER 17

THE UGLY TRUTH

About an hour later they were all standing in King's attic — except for James, who was lying on his back completely bound in heavy chains. After rereading the Monster Tarot description of the Snarf several times, Melissa had decided to reinforce James's bindings. The full-grown Snarf was formidably strong, she pointed out, and they shouldn't be taking any chances. Morton was forced to agree this was a good idea, although it broke his heart to see James bound up like a prisoner.

The five candles flickered in the dusty air, throwing dancing shadows across the conical ceiling. In the center of the room the gargoyle sat ominously on the stone font, and Melissa was pacing nervously around it, holding one of the slender medieval swords that she'd retrieved from her closet. Mr. Brown was nowhere to be seen.

"Maybe I should go and find Mr. Brown," James said, pulling himself into a sitting position.

Melissa scowled at him.

"No, really," James said. "I can see in the dark, and I'll be able to smell him. If you'll just take these chains off . . ."

"We can't do that, James," Melissa said, looking guiltily away from him.

"I'm fine now. I promise. I don't even feel hungry."

"Not going to happen," Melissa said. "If Brown doesn't show, we're going to have to resort to plan B."

"Plan B?" Morton asked. "What's that?"

"We hide James in my closet. There are plenty of monsters in there now, so we'll feed him on those. Not sure what we're going to tell Dad though."

Morton was speechless.

"Maybe we could do the ceremony without Brown," Wendy cut in, with a tone of desperate optimism. She turned to face Morton. "Did he tell you anything about what you have to do to reverse the wishes?"

"No," Morton said. "He just said we needed the fingers and it was all described in King's book and . . ."

Morton stopped in midsentence and stared blankly ahead of him. A very troubling thought had just popped into his head.

"What is it?" Melissa asked.

Morton raised his hand. "Wait! I need to think," he said. The room fell silent, and Morton began to shuffle the events of the last few days around in his brain. Something was not quite right. He thought that if he could just move one piece of the puzzle, then everything would make sense. Like Copernicus, he thought, moving the Earth from the center of the solar system and replacing it with the sun . . .

"Ahoy there, shipmates!" a voice called from below. Morton felt his stomach lurch violently. It was Mr. Brown's voice, and suddenly Morton had an irrational urge to close the hatch and lock him out, even though they'd been waiting anxiously for him all night.

"Permission to come aboard?"

Brown's face appeared through the opening in the floor. Morton had never seen him in casual clothes before. He wore a loose-fitting black cotton shirt with a colorful dragon printed on the back and a pair of tattered jeans.

"What happened to James?" Brown asked at once, spotting the tangle of chains on the floor.

"He's turning into a monster," Melissa said bluntly.

"Then we'd better start," Brown said, passing his walking stick to Morton and squeezing himself up through the hatch. As he struggled to his feet, Morton noticed he had a large green velvet bag tucked under his arm that held a heavy solid object.

"The Book of Portals," Morton gasped.

Brown looked over and nodded. "Perhaps the most valuable book in existence," he said, patting the bag proudly.

"You're late!" Melissa said, eyeing Brown with a cold, suspicious eye.

Mr. Brown turned and looked at Melissa. "I was busy making preparations for tonight's festivities," he said, seemingly unoffended by her harshness. "You must be Morton's sister," he added cheerily. "The de facto matriarch of the shrinking Clay clan."

"The de whato?" Melissa replied, screwing up her face.

"Oh, never mind. It's wonderful to meet you at last. Robbie and James, I know of course, but this young woman . . ."

Wendy stepped forward nervously. "I'm Wendy, Melissa's neighbor."

"Really?" Brown said. "I hope all the neighborhood kids don't know about this."

"No, just me," Wendy said.

"Good," Brown said, surveying the attic for the first time. "You have the gargoyle in the right place, I see. And you have the fingers?"

Melissa held up a small leather pouch that was strung around her neck like an oversize locket. "Of course. What we want to know is how all of this works."

"It's fairly simple," Brown said. "All you have to do is put the fingers back on the gargoyle."

"It can't be that simple," Morton said. "There has to be a counter verse."

"Let me finish," Brown said. "First, you have to do it on the full moon. Unless the moon is actually in the sky it won't work. And, yes, you have to recite the counter verse, word for word, but the most important thing is the order of the fingers. Here, hand them to me and I'll show you."

He reached for the pouch around Melissa's neck, but Melissa pulled away. "What do you mean by the order of the fingers?"

Mr. Brown stared curiously at Melissa. "Well, why don't I just read it out to you," he said after a long pause.

He limped over to the lectern and loosened the string from the neck of the large velvet bag. He took out a tattered and ancient leather-bound book with a large dark jewel set into the front like a bulbous black eye.

Morton's mind began swirling at double speed. There was something familiar about that book. A book with a black jewel mounted to the front was not something you easily forgot. He knew he had never actually held such a thing, and yet it was as familiar as his own lunchbox. Had he dreamed about this book? Had he read about it in a comic? Had he seen it on Mr. Brown's bookshelf without really realizing it? That seemed right. It felt right. He had seen it on a shelf — but not alone, it had been among hundreds of other books. And Mr. Brown didn't have any books in his office. . . .

A storm of images burst into Morton's head like fireworks exploding in the sky. His mind raced from one recent event to another, replaying everything that had happened right from the day they'd arrived in Dimvale. The sensation was so overpowering that he literally felt dizzy and had to steady himself on one of the large stone candleholders. The candle swayed dangerously, spilling a pool of hot wax onto his hands. For a brief moment he found himself looking directly into the candle itself. He thought about John King's obsession with working by candlelight, with staring at the very heart of the flame, just as Morton was now staring into that black void. And then somehow Morton knew. It was just as King had described: The answer seemed to pop right out of the blackness.

It was funny, he thought, that the truth had been there all along, but he couldn't see it for the clutter of emotions and fear and false facts. In the end, he realized, truth was just the thing left over when you took everything else away. It was a small thing, beautiful in its own way, but also a little bit sad and, in this case, a little bit frightening.

"You said that was King's book," Morton said to Brown, regaining his balance.

"King's book?" Brown said, smiling. "You're confusing the story. King approached me because he knew I had it. It was my book. I bought it in an auction, remember?"

"I remember that's what you said. But later you said it was King's book."

Everyone turned to face Morton. Mr. Brown's smile wavered slightly. "Oh, did I? Well, a slip of the tongue, I guess."

"That's what I thought at first," Morton said, "until I saw the book."

"What is it, Morton, what's wrong?" Melissa said, recognizing the shift in the mood.

"I've seen that book before," Morton said. "We all have."

Everyone began glancing at one another in confusion.

"Remember the magazine article that Wendy found?" Morton went on. "The one with the photo of Dad's office?

That's how we found the hatch, right? Well, there were hundreds and hundreds of books in King's office, but right behind him, sitting on top of a pile on his desk, was this one. This strange old book with a black jewel mounted on the front."

Brown wasn't smiling now. He was shaking his head and frowning. "It must have been another one."

"Another book with a black jewel on the front?" Morton said. "I don't think so. I've been trying to figure it out since this afternoon. Your story sounded right but it also sounded wrong. It could have happened the way you described it, but the truth is you've taken the facts and jumbled them up to suit your needs."

"Melissa," Brown said urgently, "Morton's wasting precious time. Hand me the fingers, and we'll reverse these wishes before it's too late."

Melissa didn't budge. Her hand tightened on the pouch around her neck. "Keep talking, Morton," she said.

"It's just like Dad said, about the solar system," Morton went on. "If even one fact doesn't fit, then the whole theory has to be wrong."

"Look, the moon will set soon," Brown said, stepping toward Melissa. "And then it will be too late for James! Now hand me the fingers."

Melissa turned, suddenly grabbing her sword and pointing it directly at Mr. Brown's rotund belly. He stopped dead. "Let Morton finish," she said with a dark, dangerous glint in her eye.

"This is madness. We're running out of time," he said in a pleading tone.

"It should have been obvious," Morton went on, looking at his teacher, "because you don't collect books. You don't *like* books. You don't have any in your office. The only book you ever bring to class is the textbook assigned by the school board, and you're not even interested in that. King was the one who loved books. He had a passion for books bigger even than his passion for drawing. The very idea that King would come to you looking for a book is ridiculous. He didn't come to you. You went to him."

There was a long silent pause, and Morton could hear wax boiling away at the tips of the giant candles.

"So? What if that were true?" Brown said, his tone even. "It wouldn't change anything. You need to reverse the wishes and you need to reverse them now."

James suddenly pulled himself to sitting position. "It changes everything," he said.

Morton nodded in agreement. "All along we've thought that King was behind this whole thing. We even thought he might still be alive. I secretly wished he was alive because more than anything I wanted to meet him. But King is dead, isn't he?"

"I have no idea," Brown said.

"Yes, you do," Morton said, "because you killed him."

"He killed John King?" Wendy said, in abject horror.

There was a sudden swish of steel as Wendy and Robbie lifted their swords and joined Melissa, pinning Brown on all sides with gleaming blades like the spokes of a silver wheel.

"Let's not get carried away," he said, raising his hands higher. "What would be my motive?"

"Three wishes," Morton said simply. "That's anything you want — riches, fame, immortality even. I can't think of a better motive. Even the most saintly person in the world would be tempted. That's why King fell for it, isn't it?"

"King was no saint!" Brown spat, losing his calm for the first time. "He was a madman. That much is obvious to anyone."

"No, he wasn't," Morton said, at last feeling completely confident about the facts. "I should have listened to my instincts all along. King wasn't a murderer or a lunatic. But then, he wasn't an infallible genius either. He was just a regular guy, struggling through life like the rest of us."

"Regular guy!" Brown scoffed. "What kind of 'regular guy' locks himself in a room staring at candles and writing creepy stories for kids?"

"The kind that you needed to make the gargoyle's power come to life," Morton said. "The story you told was almost true but it was upside down. It wasn't your book. You were the one who stole the gargoyle from the museum of course — a blind man couldn't have done that — but you didn't know how to activate the magic. Somehow you found out that King had the only existing copy of The Book of Portals. You moved to Dimvale, got a job as a history teacher, and then made your move on him. You told him about the gargoyle and the wishes. You needed him, for the book, and he needed you, for the gargoyle. No doubt you promised him one of the wishes, the only wish he'd want: to get his sight back. That would be enough to tempt him. But you didn't tell him about the human sacrifice, and he wouldn't have known because he was blind. He couldn't read his own books anymore. But you could. At the last minute you tried to kill him. But King must have been quicker or smarter than you expected. There was a struggle, and somehow he overpowered you and managed to get away with the gargoyle. No doubt he buried it in a hurry because he wanted to hide it from you forever. I'm not sure what happened then. I think you probably caught up to him and maybe he wouldn't tell you where he'd hidden it, or maybe he told you he'd thrown it down the well. Either way it ended up the same. You pushed King down the well that night."

As Morton finished the story he felt a tremendous sense of relief and stood up straight, looking Brown directly in the eyes, daring him to deny the charge. Brown surprised him by snorting through his nose dismissively, as if Morton had just told him nothing more shocking than the fact that his shoelaces were untied.

"For a tiresome little boy you certainly are observant," he said dryly. "I'll plead guilty to everything else, but I didn't mean to push old King down the well. The rest was pretty much as you described. I stole the gargoyle and convinced King to help me. Oh, he refused at first, tried to tell me there was no such thing as real magic, but I knew he'd come around eventually, and sure enough he did. After months of sitting in the darkness of his sad, lonely life, he saw the light, if you'll pardon the pun.

"We did everything it said in the book. We sacrificed the five pigs, we burned the roots of a laburnum tree, and we recited the words of an ancient summons to the creatures of the underworld. King was sitting in the center there. It should have been so easy. I had the knife in my hand, I raised it silently, but it was almost as though he had a sixth sense. He caught my hand as it was coming down. I'll never know how he did that. And he was strong. He twisted the knife right out of my grip and smacked me over the back of the head with the handle. The next thing I knew, he and the gargoyle were gone and my head was throbbing. I ran outside looking for him, and there he was, standing by the well with his hands inside it. 'Stop or I'll drop it,' he said. I panicked. I jumped for him, and then I heard a loud clatter as something fell down the well. I thought he'd dropped the gargoyle. What else could it have been?"

"A shovel," Morton said. "The shovel he'd used to dig the hole."

Brown nodded gravely. "If I'd been a bit calmer, I might have gotten that information out of him. As it was I throttled him. There was a struggle. He slipped . . ."

"You pushed him, you mean!" Robbie erupted, his hatred boiling over.

"Pushed? Slipped? What does it matter?" Brown went on without remorse. "Either way, he fell. I managed to calm down after that. I thought it through very carefully. I decided to burn his diaries and put the cover back on the hatch to the attic. Nobody would ever know to look up here, and that's where all the evidence was. Take all that away, and this book, and all that's left is some crazy blind old man falling down his own well.

"I have to thank you, Morton, for finding the gargoyle. If it hadn't been for you, I would have lived out the remainder of my days thinking that all hope was lost forever."

"All hope *is* lost for you," Morton said fiercely. "We're going to tell Sharpe everything."

"Before or after you reverse the wishes?" Brown asked casually.

"After!" Wendy said. "We have to reverse the wishes now. If the moon goes down James will . . ." She couldn't bring herself to finish the sentence.

Melissa nodded in agreement. "What do we have to do?" she said, looking hopefully at Morton.

"Oh, how sweet," Brown chuckled. "Everyone's pinning their hopes on the comic book expert. But I'm sorry to tell you, Morton doesn't know how to reverse the wishes, and as you already guessed, I'm not going to reveal anything. I'm just here to get my hands on the gargoyle and the fingers. I'd like to say, give me the gargoyle and nobody gets hurt, but that won't work. I'm going to replace the fingers myself, then use one of you as a sacrifice to reactivate the gargoyle. The rest of you, sadly, will probably end up down the well with dear old King."

Everyone exchanged quizzical looks. Melissa prodded Brown's belly threateningly with the tip of her sword. "You're definitely missing the point, if you'll excuse *my* pun," she said. "There are five of us, and we have swords. There's one of you."

"Did you know that choosing the person to sacrifice is an art?" Brown said, smirking at Melissa. "A certain flavor of the victim's character permeates the wishes. I think I'm going to choose you."

"You disgusting old —" Wendy began, but Morton cut her off.

"Don't!" he said, raising his hand to stop her. "He's just trying to make us angry. Hoping we'll make some mistake. He's desperate, that's all."

"I'm far from desperate," Brown said in a gloating voice. "In fact, I'm just beginning to have fun."

Brown then snapped his fingers, and the next moment a deep gurgling growl echoed from the room below and a ghastly dark shadow rose through the open hatch in the floor.

Wendy screamed.

Morton's heart started hammering against his ribs as an oily black form stood breathing heavily in the flickering light, separating him from the others. He recognized it at once and realized in that same instant that he had grossly underestimated Brown. The immense two-legged lizard with a bird's beak, black leathery wings, lifeless white eyes, and huge, fierce talons for hands leered slowly around, as if taking in the situation.

"Let me introduce a friend of mine," Brown said. "I'm quite proud of it. It's my first other-dimensional beast."

"It's a Galosh," Morton said, determined not to let fear consume him.

"Galosh!" Melissa scoffed. "What is that, a rubber-boot monster?"

Brown chuckled. "You like it? I summoned it using King's book."

"So that's the real reason you were late," Morton said, trying desperately to remember if a Galosh had any known weaknesses. "You were summoning monsters!"

"Among other things," Brown said with a mysterious smile. "You didn't really think I'd come here unprepared, did you?"

Everyone remained frozen. Brown was still pinned at the center of a wheel of swords, but now all eyes were on the growling, powerful creature.

"Now," Brown went on. "I think you better hand the fingers over to me and stand back before someone gets hurt."

Melissa glanced back and forth between Brown and the black beast, as if searching for a way out.

"Morton," she said, "you know all about this voodoo magic, right?"

"It's not voodoo," Morton said, backing away from the creature and reaching quickly for a sword.

"Well, whatever! What do we do?"

Morton wiped sweat from his eyes and focused his mind like a laser on the task at hand. Killing a Galosh was very difficult. Their leathery skin was more than an inch thick and even when severely wounded, they didn't feel any pain. That's why they were the first choice as foot soldiers in large-scale inter-dimensional wars. The only possible way to stop it would be to . . .

"Well, what is it?" Melissa demanded from across the room. "Come on! I can see that little brain of yours churning!"

"Well, if Brown summoned this thing, then it's tied to his life force," Morton explained reluctantly. "If Brown dies, the beast returns to its own dimension."

"Aha! Just as I thought," Melissa said almost gleefully to Brown. "Your leather buddy is not invulnerable after all. So, the question is, Brownie, how fast do you think he is? Do you think he can make it across the room before I can push this blade through your black heart? Because that would have to be pretty fast, wouldn't it?"

The creature let out a fierce growl and took an angry step forward. Melissa immediately pushed the tip of the blade harder into Brown's shirt.

"Stop!" Brown yelled at the beast.

The Galosh did so immediately.

"Very wise," Melissa said. "Now, if you want to live, you better tell your beastie to go have time out in the basement until we're finished here."

Brown stared defiantly back into Melissa's eyes, still smirking.

"If you think I'm bluffing," Melissa said, "then you don't know me very well. I've killed a lot of monsters in the last few weeks."

"But you've never killed a human," Brown said tauntingly.

"No, but in your case I'll make an exception," Melissa retorted. "You're worse than a monster anyway. Monsters don't have any choice but to be what they are, but you do."

Brown shrugged, seemingly still unafraid of the swords.

"On the count of three, then," Melissa said adjusting her sword so that its tip sat neatly between his ribs. "One Mississippi."

Morton swallowed hard. Would Melissa actually do it? The Galosh began snorting furiously, stamping its clawed feet like a bull, ready to charge.

"Two Mississippi . . ."

The beast let out a terrifying roar, causing Wendy and Robbie to flinch, but amazingly, Melissa held firm.

"Three Miss —"

Several things happened at once. Brown yelled, "Now, Galosh!" and at the same moment dropped to his haunches. Morton thought he was trying to dodge the swords, but the swords were now pointing at his head, which made him even more vulnerable. The Galosh, meanwhile, was sprinting on its powerful reptilian legs toward Brown. Morton was sure Melissa would have no choice but to pierce Brown's throat, but Brown then did something completely impossible. He sprang like a gazelle high into the air so that his feet cleared the swords, and kept going up — four, five, six feet high above everyone's heads. He then somersaulted in midair, dropped his walking stick, and seemed to bounce on the ceiling like a flabby helium balloon, giving Morton the illusion that the room had suddenly been turned upside down. Everyone was staring up in shocked confusion when the beast flung itself into the ring of swords, spinning like a black tornado. In the blink of an eye the powerful creature had knocked the swords aside. Melissa, Wendy, and Robbie were left lying on their backs in a dazed heap. Only Morton, on the other side of the room, was still standing. The beast let out a fierce roar, and Morton lifted his sword and pointed it defiantly at the creature.

Brown began to laugh hysterically. Morton dared to pull his eyes off the Galosh to see his teacher clambering spider-like on the ceiling. "That was even easier than I thought. I have to say, once you get the hang of it, King's book is lots of fun!"

A terrified silence filled the room.

"I'd love to stay and chat, but the moon is setting and I have a life of eternal riches to get on with. Or should I say, an eternal life of eternal riches."

Brown scuttled higher toward the peak of the conical roof, clinging impossibly to the rafters. "Save one of them, kill the rest," he said coldly. "And be quick about it."

CHAPTER 18

A FURRY FURY

The creature raised its fearsome talons and leaped for the huddle of kids on the floor. They rolled and scattered like startled pigeons, only just escaping as the beast's left claw smashed into the floor with devastating force right between Robbie and Wendy, missing them by a mere inch. Morton struggled to lift the point of the heavy sword and jumped forward, but the Galosh was faster than he expected and it swung its arm around, smashing him in the chest.

Morton felt as though he'd been hit by a train. The sword flew out of his hands and he crumpled in agony to the old wooden boards. The creature lumbered across the room on its clawed feet and towered over him. Robbie ran in to attack, but the Galosh kicked him away effortlessly. Then Melissa grabbed her sword again and leaped forward. She had the most experience with monsters, but she made the almost fatal mistake of taking her eyes off the Galosh to see if Morton was okay. In one downward blow, it shattered her sword. Then it lifted her up, pinning her neck in one of its birdlike talons. She thrashed about, pounding on the leathery body, but it was no good. The creature didn't even flinch.

Morton scrambled on all fours to grasp his sword again but froze suddenly when a horrific inhuman growl filled the attic. It wasn't the Galosh. Everyone turned in unison to see James standing on the other side of the room. He let out a second terrifying roar, and Morton watched with disbelief as he snapped his chains like strings of licorice. His eyes cast a dim green glow, and Morton could see his back arching as spines tore through his clothing and erupted all over his hands and face. It was the most terrifying apparition Morton had ever seen.

In a sudden blur of motion James threw himself at the beast. It dropped Melissa and turned to defend itself. James and the Galosh collided in the center of the room and began tearing at each other's flesh in a whirlwind of savage blows. James was formidably strong and threw the Galosh to the floor several times, but each time the Galosh leaped up and resumed the attack, showing no signs of fatigue. Morton knew why. The only way to kill a Galosh was to hack it to a thousand pieces. If James had been a fully transformed Snarf, he might have stood a chance, but being part human, he was tiring quickly. After a few more minutes of terrifying struggle, the Galosh drove one of its talons right into a vulnerable part of James's shoulder, then spun him around and threw him clear across the room. James landed in a bruised heap and didn't get up. The creature inched toward him.

Brown raced in agitated circles around the peak of the ceiling. "Finish him!"

Morton watched helplessly as the Galosh locked its empty eyes on James. The creature was about to deliver a final deadly blow when a high-pitched, painful scraping noise reverberated around the attic. It sounded like a nail scratching along an immensely long chalkboard. The Galosh stopped and looked around. The noise came again. A long, grating rasp. Then there was a different sound, a series of soft thumps that sounded to Morton as though a rain of tennis balls was landing on the roof outside. The noise grew in intensity, turning into a veritable storm. Brown began crawling around randomly like a frightened upside-down dog. The sound became so loud that Morton and the others pressed their hands to their ears. Something was landing on the roof and scraping at it with sharp claws. It was as if a hundred . . .

Cats!

Morton suddenly realized what was happening. Hundreds upon hundreds of cats must have been scampering over the turret roof, their claws gripping onto the slates as they scratched and slipped around. The Zombie Twins, Morton thought. They were herding the cats onto the roof. But why? Had they come back for the gargoyle?

The scratching grew more furious until quite suddenly one of the black slates flew off, revealing the starlit sky beyond. The hole filled instantly with a dozen snarling feline faces. Morton gasped. He'd never seen cats looking so fierce. Brown raced down from the peak and, in a mind-bending defiance of gravity, stepped onto the floor just behind his demonic creation.

"Quick, get the fingers!" he ordered.

The Galosh shot toward Melissa. She attempted to run but there was nowhere to go, and a second later the Galosh hooked the pouch from around her neck, snapping the leather string.

More slates flew from the highest part of the roof as the cats clawed their way into the attic. They began to throw themselves through the square holes and into the enclosed space, spreading across the floor, hissing and screeching.

Brown shouted at his beast again, "The gargoyle too, you idiot!"

Morton looked over to see that Brown was now standing at the open hatch beside the Galosh. It would have to wade through an ocean of cats to reach the gargoyle. It hesitated, glancing around at the increasing chaos.

"Now!" Brown ordered fiercely.

Then it ran. In three heavy steps it cleared the distance to the font in the center of the room, where it grabbed the gargoyle and tucked it firmly under its arm. The cats swarmed instantly up the creature's leathery legs like a living fur coat, sinking hundreds of pairs of teeth and thousands of claws into its tough skin. A dozen gashes opened up on the beast's body, and rivulets of watery blue blood spilled to the floor, but the creature didn't slow down. In three more strides it was back at the hatch, and in one enormous leap it vanished down the hole. Brown dove after it and slammed the ebony panel shut. Morton's heart sank as he heard the clunk of the heavy latch below. They were locked in. He spun around, expecting the cats to begin attacking them, but the cats didn't even seem to notice they were there. They milled around in passive confusion.

Wendy ran immediately over to James and crouched beside him. "James!" she cried.

James's eyes fluttered open. "I'm fine," he said.

Morton breathed a sigh of relief. He'd thought James was too far gone to be able to speak but, judging by his voice, there was still something of the old James left after all.

"You don't look fine," Melissa said, gesturing at the wound on his shoulder.

"Hey, I can battle a tank and win, remember," he said, sitting up and looking around. "Why aren't the cats eating us?"

"I don't know," Wendy said. "They look hungry enough."

Morton then noticed that the cats were scratching at the hinges around the hatch.

"They're helping us escape!" he said incredulously.

"I thought you guys said the Zombie Twins were controlling the cats," Robbie said, looking around in exhausted confusion. "Why would they want to help you?"

Morton shook his head. "I'm not sure. The Zombie Twins are really evil in the comic."

The scratching got louder and more frantic until, with a sudden crash, the ebony panel fell through its own jamb, bounced off the aluminum ladder, and landed with a thud on the floor below.

Morton ran over to the hole and gazed down in amazement. The cats began jumping down and sprang purposefully out of Dad's office as if guided by a powerful beacon.

"Quick!" Melissa yelled. "Get Brown!"

James leaped to his feet and was the first to clamber down the ladder to the floor below.

Everyone followed James amid the endless waterfall of cats and ran down the stairs to the kitchen.

They all burst through the screen door onto the porch at about the same time and came to a sudden halt. Morton had half expected to find Brown speeding away down the driveway in his car, but the teacher hadn't escaped at all. He was standing motionless in the middle of the lawn beside his wounded beast, completely surrounded by cats. Hundreds of green eyes glinted in the moonlight as the cats stared unblinking, scowling and hissing. Morton had never seen so many cats in his entire life. It was a wholly unnatural and chilling sight.

Then, with eyes glowing so fiercely they cast a red glow on the cats below, the Zombie Twins drifted to the front of the pack accompanied by several sinewy Gristle Grunts, a clutch of Acid-Spitting Frogs, and the four-headed Hydra Snake that Morton had battled in school.

"What's going on?" Melissa asked, rubbing the back of her neck.

Morton shrugged. He had no idea.

"You better call off these toys of yours, Morton," Brown yelled as soon as he saw them, "or you'll regret it!"

"What's he talking about?" Robbie whispered.

"He thinks I'm controlling the Zombie Twins," Morton said.

"You're not, are you?" he said uncertainly.

"No!" Morton exclaimed.

"Then who is?" Robbie asked.

Morton could think of only one answer, and as soon as the idea came into his head he realized it had to be right. "King," he said. "King's controlling them."

"King?" Melissa hissed. "Make up your mind. I thought you said he was dead."

"He is," Morton said, "but I think I finally figured out what's —"

He didn't have time to finish. Brown commanded his beast to run. In a surge of motion, the creature grabbed the gargoyle by one of its three legs and used it like a club to smash its way through the cats. The animals began yowling and hissing and leaping aside as the beast bludgeoned a path through the angry brood. Brown followed, racing through the clearing to the bottom of the yard until he reached the well. He then bounded up onto the circular stone wall while the beast stood below, swinging the gargoyle mercilessly at the approaching cats. But the cats kept coming, surging relentlessly toward the Galosh.

Brown's face turned to terror and he quickly fumbled in his pocket, pulled out the small leather pouch containing the stone fingers, and raised it over the black, bottomless well. "Call them off!" he yelled. "Call them off or we all lose!"

"We can't stop them!" Morton shouted.

The cat pack was growing even more savage now. They climbed over the Galosh, leaping onto its back, shoulders, and head. Two Gristle Grunts sped over like trained dwarf soldiers and grabbed each of the beast's legs, causing it to collapse to the ground. The beast let out a fearful wail of anger. It pounded a few more times, using the gargoyle as a weapon, but the odds were heavily against it. In one swirling motion the cats swarmed over the crippled creature, burying it completely in a mass of fur that writhed and churned like a giant hairy wave on Dad's perfect green lawn. The noise was deafening. Like a thousand cat fights all happening at once, yowling and mewling and spitting. And then, just as suddenly as it had started, it stopped. The cats dispersed and, impossibly, the Galosh, foot soldier of the underworld, was gone. There were no limbs, no tatters of flesh, no scales or bones. All that remained was the lifeless gargoyle, lying facedown in the grass. Morton felt suddenly sick.

Brown's face went as pale as the moon. "I said call them off!" he yelled again. "Or I'll drop the fingers."

Instantly, as if obeying some unheard command, the animals became calm. The Zombie Twins floated over the pack and settled a few feet from Brown, staring mutely up at him.

"What just happened?" Melissa said, trembling visibly.

"I think the Zombie Twins are on our side," Morton said.

"Are you crazy?" Melissa exclaimed. "They set those flying snakes on us."

Morton shook his head. "I think they were trying to hide the gargoyle in the closet to keep it safe," he said. "That's why they didn't just steal it. And they rescued us in school by taking the monsters away before they could hurt anyone."

Melissa's face changed from disbelief to realization. Morton looked back at Mr. Brown still holding the pouch over the well. "Brown thinks I'm controlling the cats," he said. "I'll go talk to him."

"You can't go out there!" Melissa exclaimed, grabbing firmly on to Morton's shoulder. "Did you see what those cats just did to that rubber-boot monster?"

Morton paused on the edge of the porch and looked out at the sea of cats.

"I don't think they'll eat me," Morton said.

"It's not worth the risk!" Melissa insisted.

"But the moon's getting low in the sky," Robbie said. "We have to do something."

Morton looked over at the half-human form of James, who was staring in bewildered silence, panting heavily.

"You're going to have to trust me," Morton said, looking back at Melissa.

Melissa chewed her lip nervously, then nodded and released Morton's shoulder. "Okay, you're right," she said. "Do what you have to do."

Without another moment's pause Morton marched bravely across the lawn. More than a hundred heads and two hundred ears were swaying and twitching patiently, like one giant four-hundred-legged pancake of fur. He stepped right up to the edge of the pack. The cats seemed oblivious to his presence. Every glowing eye, be it cat, Grunt, Hydra Snake, or Zombie Twin, remained fixed on Brown.

His heart pounding, Morton pushed his right foot into the hot mass of bodies. The animals didn't stir. He then did the same with his left foot and the cats merely shifted aside. Breathing a sigh of relief, he continued to push his way silently through the cats. After what seemed like forever, Morton eased his way out of the other side and stood within arm's reach of Brown.

"Nicely done, Morton," Brown said, regaining some of his composure. "But you haven't won yet. I'd say we have a stalemate."

Morton looked behind him. A galaxy of green eyes glittered back. There was no escape for Brown.

"I can't call them off," Morton said, turning to face Brown. "I'm not controlling them."

"Don't try to bluff a con man, Morton. I know those red-eyed little men are your toys."

"Yes," Morton said. "They are my toys, but I'm not controlling them. Please, you have to believe me."

Morton glanced desperately up at the moon again, the bottom of which was now dipping behind the rooftops.

"If not you, then who?" Brown said, also noticing the moon's dangerously low position. "Wait, don't tell me," he hissed angrily. "It's King, isn't it? The mad, dead fool come back to haunt me."

"I think so," Morton said.

"How? How could he have come back?"

Morton shook his head nervously. "I don't know for sure, but I have an idea. You said yourself that the sacrificed person puts their mark on the wishes."

"Not to that extent," Brown said dismissively.

"I know, but the more I think about it, the more it makes sense. You see, King was the human sacrifice that activated the gargoyle and then, in a weird way, all the wishes were wishes that came out of his imagination."

"How so?"

"We all wished for things from the comic, from his comic. James wished to be a Snarf, which is a mythical creature King invented. I wished all the other monsters he invented to life, including the Zombie Twins, and Melissa wished for an infinitely large closet, which it turns out was an idea she got when reading another one of King's stories. So in a weird way King is tied up in the whole thing, and I think, well, I don't know how, but I think he's controlling the Zombie Twins. And I hate to say it, but I think he's really mad at you."

Brown swallowed hard, the smug expression completely gone from his face. His eyes began to dart wildly in his head. "If that's true, then I might as well throw these down the well," he said bitterly, swinging the pouch in his hand. "King would never let me leave here alive."

"No!" Morton said. "I don't think that's true. If there's one thing I learned from his stories, it's that two wrongs don't make a right, ever. King didn't believe in revenge."

"You're just saying that!" Brown spat.

"No, it's true. In all the stories where people tried to get revenge, they ended up dead or worse. Look, the cats are calm now. If he wanted you dead, you'd be dead already. I think if you get down, ever so slowly, and take my hand, maybe we can get you inside where it's safe, reverse the wishes, and then it will all be over."

"You'll turn me in though!" Brown said hotly.

Morton nodded. "Yes. Yes, we will. But we can vouch for you. We'll tell them you did the right thing in the end. Everyone makes mistakes, right?"

"So you'll throw me to Sharpe instead of the cats?"

Morton held his gaze. "I think even you'd rather take your chances with Sharpe this time."

Brown looked back at the moon and then at the two skull-faced creatures hovering just in front of the now-silent cats.

"Is that true, King?" he called tauntingly. "Are you hiding behind those red eyes, laughing at me? Always one step ahead, weren't you?"

"We don't have much time," Morton said anxiously.

Brown nodded. "Fine. Let's get this over with."

Morton reached out to grab Brown's arm. Brown hesitated.

"It will be safer if we're together," Morton urged. "Just don't make any sudden movements."

"Sudden like this!" Brown said, kicking Morton in the stomach and sending him reeling backward into the soft living mattress of cats behind him.

"No!" Morton yelled, but Brown was already running, despite his bad leg. He hobbled to the side of the house where he instantly leaped up and once again, like a human fly, clambered impossibly up the vertical wall.

The cats went suddenly berserk, hissing and spitting with insane fury and throwing themselves against the wall of the house. But he was already several feet above the ground and climbing fast. The Zombie Twins' eyes burst into red beacons that shone like searchlights onto the rapidly escaping Brown. Brown didn't look back. He kept on climbing and was almost at the roof of the house when he stopped and gasped with fear. Morton, still lying on the lawn, could see everything. Two venomous giant spiders, each the size of a baseball mitt, with grotesque hairy pincers and six glassy, emotionless eyes, crawled from the gutters and darted toward Brown. He screamed and twisted clumsily sideways, lost his grip, and tumbled to the ground, landing with a loud thump. Morton thought for a horrible moment that he'd broken his back, but a second later he was on his feet again and attempting to run.

That was the last mistake Rodney Brown ever made.

In one efficient and chilling motion, a hundred cats washed over him. Morton heard a muted scream from beneath the deadly mound of fur, saw Brown's flailing form thrash hopelessly, and then, like the final ghastly act in a demonic conjurer's trick, the mound shrank to nothing and the cats slipped away, leaving not so much as a single hair behind.

For the second time the previously ferocious animals resumed passive sitting positions and began licking their paws and cleaning their whiskers like perfect pets in a TV commercial. The Zombie Twins drifted forward and hovered over the spot where Brown had once been.

"The fingers?" Melissa yelled. "Where are the fingers?"

Morton leaped to his feet and raced over to the center of the preening circle of cats. Relief flooded through his entire body when he saw that the Zombie Twins were floating just beside the now-tattered but still intact leather pouch as if guarding a trophy.

"They're here," he yelled.

Melissa burst out from the porch and ran over. "Well, don't just stand there," she yelled back, pointing to the moon, which was almost completely hidden behind the roof of the house.

"We need to get the gargoyle into the attic," Robbie said urgently.

"No time," Melissa snapped. "Just grab the book and bring it down here."

Robbie nodded and tore off into the house.

Morton picked up the soggy pouch and fished the three fingers from inside. He clutched them tightly in his fist and followed Melissa over to the bottom of the yard where the gargoyle lay abandoned, facedown on the grass.

Wendy helped James off the porch and brought him to join the others.

"What do we do?" James asked, his voice half growl, half human.

"Brown said we just put them back on," Melissa said forcefully.

"It can't be that simple," James protested.

"Maybe it is," Melissa said. "Maybe, just this once, we'll get a lucky break."

A second later Robbie practically skidded to a halt beside them, holding the jewel-embedded book in his hands. "There's a bookmark on the right page," he gasped, flipping the book open.

"Well?" Melissa said. "Read it!"

Robbie squinted at the book and shook his head. "I . . . It's too dark. Does anyone have a flashlight?"

Morton stood behind Robbie to look at the book. There at the top of the page was an unmistakable etching of the gargoyle and several paragraphs of flowing script below, but in the darkness Morton simply couldn't make out the words.

"Here," James said, holding out his spiny hands. "I can see." Robbie looked questioningly at Morton. Morton nodded, and Robbie handed him the book.

"It says the person who made the wish should replace the finger on the full moon and recite the verse:

As the Moon is full bright,
I restore my wish unto the night.
Last one first, first one last,
I replace the fingers, I forgive the past.

"That's it?" Wendy said. "Can it really be that simple?"

"It could be," Morton said, although he had to admit it sounded too good to be true.

"I guess we'll find out," Melissa said, pulling the gargoyle to an upright position.

"I broke the finger last," James said, looking down at the assortment of fingers in Morton's palm. "But how do I know which one's mine?"

"The one that fits in the middle," Morton said, remembering the day that seemed like a lifetime ago.

James seemed to have no trouble finding the finger that fit the middle of the gargoyle's hand. "Wish me luck," he said.

"Uh-uh!" Melissa said firmly. "No more wishes. Just real life."

James nodded. He leaned forward and twisted the finger until the rough edge at the base lined up perfectly with the fractured stub on the gargoyle's hand, and he recited the verse in his now deep gurgling voice. "As the Moon is full bright, I restore my wish unto the night.

Last one first, first one last, I replace the fingers, I forgive the past."

For one horrible, heart-stopping moment Morton thought nothing was going to happen. James looked at them sadly, but then, there was a sudden crackling sound and blue light flashed in a ring around the severed finger joint. Morton saw the crack around the base of the finger vanish completely.

James let out a terrific howl of agony and fell backward into the damp grass. He rolled and yelled until he finally curled into a ball and began trembling and making small sobbing noises. Melissa rolled him onto his back. His skin had lost its silver-gray pallor and the spines had vanished completely and his eyes . . . Morton almost wept with joy. His eyes were a clear deep blue. That's when Morton realized that even though tears were streaming down James's face, he wasn't sobbing at all, he was laughing.

"Are you okay?" Melissa asked.

James pushed himself up onto one elbow and waved his arm.

"Never better," he said. "Now hurry!"

Melissa stepped forward and took her finger next. She glanced longingly up to her bedroom window. After a brief internal struggle she dutifully put the finger in place on the gargoyle's hand and recited the verse. A second spark of blue fire spun like a healing ring around the cracked stone, and an instant later the finger was fused back into place as if it had never been broken. A light burst out from Melissa's bedroom window like a small, silent explosion and then faded quickly to darkness.

Melissa sighed sadly.

Morton gripped the last of the fingers and turned to face the Zombie Twins, who were floating attentively nearby. "I'm sorry about this," he said, feeling suddenly sad.

Melissa dropped her jaw in disbelief. "Morton! Don't apologize to those things!"

"They saved our lives! King saved our lives."

"They have to go."

"I know. It's just . . . well, it wasn't all bad, was it?"

"No, but if there's one thing we've learned about magic," Melissa said, "it's that you can't control it. So hurry up and put that finger back."

Morton nodded gravely and put the finger back in place. After reciting the verse a third ring of fire flashed around the break and then faded, leaving the final wound magically healed.

Slowly the Zombie Twins' red eyes grew dimmer and they seemed to lose their ability to hover. Like deflating balloons they keeled sideways and settled to the grass. One of them raised its right hand and pointed at the moon and then it froze. For a moment Morton felt sure he was looking into the eyes of the legendary John King, but then the eyes went out and whatever spirit had animated its tiny body was gone. The Grunts too toppled over, lifeless foam toys once again and, from somewhere up on the house, the King-Crab Spiders fell limply through the air, landing with a soft thump in the shrubbery below.

Morton turned to look at the impossibly large swarm of cats. Quite suddenly they all began hissing and screeching at one another, no longer happy to be so closely packed. A few savage fights broke out, and more violent yowling filled the night, but this time it didn't last long. Very quickly the cats began to disperse, running in every direction off into the night.

"It's over," James said, looking at his hands. "It's really over."

CHAPTER 19

A NEW LIFE

Morton realized he was trembling, as if the stress of the night's events were only now taking hold, but he was determined not to give in to it. There was still a lot to do. First he got Robbie and Wendy set to work shooing away the remaining cats because, as he pointed out, it wouldn't be good if the entire town's cat population was discovered on their lawn the next morning. Then he went to check on James, who was sitting in a daze, rubbing his arms and legs.

"Are you sure you're okay?" he asked.

James smiled broadly. "I feel great, but you'll be glad to know I don't feel so great that I want to sing."

Morton laughed and gave James a big hug. He really was back this time, no doubt about it.

"We still have to decide what we're going to do," Melissa said. "Should we come clean and tell Sharpe everything?"

"Well, I for one am sick of lying," James said, and Morton couldn't have agreed more.

"I'm not sure honesty is the best policy this time," Robbie said.

"Why not?" Wendy said, looking confused.

"What will you tell her?"

"The truth," James said.

"Do you have any idea how ridiculous that's going to sound?" Robbie asked.

"Yeah, but . . ."

"She'll want proof," Robbie added.

"So? We have all kinds of proof," James said. "We've got the book, and the gargoyle, and —"

"Robbie's right," Morton cut in, realizing suddenly where Robbie was going with all of this. "If we tell the truth, they'll take the gargoyle and King's book away from us as evidence. And after what we've just seen, can we really trust anyone not to use the wishes themselves?"

"Are you suggesting we keep the gargoyle?" James said.

Wendy shook her head. "We can't keep it. I don't know if I could ever trust myself with that thing always lurking in the back of my mind. It's like putting a giant chocolate bar on your desk and telling yourself you can never eat it."

Melissa nodded vigorously. "Wendy's right. We have to get rid of it."

Morton looked down at the fully restored gargoyle. "So are we agreed? We get rid of the gargoyle forever?"

Everyone nodded.

"Right," Morton said, hoisting the heavy statue into his arms. "If King's body was lost in that well, then I guess that's the best place to put the gargoyle."

He marched quickly over to the well and without

pausing, without giving himself a chance to think about it for one more second, he dropped the gargoyle into the inky black depths and watched it tumble silently until it vanished from sight forever.

Nobody spoke for several minutes. Only now that the gargoyle was gone did they each realize just how heavily it had weighed on their minds. Morton knew that the others were, like him, thinking of all the good things they could have wished for. But he knew that, in truth, nothing genuinely good could come from dark magic.

"That only leaves the book," Morton said at last.

"We'll burn it," Robbie said.

"We can't do that," Morton said, surprising himself.

"Why not?" Melissa said.

"You know what Dad says," Morton replied. "Nobody should ever burn books, no matter what's in them."

"I don't get it," Melissa said. "You get rid of the gargoyle but you want to keep the book? They're both the same aren't they?"

"I agree with Morton," James said. "The book contains knowledge. Maybe it's knowledge that's too dangerous for us to use right now, but it's still knowledge."

"King wouldn't have burned the book," Morton added.

In the end they took a vote, and only Melissa and Robbie wanted to destroy the book.

"So what do you propose to do?" Melissa asked gruffly.

"We hide it in King's attic, cover the hatch, and never go in there again," James said.

"Then that only leaves one problem," Robbie said. "What are you going to tell Sharpe?"

"We're not going to tell her anything," James said. He yawned fiercely. "There's no evidence left now. Even the cats will probably find their way home by morning."

Morton wandered across the garden and picked up the soft, foam Zombie Twins. He looked at them and sighed heavily. "You know, I only wish that —"

Morton never finished his sentence. James and Melissa bounded over to him and clapped their hands over his mouth.

"No more wishes!" they chorused.

The next morning the sun shone crisp and golden through Morton's bedroom window. He bounced out of bed and flung the curtains wide, basking in the cool bright light. He'd expected to be tired beyond words. It had been almost dawn by the time they'd finished putting the house back in order. Yet Morton found that he was bursting with energy. Today, he thought, was going to be a completely normal day. What an exciting idea.

Morton arrived at the breakfast table to find James and Melissa were also wide awake and chattering energetically.

Dad bustled in from the kitchen with a large jug of orange juice and a steaming pot of tea.

"Morning, Dad," Morton said, smiling.

Dad returned the greeting and they settled down to what Morton thought was a completely ordinary breakfast.

After a few minutes, however, Dad began scratching his head and looking curiously at all three of them.

"Has somebody stolen my children and replaced them with aliens?" he said lightly.

"Huh?" everyone said.

"Well, not only are you not arguing but I also just heard James ask for the milk, and not only did he say 'please,' but Melissa passed it to him and then James said 'thank you,' and Melissa said 'you're welcome.'"

"We're always polite, Dad," Melissa said teasingly.

The kids giggled, and Dad scratched his head again. "You know, I might be slow, but I'm not stupid. Something is going on here, and I intend to find out just exactly what it is."

"Actually, Dad," James said, "for once you're dead wrong. Absolutely nothing is going on. That's what's so great about today."

Dad looked even more perplexed.

Melissa got up from the table and kissed him on the head. "Don't worry about it, Dad. You should save your brain for more useful things, like figuring out why the universe is expanding, or how old the galaxy is."

James too got to his feet. "Come on, Morton. We better get to school. It looks like Dad needs his beauty sleep."

Morton ran over and threw his arms around his father. "I love you, Dad," he said, before heading to the door.

Dad smiled, but looked more confused than ever.

"Bundle up," he said. "It might be sunny, but it's getting wintry out there."

A moment later the three kids stood outside on the porch ready for their first normal day of school. The air was indeed quite cold, and Morton noticed with some lament that the last of the leaves had fallen from the trees, leaving them utterly bare.

"It's Halloween in a couple of weeks," James said as they paced down the driveway.

"That's right," Morton said. "I can't believe I keep forgetting that."

"Well, I for one am glad nothing magical is going to happen on Halloween," Melissa said. "Although, we could have gotten some pretty awesome costumes from my closet. . . ."

Melissa fell silent. They were just crossing the lawn, and she had stopped in the very spot where Brown had fallen to his doom. "It's a pity about Brown," she said solemnly.

"Pity?" James said. "I thought you wanted to stab him through his 'black heart.'"

"Well, obviously I was bluffing."

"You were?" Morton and James said in unison.

Melissa began to wriggle uncomfortably. "I . . . I think I was. But, I mean, even if I wasn't, that wouldn't make me a bad person, would it? We were in a tight spot, right? We had to reverse the wishes. We did the right thing, didn't we?"

"*You* did the right thing," James said, putting his hand reassuringly on Melissa's shoulder. "I won't forget that."

Melissa looked back into James's eyes and then quickly looked away. "We better get going," she said, pacing off toward the street. "Don't want to be late."

Morton and James followed.

"I think I'm going to be a Zombie Twin," Morton said, changing the subject back to the topic of Halloween.

Melissa stared at him in amazement. "You are joking, aren't you?"

"No!" Morton said. "The Zombie Twins saved our lives! I can't wait to reread all their stories now. They're my new heroes."

"I guess some things don't change," Melissa said. "What about you, James?"

James shrugged. "I don't know. I'll have to think about it."

They reached the foot of the driveway and found Wendy sitting on the wall, waiting. Morton noticed that James straightened his hair with his hands and smiled broadly at her. She gave a little wave and then turned to walk off with Melissa.

The boys ambled away in the opposite direction, and Robbie came running up behind them soon after.

"Hey! It's Halloween in a couple of weeks. You wanna buy some cool decorations? I've got a basement full of the stuff, including a life-size Sweeney Todd that —"

"No, thank you!" Morton and James chimed loudly.

"Oh, uh, right. I guess not," Robbie said, looking suddenly embarrassed.

Just then they all heard a high-pitched squeak and looked over to see a perfectly normal white cat chasing what looked like a two-headed rat along the gutter on the other side of the street. The rat squealed and shot down the nearest drain, and the white cat perched on its haunches, meowing hungrily and peering down after it.

"Was that a two-headed rat?" James said.

"It was," Robbie replied. "I'd recognize those nasty teeth anywhere."

"But shouldn't it have turned back into a toy?"

Morton scratched his chin. "I wonder if that was one of Timmy's rats. I mean, reversing my wish might not have affected those."

"Well, let's hope the cats finish them off quickly," James said.

They were about to start walking again when Morton spoke up. "Wait a minute! Doesn't that cat look familiar to you?"

James and Robbie exchanged quizzical glances.

"Yeah," James said. "I've seen that cat before because I've seen every cat in Dimvale. They were all in our yard eating Mr. Brown last night, remember?"

"No," Morton said. "That's not just any cat." In fact this was the little cat he'd seen on the poster, the one with eyes of green like jelly beans. "It's Squiffy," Morton went on. "Willow's cat. Do you think he's lost?"

"Well, cats don't usually get lost," James said, "but

maybe you should bring him along, just to make sure he finds his way home."

"That's what I hoped you'd say," Morton said, and he ran across the road to scoop the small white ball of fur into his arms.

A few minutes later the three boys arrived in the school yard to find it boiling over with excitement. It seemed everyone had a story to share about how their cats came home in the night.

"Marmalade woke me up at six o'clock scratching on my window."

"I couldn't believe it! I tripped over Tibbles walking out the door this morning."

"And then I heard this meowing from the tree and I looked out and there was Monte, looking fat as a ham and licking his lips like he'd had the biggest feast of his life."

Morton couldn't help grimacing at this. He wondered how the doting cat owners would feel if they knew just exactly why their beloved animals had returned to them so well fed. A few moments later he spotted Willow standing in the crowd, listening to all the stories, but looking forlorn and teary-eyed.

Morton snuck up behind her and tapped her on the shoulder, holding the fuzzy white ball in his hands.

Willow turned, popped her eyes open wide, squealed like a banshee, and jumped up and down like a kangaroo.

She yanked Squiffy from Morton's arms and squeezed her cat until it looked like he might burst. Then she put Squiffy down and hugged Morton so that he too felt like he might burst, then she let go of Morton and hugged Squiffy again.

And that wasn't the end of the good news. Later that morning, just after recess, Robbie ran up to Morton with a bright beaming smile that Morton didn't think he'd seen on his face before.

"You'll never guess what happened," Robbie said.

Morton shrugged. "I'm not even going to try."

Robbie chuckled. "Well, Nolan Shaw just asked me if I want to be the lead singer in his new band, Shatter Box."

Morton's jaw dropped like an anvil. "But . . . But can you even sing?"

"A bit, but that's besides the point. Nolan says I'd be perfect because, according to him, I'm the school's new most popular 'bad boy.' Apparently everyone's been talking about how we fought off the monsters in the hall and stood up to Brad and stuff. He thinks I'd make his band an instant hit. Says I'd be really popular with the girls."

"Girls?" Morton exclaimed, feeling very confused.

Robbie shrugged. "That's what I said. I don't even know any girls."

Morton found himself suddenly fumbling for words. "But, are you . . . ? I mean, are you going to do it?"

"Of course not," Robbie laughed. "But it's nice to be asked."

Morton suddenly found himself laughing too. "I guess that counts as a happy ending, then," he said.

"Almost," Robbie said. "We still need to get Sharpe off our trail."

Morton nodded in agreement. He was quite certain that Sharpe would come and drag them out of class eventually, but in fact nothing remarkable happened that day except that Finch was seen racing through the hallways trying to figure out where Mr. Brown was. By the time history class came around in the afternoon, Finch had successfully appointed a substitute by the name of Miss Francis.

After a week Morton began to accept that Sharpe was never coming. The reappearance of the cats and the simultaneous and utterly mysterious disappearance of Mr. Brown had given her new leads to follow. In fact, rumors began circulating almost at once that Mr. Brown had fled town because he was somehow responsible for the cats and all the other odd goings-on in Dimvale. Morton wholeheartedly encouraged the rumor, because it was almost true, and it wasn't long before the whole subject of the cat thief and Timmy's bag of monsters faded from fashionable conversation.

James seemed to be the slowest to recover, but that was hardly surprising. Morton couldn't even begin to imagine what emotional and physical traumas he had struggled through. It had no doubt been worse for him than for anyone else, although James never complained about anything.

"So, did you decide what you're going to be for Halloween yet?" Morton asked him as they walked home from school a week later.

"Yes," James said firmly, "I'm just going to be a boy. A normal, boring, humdrum boy."

Morton smiled. You could never be that, he thought. You're my brother and you'll always be one of the bravest and most extraordinary people in the world.

ACKNOWLEDGMENTS

First acknowledgments go to my lifelong friend Eddie (Hed!) Smith for the inspiring, mad conversations that started in the school yard and still go on today over the Internet and an occasional pint when we manage to be in the same country. I'm sure seeds for this story germinated in those school yard ramblings.

I'd like to thank Lois O'Neill for her feedback with a very early draft of this book and for the encouragement that gave me the confidence to keep going. Margot, of course, who has been there since the beginning of everything, for the things that cannot be counted and for which words are utterly inadequate. Meghan Marentette, for her truly awe-inspiring editorial notes. Nick, my editor at Scholastic, for his infectious enthusiasm and sound guidance.

My agent Rosemary Stimola and her editorial assistant, Allison Remcheck, I cannot thank enough for seeing the book you hold in your hands long before I ever did, and for patiently guiding me through many rewrites until I finally discovered it.

And last, but not least, I'd like to thank Heather Young, my secret weapon, for her utterly honest and invaluable story advice and penetrating feedback on at least three drafts of this novel. Heather rocks!

ABOUT THE AUTHOR

Sam Fisher was born in England, and decided at the age of five that he wanted to be a writer. He now lives in Canada, where he teaches screenwriting, invents gizmos, and builds things out of wood. He wrote *Scare Scape* for his three fantastic children.